Duce slipped the key into the metal door. The door opened, revealing a corridor with hallways branching off to the sides and a table with a lockbox and pile of white packets. A gunman in the corridor, an ex-linebacker with an Uzi, looked surprised, his mouth opening slowly to yell a warning to someone in a room behind him. That was all Duce needed to see.

He raced past the gunman—muscle fibers pulled steel-wire taut and stitched against his skin—and clotheslined the man under the chin. Bones snapped like brittle twigs. He turned to see the man hitting the ground, the pain only just registering on his face.

Duce raced to the open door in the corridor, where the vacant glow of a television emanated. One man, nothing Rastafarian about his Vietnamese features, was in the process of standing up from a rocking chair, pulling an Ithaca shotgun. Terror flowed like molasses across his face.

Between one heartbeat and the next Duce was at the chair, grabbing the man by the front of his shirt. One push sent him flying backwards into the bedroom wall. Before the ganger could hit the floor, Duce grabbed him again and rebounded him into the wall a second time for good measure, leaving a deep dent in the sheet rock and a trail of blood as the body slid to the floor.

"Uh-uh, bitch…"

Duce turned toward the voice—

"…this is my house."

—and found himself looking at a well-built, shirtless man with light black skin. Gang tats covered his arms, and a full beard and natty dreads spilled out over a black headband. The Skorpion submachine gun in man's hands erupted in a staccato roar, punching a line of bullet holes across Duce's chest and right shoulder.

ISBN 1-58846-866-6
First Edition: February 2005
Printed in Canada

White Wolf Publishing
1554 Litton Drive
Stone Mountain, GA 30083
www.white-wolf.com/fiction

Blood In,
Blood Out™

Lucien Soulban

Vampire
THE REQUIEM

Vampire
THE REQUIEM

Prince Maxwell Clarke rules the Kindred of Chicago with a stern but steady hand, balancing the interests of the city's diverse population against the dictates of Kindred law and the ancient Traditions. Recent events in neighboring Cicero (where a newly Embraced vampire endangered the Kindred's law of secrecy by attacking his family and later a police officer) have increased tensions between several of the vampiric *covenants* in the city, with the aristocratic *Invictus* and their allies, the *Lancea Sanctum*, contending with unrest from the populist *Carthians*. The Carthians, who ruled the city until a disastrous turn of events in the late 1800s, have since chafed under the authoritarian rule of the Invictus, and their Prefect, Duce Carter, must walk a fine line between calls for revolution within his own ranks and the need to preserve the peace in the city. Things are equally difficult for the Prince, as his only progeny, Persephone Moore, has displayed a rebellious streak of her own. Her frequent flirtations with the Carthians have been a source of embarrassment for Maxwell and a constant irritant among the Invictus, who view the Carthians as a mob of troublemakers that must be dealt with by any means necessary. To make matters worse, Solomon Birch, the Prince's most senior advisor and the head of the Lancea Sanctum, views Persephone as an abomination against the laws of his covenant, and his feud against her has already resulted in bloodshed between the two. This has only served to drive Persephone further from the Prince and into the orbit of the Carthians. The Danse Macabre continues.

This is dedicated to my parents and my sister, who supported me at my best and at my worst with equal love. This is for Jean Carrieres, who never stopped believing in my abilities, and never let me doubt myself. And this is for Richard Dansky, who always supported my efforts with encouraging words and a wise eye.

Prologue

The dispute was heated, the participants arguing with their hands as much as their voices. Duce Carter sat back in a leather office chair and tried to appear supportive, hiding his impatience behind a pair of Ecko shades and an impassive expression that smoothed the lines of his face. It was all for show, though; he was quickly losing patience with this matter.

The man pacing around the abandoned restaurant's office, and the source of Duce's agitation, was Edgar Welby. Edgar was obviously trying to vent his frustration, and while Edgar was slight in every physical sense—with a small-boned, almost birdlike frame and a balding scalp swept by long fragile strands of gray hair—Duce knew better than to underestimate Edgar or the other man present, Adrian Fulsome. All three men were vampires, born of the same predatory instinct, the same thirst for blood. It drew them together and yet made them distrust one another. The hunger for blood was like a living thing coiled in their unliving bodies, a Beast that most vampires fought a nightly battle to control. Duce watched the little man pace, and he wondered how close Edgar was to letting his own Beast slip free.

If Adrian Fulsome was feeling nervous, Duce couldn't see it. Fulsome sat on the edge of the office desk, as calm as ever. The rumor among the vampires of Chicago was that Fulsome never lost his cool, never succumbed to the madness of his inner hunger, even when provoked. Duce didn't believe it for an instant. No vampire was safe from his own urges, not ever. Fulsome probably just made sure no one ever got the chance to see it.

lucien soulban

Adrian was in his late 20s, with well-groomed blond hair, hazel eyes and perfect teeth. He looked well-behaved and reserved, but his wry smile and calm stare suggested unfaltering confidence. Fulsome regarded Duce with just such a look and smiled. "You're wrong, Duce. You're making a serious mistake here."

"That's what I'm saying," Edgar said.

Duce shrugged. The decision was his alone, as leader of the city's Carthians. It was bad enough vampire society was divided into different factions, different loyalties, but that he also suffered rebellion in his own house was unacceptable. The Carthians advocated change, bucking against centuries of stagnation that bound vampires in a web of outdated ideas and an oppressive society. *That doesn't mean I have to put up with this kind of bullshit*, Duce thought.

"What you're proposing is dangerous and flawed," Duce said. "It's a stupid idea."

"Stupid? It'll work!" Edgar said, growing more frustrated.

"I agree," Fulsome said. "At least give it a shot."

"Give it a shot?" Duce said, straightening in his chair. He brought the shades down far enough to stare at the two from over the rim. "You want me to risk everything we've gained on a gamble."

"Gained?" Edgar said. "You haven't gained anything. The Invictus are stringing you along, Duce. No way they'll ever share power with us."

"They're the top dogs," Duce replied, "I'll admit that, but stepping on their feet like this isn't the way to do it."

"And what *is* the way to do it?" Edgar shot back, "Acting like their bitches? Bending over a table and taking—"

"Pinch it off right there," Duce snarled, his impatience finding expression. "I expect some respect as your Prefect. I've never asked the Carthians to grab their ankles, and I won't take that from you, the Invictus, the Sanctified, the Prince or any other vampire."

"Duce," Fulsome said, "you have to admit that we haven't accomplished much these last few years. So we won the right to free assembly and freedom of speech from Prince Maxwell—the social disparities that brought us together still exist. We still haven't brought equal power or equal representation to the Kindred in this city. The Invictus and the Lancea Sanctum still manipulate us under the guise of the Masquerade. The Masquerade is nothing more than a tactic to control us, to keep us a feudal society."

"First off," Duce said, "the Masquerade is necessary. It teaches us to keep hidden from a public that would destroy us if they knew we existed, and it prohibits the indiscriminate creation of other vampires. There's nothing wrong with that. And secondly, feudal societies required decades—fuck, *centuries*—just to make the changeover to a democracy. Yet here you are, trying to push progress by kick-starting it in the nuts."

"We got to start somewhere," Edgar said.

"We already started!" Duce said. "I'm negotiating more rights through Prince Maxwell. And what he says goes for the Invictus and the Sanctified. I won't screw that up through blackmail."

"This is more than just blackmail," Fulsome said. "We have a member of the Invictus who created a vampire out of turn and then tried to hide her, in direct contravention of the Second Tradition: *Embrace others at your peril*. Steinitz will do anything to keep that secret. It's worth the risk."

"No, it isn't!" Duce said, tired of the argument. "I would destroy anyone who tried to use my own progeny to blackmail me, and so would you."

"Kill one of us? Fine! But there's no way Steinitz can stand up to the Carthians as a united front."

"We don't have shit on Steinitz," Duce said. "So he Embraced progeny without permission. So the fuck what? He'll go to Prince Maxwell to recognize his offspring, and ask for forgiveness. Then he'll fuck over whatever progress we've made."

"No way. He's got too much to lose. Steinitz will cave," Fulsome said.

"And you're underestimating him. He's a proud man, and I guarantee you that his first reaction will be, *if I'm going down, you're going down too*."

"That's an assumption."

"No, that's an observation. And the Invictus will close ranks around Steinitz rather than let us have an in through him."

"If they found out."

"Steinitz will come clean, Masquerade or no Masquerade," Duce snapped. "So the answer is no. We're seeking a higher ideal here, and we won't get there by crawling through the mud. End of fucking discussion."

"Wait," Edgar said. "That's it? Don't I get the right to debate this? Don't the Carthians get to vote on this? Adrian, you're the Myrmidon. Aren't you arbiter when two parties disagree?"

"Yes, I am—"

"He's also supposed to be neutral," Duce said, interrupting, "which he isn't right now. And the fact is as Prefect and chair, I have the right to veto whatever issues come up before the Carthians if I consider it a waste of time. I won't bother the covenant with this nonsense. Your time is up." Duce stood, ready to leave.

"Don't do this, Duce," Fulsome said. "Too many Carthians have their hopes riding on this."

Duce turned around, shaking his head. "Now I *know* you didn't just say that," he replied. "*Tell* me you didn't tell our brothers and sisters about the plan without discussing it with me first. Tell me you didn't get their hopes up with that foolish-ass idea."

"No," Edgar said, "he didn't. But I did."

"Then you stepped out of line," Duce said. "This is the exact shit I've been trying to avoid," he said to Fulsome, indicating Edgar with a wave of his hand. "We can't go running around doing whatever we feel like. We've got to act united. The Carthians have got to stop acting like children looking for a fight."

"Look," Fulsome said, "Let's call a truce here. It's been a long night and you're late for your next meeting, aren't you?"

Duce checked his watch and grimaced. "Shit, yeah."

"I'll talk with Edgar about the need to go through proper channels," Fulsome said evenly, nodding to Edgar. "And you go meet…who's it you're meeting?"

"Tania," Duce said, smiling.

"Go have a pleasant night with Tania. I'll sort things out from here."

"All right, then. Later," Duce said, eager to walk away from the aggravation. With a curt nod he headed out the back door of the restaurant. Tonight was his third rendezvous with Tania, and he was actually looking forward to her again. She was smart, passionate and an activist in local African-American lobby groups. By the time he reached his black SUV, he'd mostly forgotten about Edgar and his plans.

They heard the SUV's engine start. Fulsome pulled the curtain back a fraction to peer through the grime-covered window. He watched as the lights of Duce's SUV vanished into the dark.

"So," Edgar said, still fuming. "That's it?"

"No," Fulsome said. "That's far from it. You're right. This has gone on long enough."

Edgar cocked his head one side. Fulsome smiled at the confusion evident on his face.

"What're you saying?" Edgar asked.

"Time to shake things up." Fulsome let the curtain drop back into place. He fished a micro-cassette recorder from his pocket and pressed the stop button.

Fulsome had everything he needed to start.

Part One:

Blood In

"The first step in any revolution is learning how to use the establishment for one's own ends."
—Duce Carter

Chapter One

Six Months Later

The club bounced to the bohemian stylings of funk-master D-Lish, Chicago's hottest import, and there was little elbow room left on the dance-floor. Rap'sody was in the North End of Chi-Town, a handful of blocks from the Magnificent Mile. It was *the* Saturday nightspot for the young and hip, though the occasional islands of older sub-urbanites danced in tight circles around their purses, slumming and daydreaming of their unmarried days. The atmosphere was smoky and intimate; club-goers slipped past each other, brushing hips and passing an almost electric charge through one another...a circuit of flesh never entirely broken or complete in the sea of grinding bodies.

That was why Duce Carter liked it. The energy was liquid; caffeine dew on mortal tongues.

Duce slipped past hot, anonymous bodies, maneuvering his date through the crowd. Whenever he looked back at her, Tania would smile in return. She seemed happy, but Duce only felt confused. He knew that to hear her talk, he was a handsome specimen of genus African-Americana. To hear her talk, he was a fine brother with silky skin, cheekbones reminiscent of the Masai, and a nice dresser in his dark silks and leather shoes. Prada, Versace, Hugo Boss, Timberlands; they all rolled off his tongue like he was born to the style. Lord knows he practiced enough. Most of all he acted respectfully, and she loved him for that.

But it was all still just talk. Duce felt caged tonight, unworthy even, of such adoration. She was beautiful — her skin darker than any sister he'd ever seen, her face angelic and her afro cut short in a smart, Parisian style. He felt inadequate under her expectant gaze, those large black eyes watching, waiting for something he bet she couldn't quite articulate.

Most mortals had that look around Duce's kind. They mistook a Kindred's intensity for real passion that was about to erupt and engulf them. They wanted that storm of emotion, but there was a thin difference between passion and violence, love and hate. Few mortals understood that dangerous, razor-thin edge. Few Kindred did, either, Duce admitted, and that was why flirtations with mortals almost always ended in blood.

Still, it bothered Duce, her demanding more than he could deliver. He wanted to give her more, but he wasn't sure he was willing to bring her to the next step. For her, that meant moving in together. For him, it meant revealing his nature and addicting her to his blood. That way, she'd do anything to protect him.

It was forced love.

It was slavery, and Duce could not abide slavery.

"Duce!" A muffled voice cried out over the whumping bass.

Duce looked around, craning his neck to see over the sea of heads. He spied a patch of white hair nearby and an arm waving him over to a small booth against the wall.

Patrick Morneau was older than Duce, his white dreads pulled into a ponytail and crows' feet scratched into the corners of his eyes. His skin was light, his eyes green, but there was no mistaking him for anything other than a brother. Duce clasped Patrick's hand and drew him into a quick half-embrace. They clapped each other on the shoulder, firmly, just in case they needed to push off each other. Duce trusted Patrick implicitly, and he distrusted him. That was the nature of their relationship, the nature of their species.

"Didn't figure you'd be out tonight," Patrick said. "Hello, Tania."

"Nice to see you again, Pat," Tania said with a smile.

They settled into the black-vinyl booth. Duce noticed that Patrick had blown out the table's small candle. Not that he blamed him. The darkness was comfortable and safe. Fire, even the small flame of candle or match, was a reminder that for all their power, the existence of a vampire was always a precarious one.

"Felt like going out," Duce said. "You know how it is. What about you? You normally don't hang here."

"Wanted to be among my own people," Patrick said, trying to hide a tinge of bitterness with an easy grin.

Duce smiled and nodded, catching Tania's bemused frown. This was a mixed club playing safe hip-hop for an upscale crowd. Not as many African-Americans here as in other venues, but then, that wasn't what Patrick was talking about. Tania wasn't looking in the right shadows. Duce looked around and noticed a few booths immersed in gloom, their candlelight guttered out. He sensed the predators in the club, searching for the easy mark, searching for the open throat, the same as lions sunning on the savannah. Casual. Hungry. Vigilant. Duce knew they were there thanks to every vampire's innate awareness of one another. It was a predatory acknowledgement.

The silence at the table lingered uncomfortably for a few long moments before Tania abruptly slid out from the booth. "Looks like you two might want to talk," she said. "I'm getting a drink."

"Sorry, boo," Duce said. "Do you mind?"

"Not at all," she replied, attempting a smile. "Can I get you anything? No? Patrick?"

"Nothing, thank you," Patrick said.

As Duce watched Tania leave, he realized someone in the crowd was watching him. Persephone slipped through the crowd, trailing mostly male lackeys and admirers in her wake. A platinum blond with a fake mole on her cheek, she'd plucked another evening's couture from the sense and sensibilities of the 40s, her new passion. Her trim physique fit well into tonight's surprisingly demure outfit; a black, knee-length skirt and hip-length flared jacket with stiff collar, gold buttons and long sleeves that ended where black gloves began. A black brimless felt hat crowned the ensemble. She winked at Duce as she passed, a coy smile breaking her mask of indifference.

"Sorry, what?" Duce said. He'd missed Patrick's comment.

"I said, I like Tania a lot."

"So do I," Duce replied.

"You drink from her yet?"

Duce knew where this was heading. "Nah, man," he said, shaking his head. He felt exasperated and maybe a little confused at his feelings. He wanted to sigh, but it was just another mortal affectation he no longer needed. He rubbed his head instead. "I don't know, Patrick. I love her 'n all, y'know, but...."

"Yeah. I know. I can see how she looks at you. You plan on taking her?"

"C'mon, Patrick. I wouldn't do her like that."

Patrick shrugged. "Sometimes you got no choice. So. She doesn't know what you are, does she?"

"*Who.* She doesn't know *who* I am."

"Bullshit. *What* you are. She thinks she's dealing with a person. Man," Patrick said, shaking his head, "cut her loose. She doesn't deserve what you got to offer. Cut her loose before you hurt her. I mean *really* hurt her."

"Patrick, that's your answer to everything."

"Let her go, let her have her beautiful mortal children and her beautiful mortal life."

"I don't know. I'm still thinking about it." And he was. Duce liked her, and he half entertained the notion of binding her to him with his blood. But again...it was slavery. Vampire blood was addictive, and it invariably twisted the drinker into feeling false love and loyalty toward the vampire. Duce didn't want a puppet. He loved Tania for her independence.

"Man, she doesn't have time for you to make up your mind," Patrick said, almost as if privy to Duce's musings.

"What's that supposed to mean?"

"It means don't string her along. It means you got far more years than she can afford to waste waiting for your ass.

It means make up your motherfucking mind. This isn't like you. Bounce her or bite her, but don't be a pussy about it."

Duce laughed. "Man, you're harsh!"

"Gotta be what I am," Patrick said with a grin and a shrug. "I just see you tripping over the same hurdles we all got to jump. Besides, you got bigger fish to fry."

Duce frowned. Patrick had been a Carthian for a long time, and there wasn't much that went on in the covenant that he didn't know about. "What have you heard?"

"Welby's still missing, and Beth's bitching about you to anyone who'll listen."

"Yeah, well, we'll see who's listening to her bullshit."

"Duce, that's the problem. A lot of folks are listening to Beth. The people are losing faith in you, man. You got to nip this shit in the bud."

"I can't censure her right to preach," Duce said. "I don't like the shit coming out of her mouth, man, but the minute I start censoring her, I go against everything we're trying to do. I'd be no better than the Invictus."

"If you really think the Invictus are that bad, then why you negotiating with them?"

"Because they're in power," Duce said, then caught himself. Tania was back, nursing a neon-blue drink through a straw. Patrick smiled and slid out from the booth.

"Take my place, it's time I got going," Patrick said, giving his friend an upturned nod before vanishing into the crowd. Tania slid into the seat next to Duce and snuggled into his arms, but Duce was distracted by the scent of her skin. He resisted the urge to push his teeth into her neck and taste her blood.

He so wanted to taste her blood.

Patrick maneuvered through the crowd, gently pushing past people on his way to the door. He spotted two vampires, both dressed in FUBU team jerseys. One in a black Scully cap flashed Patrick a gold-toothed sneer. Patrick ignored him and walked past him.

"What's up, Chocolate Milk?" the vampire said. "What's up, beeyatch?"

His companion laughed as they headed deeper into the club. Patrick didn't bother turning around. He headed out the door and into the night.

So much for my own people, Patrick thought, his mood suddenly bitter.

Tania laid her head back on Duce's shoulder and smiled, but she could feel the tension in his chest and arm. She sighed and put her drink down.

"Is everything okay? You seem distracted."

Duce locked eyes with her, the same passionate intensity she'd expected of him blazing in his deep, dark eyes. "I am," Duce said, grasping Tania's hand. Whether he was ready for the answer that was about to pop out of his mouth, he wasn't certain. He was just going to start talking — stream of consciousness passion, as it was — and see where that led him. "We need to talk, but not here." Duce pulled Tania out of the booth.

"But my drink—" she protested, but they were already heading for the door.

Halfway to the exit Persephone seemed to appear from nowhere, blocking their way. Her entourage stopped as well, suddenly leery of Duce. She wasn't the sort who typically sought people out.

"Hiya, Duce," Persephone said, before eyeing his date. "What's with the training wheel?" Duce laughed before he could stop himself. A small part of his mind was horrified at the casual cruelty. It seemed to happen more often with each passing year since his Embrace. Tania looked hurt, her expression instantly wounding Duce.

"Training wheels?!?" Tania replied, giving Persephone the once-over. "I suggest you drop the attitude, Miss Heifer!"

Persephone smiled and Duce immediately knew Tania was in trouble. Persephone didn't back down from situations. She wasn't a bitch normally, but she was a predator, feeding off the rush of her own blood when instinct took over and her senses narrowed into killing points. She was one of the Kindred, and Tania was nothing more than prey.

Duce quickly stepped in the way. "Not now, Persephone."

"No, no," Tania said. "You find her funny? Go on and play with Miss Heifer." She stormed away. Duce growled and pushed through the crowd to catch her.

Tania was outside the neon-lit club by the time Duce caught up to her. He spun her around and was met with a sharp slap across his face. It stung far worse than it should have, but Duce knew he deserved it.

Folks standing in the line-up outside the club chuckled. A few women cheered. He ignored them.

"I'm sorry," Duce said.

"Fuck you," she said, hailing a cab.

"You have every right to hit me," Duce said, turning her around again. "I didn't mean to hurt you."

"Well you did." Her voice was hoarse with swallowed tears.

"And I'm sorry. It slipped out, but it's a part of me I'm trying to change...trying to turn my back on. You know I respect you, right?"

"I guess," Tania whispered.

Duce took Tania into his arms and held her. She sniffed into his shirt.

"Don't be messing my shirt, now," Duce said softly. Tania laughed.

Somewhere on the street, car tires squealed. Duce looked up in time to see a Buick pulling into view, the windows rolled down, angry faces screaming. Gloved hands held out matte-black submachine guns.

Duce knew it was bad from the minute the car tires squealed. A flashback — of drive-bys past — worthy of a war vet. Next came the gangbangers hanging out the window, guns blast-ing, their faces contorted as they shouted for his blood, but Duce couldn't make out the words at the time. Everything seemed to happen in slow motion, the sounds distorted by the roaring in his temples and the hammering of gunfire.

The tires screeched and the next thing Duce realized, bodies were dropping to his immediate left along the sweep of the guns. The line-up into the club was long, not to mention the players hovering outside waiting to cut in line, score some medicine or scope the local talent. Duce didn't remember going low, only that bodies fell slowly to the ground; he was moving in a blur, his nerves burning like the long steady drag off a cigarette.

Not that anyone noticed.

They were too busy bleeding, dying.

Three bullets punched through Duce's upper chest, catch-ing him by surprise, but he was still on his feet despite the pain. The smell of blood hit the air, and survival and hun-ger rolled up into a fist inside Duce's gut. He staggered on his feet, suddenly fighting the ravenous nature of the Beast. For a sickening instant, blood was all he could think about. The gangbangers sped off and took the corner hard.

He fought down the maddening hunger and compressed moments snapped back into place like a physical blow, in-undating him with images:

Tania had lurched into him from a bullet's impact. She was on the ground; writhing; painting the asphalt with her blood. She reached up for him, a pleading look in her eyes.

At least four people were motionless, more injured.

Duce was sporting holes in his chest, and he seethed with pain and an inhuman, animal need.

All he could do was stare at the blood pouring out of Tania and imagine clamping his mouth tight over her wounds.

So he ran.

Persephone leaned against the chrome rails, her back to the energetic dance floor below her. She was bored with the faux adrenaline here and the trail of sycophants. She didn't care for them much, though many times she relished the power her new existence gave her. She remembered her sun-lit days, when she was desperate to please anyone, everyone, just to belong. This was payback, if not for her, at least for every other woman that these toadies mistreated.

Liar, Persephone thought to herself. *It's a lie when you create the justifications after the fact. It's a last, desperate grab to retain your humanity against the certain truth that the malice within you needs no justification to sustain or rationalize its survival. It exists. And I allow it to exist.*

Persephone felt mildly embarrassed for what she'd said to Duce's date. The comment was on her lips before she could bite it back, riding out on a casual, jealous thought. She couldn't stop the words, or the itch for a fight. Even now, the thought of the confrontation brought an unintentional smile to her lips. She polished one of her fangs with her tongue.

The lackeys stared at Persephone, noticing her fleeting smile, waiting for her to share some intimate tidbit. They were already smiling, preparing rehearsed laughs. Persephone spun around, however, and stared down at the dance floor.

She noticed streams of people leaving, exiting for the front doors, but the black-shirted bouncers were pushing people back.

Did I miss something? Persephone wondered. She looked to her entourage and noticed another bloodsucker moving toward her. Her name was Jessie, and she was a tough little dyke in a business suit and short-cropped, spiky hair. Jessie pushed through the crowd with minimal effort and motioned to the private lounge with a flick of her head. Persephone understood and fell in stride with the short woman, leaving her groupies off-guard.

"What's going on?" Persephone asked.

"Gunshots," Jessie said. "A drive-by shooting outside. Cops are on the way. We should leave."

"Drive-by? Anyone killed?" she asked, almost too non-chalant for her own tastes.

"Don't know. But Duce was caught in the middle of it."

"What!?" Persephone said, nearly hissing. "Is he hurt?"

"Don't know," Jessie replied, "but the bouncers say they think he was the target."

Chapter Two

Persephone stepped out of the limousine on the extended hand of her chauffeur. She headed up the stairs of the five-story brownstone building and pressed the intercom button. She waved at the security camera; the door opened.

Persephone entered the building's lobby through the marble-floored foyer. It was a beautifully preserved piece of 1900s architecture, with dark lumber floors inset with a compass-point mosaic of stained woods, a grand marble staircase, alabaster columns and Victorian-era statuary in wall niches. A second-story mezzanine extended along the back wall, with doors leading to other rooms

Standing at the staircase were two guards from the Lancea Sanctum, allies to the Invictus and followers of a religious principle that tied their vampiric lineage to the Roman soldier who pierced the side of Christ on the cross. Nobody could say for certain why the Kindred existed, but those in the Lancea Sanctum were fanatical about their beliefs—and weren't afraid to use force to back them up. They stood as silent, symbolic sentinels, reminding the vampires who entered the grand building that they walked in an Elysium, a sanctuary where the business of the domain was conducted and violence of any kind was forbidden. Newcomers ignored the warning at their peril.

There were several such sites across the city—the Shedd Aquarium in particular was host to the Prince's regular Court and hosted its most important gatherings. The brownstone was a much smaller affair that primarily served

as a site where the business of the Prince's domain was conducted on a nightly basis.

Persephone had barely waited a minute before Robert
walked down the stairs. He was the Prince's chief aide and
right-hand man managing his domestic affairs. Well-
groomed and dressed in a blue cardigan sweater, the blond-
haired Robert fell somewhere between dashing and boy-
next-door.

Persephone smiled when she saw him, throwing her arms
around his shoulders. She enjoyed the warmth and smell
of his skin, briefly envying his mortality. Robert was still
alive, though he did enjoy untold longevity thanks to the
Prince's blood.

"Hello, Persephone," he said, hugging her. "What are
you doing here?"

"Little birdie told me about a meeting of the Primogen
concerning Duce Carter?" Persephone asked, referring to
the city's council of its most influential vampires. She tried
to sound casual, but her stare was sharp and intent.

"Not a good time," Robert said, looking around. "Listen dear. I suggest steering clear of this matter with Mr.
Carter."

"Oh," Persephone said, affecting a bemused grin. "Is
that an official edict from on high?"

"No," Robert said. "It's a suggestion from someone who
cares for you. It's also a warning. Mr. Carter is in trouble,
and I know how the Prince feels about him. Your sire
doesn't approve of your...interest in Mr. Carter."

Persephone nodded. Prince Maxwell was the vampire
who had given her the Embrace, drawing her into the ranks
of the Kindred and their nightly existence. He was thus as
responsible for her well-being as any parent. Unfortunately, Prince Maxwell wasn't so much conscientious as he
was concerned with appearances.

"I'm just curious," she said. "What's going on?"

Robert sighed. "The Primogen have summoned repre-
sentatives from the Carthians to answer questions about
the shooting."

"And?" Persephone asked. She didn't like where this was heading.

"And," Robert said, "it looks like the Carthians are turning their backs on Mr. Carter."

Before Persephone could press Robert for more information, a retinue of the city's oldest blood made their way down the stairs, their marble faces stern and unforgiving. Robert offered Persephone a quick nod, then hurried away to the elevators, obviously anxious. The vampires barely paid Persephone a glance before they swept out into the night, their drivers waiting outside.

Next down the steps were Adrian Fulsome and Bethany Adenauer, two of the highest ranking members of the Carthians after Duce. While she was ambivalent towards Adrian Fulsome, she hated everything about Adenauer, from her short, trim stature to the look of contempt she afforded everyone who wasn't a part of her own social circle. She caught Persephone's eye and gave her a smug little smile. *Bitch*, Persephone thought, returning the gesture.

Descending the stairs after the pair was the Prince's herald, Sebastian Garin, a youthful-looking vampire with a slight, almost boyish build. It was his job to spread word of the Prince's decrees, and he would likely do so shortly. Persephone stopped him with a glance and beckoned him over. For a moment he hesitated, caught between duty and her stature as a childe of the Prince. Finally he gave up and approached her with a frown.

"What's happening?" Persephone asked in a low whisper.

"Prince Maxwell wants Duce Carter brought in for questioning concerning the drive-by last night."

"Why?"

"You should have seen it. The Primogen said it was the price we paid for letting the Carthians nest in this city. They said the covenant's nothing more than an unruly mob, a disaster waiting to happen. They stopped short of demanding action, though."

"Is Duce in trouble?"

"Oh, that's right," Garin said with a slight smile of recognition. "You and Carter were—"

"No," Persephone said, cutting off Garin. "No, we weren't." She locked eyes with Garin for a moment and the vampire's smile faded. Finally he managed a curt nod.

"Is Duce in trouble?" she asked again.

Garin shrugged. "I'm not sure. The Primogen seemed angry, but...confused."

"What do you mean *confused*?"

"They summoned Fulsome and he brought Adenauer. She did most of the talking."

"I saw the bitch. What did she say?"

"That the Carthians disavowed any knowledge of Duce Carter's actions. They agreed to support the Primogen in whatever decision they reached regarding him."

"What?" The news hit Persephone hard. She wasn't expecting this betrayal. Duce was the leading force of the local Carthians and had certainly rubbed the wrong people the wrong way, but there was no whisper of any overt dissension in the ranks. At least, nothing of this nature. It was sudden. The Carthians had effectively closed ranks, locking out Carter in a move that felt too well organized despite last night's chaos.

"Fulsome and Adenauer can't speak for their covenant, that's Duce's position." Persephone said.

"Well, they did."

Persephone shook her head. Fulsome was one of Duce's strongest allies; it was a union born of their mutual distrust for Adenauer. It didn't make sense.

"You said the Primogen are confused," Persephone said. "How? Why?"

"I'm not sure, but—"

"But?"

"Sounds like a power play within the Carthians, but before the Primogen turn on Carter, they want to determine if they can spin this to their advantage. They don't trust Carter, but I suspect they don't much like Fulsome or Adenauer either. They're not sure who to back in this situation."

"Does anyone know where Duce is?" Persephone asked.

"No. I'm supposed to inform all Kindred that Duce is to be turned over to the Prince."

"Unharmed?"

"Prince Maxwell didn't say one way or the other."

"Unharmed, then," Persephone said, locking eyes with Garin. "Please. Just that one word. I doubt Maxwell would want him injured anyway. Not if he wanted him questioned."

Garin squirmed, weighing the risk of earning the Prince's ire versus earning an obligation from Persephone. He looked around quickly, then nodded. "All right. Unharmed. But you owe me. A favor of my choosing."

Persephone nodded and hoped Duce appreciated what she'd just done. Favor-trading among the undead was dangerous commerce, especially when feuds and obligations extended outward like skeletal branches on a tree, interconnecting and intersecting in countless patterns with other people's agendas. Garin walked away, smiling.

Persephone was turning to leave when she saw Solomon Birch walking down the stairs, his eyes darting like a blade in a knife fight. He was always looking for an opening, always looking for the kill. Square-shouldered and tall, Birch adhered to the Lancea Sanctum' heavy-handed faith with frightening fervency. His position as the head of the Sanctified in the city as well as one of the Prince's chief advisors made him the second most powerful vampire in Chicago. He was a forbidding, funereal figure with a bald, scarred head and chalk-white skin, his features as grave as a martyred saint.

Persephone touched her chest, remembering the beating she'd once received at Birch's hands. He had been in the grip of a killing frenzy, an attack she'd barely survived that had occurred in front of the Prince himself. But instead of destroying Birch, Prince Maxwell had enslaved the Hound to his will. Birch had been forced to drink the Prince's blood, thus becoming enthralled and a loyal lackey to the Prince.

Not punishment enough, Persephone thought, since the blood-binding didn't protect her. Birch still despised her, regardless of her ties to the Prince, and she had little doubt that he would still hurt her if he could. He'd hurt her deeply once, and she'd responded in kind. It was an open secret that Birch believed in breeding humans like cattle, managing bloodlines over many generations to produce exceptional stock.

Birch had arranged the death of one of her best friends. She had arranged to have his prize breeding stock infected with HIV, and Birch along with them.

Despite her fierce temperament, Persephone looked away. She couldn't maintain eye contact. She turned her back and headed out of the lobby. She had other places to be, and she felt Birch's gaze stabbing her in the back as she left. She didn't dare turn around. She didn't want to know if he was watching.

Fucking cunt.

It was a simple thought that echoed in Solomon Birch's head, a raging mantra goading him closer to the feral edge, the cliff vampires never saw until they fell into the blackness that was the heart of the Beast. It wouldn't take much to leap over the cast-iron railing, land on the wood floor below him and sink his teeth into the back of Persephone's neck. He could shake her in his mouth, a rag doll caught in a pit-bull's jaws, shake her till her neck snapped. So brutal. So sweet.

But she'd like that, wouldn't she? She was daring Birch to break Elysium by presenting her backside, defying him to go after her.

Never turn your back on opponents, not unless you think them your lesser.

Birch held his temper. She'd gotten to him once before, in similar surroundings, and he'd paid dearly for it. Instead he looked to one of the Sanctified guards at the foot of the stairs and nodded towards Garin. The guard nodded and made his way over to the Herald. Birch looked down and watched the silent exchange between his hench-man and Garin. Garin's eyes widened and he quickly looked up at Birch. Garin said something to the guard and mo-tioned vaguely at the vampires milling about in the expan-sive lobby.

I have work to do, Garin claimed in the gesture. He was trying not to look at Birch, but his eyes betrayed him with quick hummingbird glances.

The guard was insistent.

They made their way upstairs.

Ah, Garin, Birch thought, so you do have something to hide.

Birch turned and walked into an adjoining smoking room with its comfortable, upholstered chairs, tables and cold fireplace. He stood and waited until the guard ap-peared with Garin. After dismissing the henchman with a nod, Birch took a slow, tortured moment to study the smaller, nervous man. Birch relished these moments, where lengthy silences implied an explosion of violence that never actually arrived. He could taste the fear in the little man.

"Persephone," Birch said through the narrow slit of his mouth, "what did she say?

"Nothing. I just told her about Prince Maxwell's—"

"Don't lie to me, please. You two talked and I want to know what she said."

Garin hesitated. He was caught between Birch's thumb and forefinger, and Birch knew how to pinch.

"I'll make this easy," Birch said, hollow pleasantries in his smile. "You're in a pickle...a real, honest-to-God pickle, here. If you lie to me—well, you know what I'm ca-pable of, and I don't blame you for being scared. And you're afraid that if you cop to anything, you're also dust."

Garin nodded, despite himself.

"But see, I'm Lancea Sanctum and you're Invictus, right? Right?"

Garin nodded again.

"Which means we're in this together. Allies, you get me? Good. So as an *ally*, I'd like to offer you one piece of advice that you Invictus rarely get from your sires. If you're going to survive this ugly, and often tragically short, existence, the first trick is to choose your enemies carefully. If you're going to cross someone, you'd better be ready to handle them when they decide to call you out. Otherwise, all you have to look forward to is a whole lot of pain. You with me so far?"

Garin nodded.

"Good." Birch put his arm around the smaller vampire's shoulder. "Now," Birch said, "I'll give you the chance to choose your enemy. Me or Persephone?"

Chapter Three

The call was simple and to the point.

"I heard what happened. You okay?"

"Yeah man, just listen. *Wait at the Division station, the platform for the Blue Line heading to O'Hare. Wait on the far end where the last door to the second-to-last car opens. Be there at 10:30. Wait for the train with an 'X' marked across the window. Get on just before the doors close, grab a seat facing the front of the train and wait. Don't look for me. Oh, and cover those white-ass dreads of yours so nobody follows you from a mile away.*"

Patrick took some umbrage at the last part, but given the situation, he was willing to let it slide. He donned a tweed cap and followed the instructions, letting three blue-trim trains speed by before the fourth slid into place, sporting a freshly painted black "X" on the window.

Doors slid open, but Patrick waited until they'd almost closed. He slipped in sideways, barely clearing through with his long black jacket. He sat facing the forward compartments, scanning faces and studying anyone who studied him back. A couple of young brothers with Black Gangster Disciple tattoos caught Patrick looking and tried "mad dogging" him with their stares. Typical intimidation bullshit. Patrick stared back, his eyes hard with death's marble gaze. They quickly looked away.

Past Damen and Western stations, and finally at California when Patrick felt the seat behind him shift under someone's weight. A shotgun spray of goose pimples peppered the back of Patrick's neck and he felt the presence of another predator. Suddenly his neck felt far too vulnerable. It took all his civilized strength not to turn around or bare his fangs.

"Chill," Duce said. The train lurched and Duce leaned forward to stare down at his own feet. Nobody could see his mouth moving. Patrick leaned against the window so his hand covered his mouth.

"You okay?" Patrick asked.

"Nah. I'm furious. I'm ready to go off like a motherfucker on someone's ass."

"What happened?" Patrick asked. "Sheriff's looking for you. Damn near everyone is. You need to step up before some trigger-happy —."

"Not yet, not yet. I need to find out who's gunning for me, first."

"What happened? All I heard was someone did a drive-by at the Rap'sody after I left. Sure they were after you?"

"No doubt. I'm talking to Tania and they cruise by and start blasting. They were looking right at me, yelling my name. They were shooting at *me*."

"Tania okay?"

"I—I don't know. She went down. So did other folks. Suddenly I'm standing in blood. Covered in it. I couldn't stay. Tania—she's bleeding and all I can think about is feeding from her. Can you believe that shit?"

"Duce, man, I warned you. That's what we are. Can't apologize for it, so we cope."

"Can you check on her? See if she's okay? Her last name's Bentley."

Patrick sighed. "I'm not visiting her. I'll check, man, but that's it."

The steady thrum of wheels on rails replaced the absent conversation. Duce sat there, staring at his shoes, trying to plot out his next course. Only when Logan Square rolled by did Patrick ask: "So? Any idea who did it?"

"No—maybe. I think it's my old set."

"Your *set*?" Patrick turned in his seat and faced Duce. Duce peered up, surprised.

"Turn around, before someone—"

Patrick interrupted him with an impatient flick of the wrist. "I'm getting tired of this *I Spy* shit. If someone's following me, they'd be on your ass by now."

"I'm trying to protect you, man."

"I don't need protecting. I'm not your Gammie. What's this about your old set?"

Duce sighed. He didn't like discussing his mortal past, but Patrick already knew some details; that Duce once ran with the Black P-Stones, a linchpin in a gang union called the People Nation. It was one of two major alliances in Chicago, both vying for the local narco-trade. What Patrick didn't know was why Duce'd split from his set... his betrayal of a good friend.

"Your set?" Patrick repeated, not budging from the matter.

"Look, Pat. I don't want to talk about it. Not here. Not now. I need to confirm something first."

"Duce, you need to come forward with this. Maxwell's treating this like a Kindred affair. You know how the Invictus are."

"Look, I don't want anyone getting in my business, all right," Duce said, a gravel pitch scraping the underside of his voice. Frustration boiled his temper fast, making him nervous, cagey. He looked out the window, trying to calm down. Apparently Patrick knew enough to back away.

"All right," Patrick said. "But you don't have much time, whether you like it or not. Do what you got to do, but you have until tomorrow, midnight."

"Why midnight?"

"Because that's when you're meeting with me and Sheriff Nguyen."

"I'm not meeting Nguyen."

"You got no choice, Duce, not if you want my help. Doesn't matter what you've landed in — a shitload of Kindred are out looking for you now, and some probably figure they got sanction to hurt your ass. And you know what, the Primogen won't even blink if you come in looking all raggedy ass because someone took a few liberties with you. Now you're a strong man, no doubt, but you can't handle them all."

"So what am I supposed to do, huh, Pat? Let some punk think he can go off on me like that? I gotta settle this."

"Then settle it, but I'm telling Nguyen you'll meet him tomorrow night—" Patrick quickly stopped Duce from objecting. "Wait, I'm not finished. Tomorrow midnight on the steps to the entrance of the Art Institute. Maybe he won't come after you until then, I don't know, but it'll be my ass if you don't show. Don't make me regret this."

Duce thought about it for a moment, but he was already shaking his head.

"I'll make sure Tania's okay," Patrick said. "I'll even visit her. But you have to be there tomorrow. Midnight. You can't run from this." With that, Patrick stood and walked to the doors as the Jefferson Park platform pulled into view. Duce still stared at his shoes. He knew Patrick was watching him, but the whole situation bothered him to hell and back. This was his problem, his fight. It was no one else's business. It was bad enough that his entire existence revolved around this forced society and friends. Duce felt like he was back in the projects all over again, a victim of prevailing circumstances with no choice of his allies or alliances. Either enlist with the people in power, or suffer.

As a teenager, Duce had joined the only real authority by default, the local Black-P Stones. They were family, more so than his parents initially. But they were only friends by nature of his environment, by demands of survival. Had he been born not two blocks over, he might have joined the Black Gangster Disciples, as eager to kill for his set as he did for the BPS. When Duce turned his back on that life, he had a choice in his new associations and social circles. Then the Kiss came, and along with it, a plunge back into a familiar existence. Suddenly, survival again dictated his choice of allegiances, though this time, he didn't join the ones in power. The notion had some-how smacked of the past.

Still, if Duce could claim to have one friend among the undead, it was Patrick Morneau. Patrick was an outsider to the Kindred community, a loner in a herd of the already-scattered. He had little power and very few acquaintances, much less friends. But it was Patrick who brought Duce into the Carthians, and Patrick who played mentor and confi-dante. That Patrick had no real influence or power appealed to Duce. He didn't have to second-guess his own motiva-tions and wonder if his camaraderie with the older vampire was based on some infernal workings of his fast-growing alien mind and its predatory politics. Patrick was a friend exactly because he offered Duce little as an asset.

"Pat," Duce said as the train slowed. "I'll see you to-morrow night."

Patrick nodded.

The train slid forward again and Duce watched the scen-ery slip away. Once at Cumberland, he'd head back into town. He had an appointment in the impoverished South End tonight, and he didn't want to be late. Not that his target knew he was coming. Duce was hunting, and he could practically taste the blood, anticipate the violent apogee of his evening's perceived trajectory.

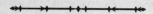

Cops called it "The Creep Zone" because of how they crept through the area, rolling on quiet treads, headlights off, past rows of shot-out streetlamps and homes with wood sheets for windows. They weren't sneaking around the South Side. Rather, they were keeping their heads low. Here, wild weed was a national flower that grew from every cracked wound in the pavement, and going GTA on cops was a national pastime. It wasn't that everybody on the South Side was criminally inclined. It was just a few bad apples spoiling it for everyone else.

Some adventurous Kindred considered the local "cui-sine" an exciting prospect. Down past 35th Avenue, how-

lucien soulban

ever, along unfortunately named streets like South Normal where life was indeed south of normal, few bloodsuckers gambled their existence for a shot at the local residents. Mortals may have been a vampire's preferred flavor, but damn if the local prey didn't balance the odds with some cold blue and a full clip of teeth.

Duce understood this world. He'd been an acolyte of its urban temples before leaving it behind for a secular existence; but his street faith never really left him. It stayed in his veins, his street-sharp instincts a perfect complement to the vampire blood whispering and drumming its tribal song in his ear.

Duce stood beneath the cradling shadows of a tree, watching hustlers and players cruise by slowly. Nobody saw him in the shadows, not even the police car that crept by, its two officers vigilant. Duce smiled. He recognized the cop in the passenger seat. Duce donned a ski mask and checked the safety on the Beretta he kept snug against the small of his back.

Empty streets made the attempt easier. Duce drew on the power surging in his dead veins, feeling it boil away like steam curling off hot water, suffusing his muscles and invigorating him for the hunt. His nostrils flared, inhaling the familiar urban stench of rot around him. He darted after the police car in jagged bursts of speed that rendered him invisible in the darkness. He kept pace with the car; it stopped, he stopped. It turned, he followed.

The white police car with its blue trim approached the edge of the Creep Zone, the familiar embrace of streetlights two blocks away. Duce had to act fast, before he was deprived of his darkness. He timed his gait with the car as it hesitated at a stop sign. In the moment before it accelerated away, Duce was at the driver's seat window, his Beretta pointed at the driver's chest. He fired three shots into the officer's bulky bullet-proof vest, spraying the interior with glass. The armor stopped the slugs, which Duce knew would happen, but the concussive force broke ribs and knocked the officer unconscious.

The cop car rolled to a stop, the driver slumped forward against the steering wheel. His partner, Duce's real target, was reaching for his radio to call for back-up and fumbling for his gun, but he was slow, too slow. The officer was bald, as many brothers seemed wont to be these days, and thick in the jaw and forehead; he hadn't changed a bit since his teenage years. Duce raced to the other side of the police car and pulled the bewildered officer from his seat before he could call for help. He ripped the radio from the cop's vest and threw the man to the asphalt where his gun clattered into the gutter.

The officer was wide-eyed, expecting to die. He back-scrabbled, looking for his firearm, but Duce was atop him, driving his knee down into the man's chest and pinning him to the ground. Hunger screamed in Duce's skull, the animal in him demanding he consummate the last act of the hunt and plunge his fangs into his quarry's throat. Stalk, pursue, kill. His every fiber pleaded for that fulfillment.

Duce hadn't planned on drinking from the cop, but surely some spoils for the victory were in order. At least enough to slake the thirst; just a taste of blood to wet his lips and calm the Beast clawing at his chest. Duce leaned down, keeping his mouth shut but drawing closer to the carotid arteries that twitched with the man's beating heart. He could hear the frightened rabbit-like patter of his prey's heartbeat echoing inside chest.

It was the same shit every night.

Feed a little, just a little. I swear that's all I want, a taste.

Kill a little, just a little. I swear that's all I want.

Who would know?

Every night the same battle raged in Duce and every night he proved himself, if not better, then in greater control of his circumstances. This was another set of conditions dictated by outside forces, another degree of enslavement in an existence where it was all he could do to separate man from Beast.

Duce pulled away from the officer's neck, silently swallowing a curse.

lucien soulban

"What up, Big Monsta G?" Duce growled, slipping a little into the slang of childhood.

The officer stopped squirming a second, long enough to study Duce's eyes, searching for some sign of familiarity. There was none, so he struggled. "Get the fuck off me! You don't know who you're fucking with!"

Duce clenched his fingers around the cop's jaw and held it tight. On any other day, he could have snapped the jaw in his grip, but he needed this fool talking. "I know who you are," Duce said. "You may have fooled the police with this reformed shit, but I know you're still Black-P Stone."

The cop quieted a little, listening. Few people knew who he was or what he was actually doing while pretending to uphold the law. Chicago admitted it had a problem with active gang members enrolling in the Police Department to help give their sets an edge. Cops killed cops, or ran protection rackets or kept their ear to the ground for the benefit of their homies. Like most gang members, though, Big Monsta G would probably need some convincing to play along.

"Black-P Stone? Don't know what the fuck you're talking about."

Duce didn't have time to play games. He slapped the officer hard enough to stun him. "Where's Law?"

"Fuck you!"

"Wrong answer, bitch," Duce said, slapping the officer again. "Where's Law?"

"Fuck-"

Duce slapped the cop a third time, hard enough to rattle the teeth in his skull. "*Damn*, you're bad at this game! Where's Law, and if I have to ask again…" Duce said, brandishing his Beretta.

"Shit, man!" the cop said, his courage shaken. "Awright! Awright!"

"Where?"

"The high rise jets over on 14th. West Side. I heard he got a crib there, but I don't know the address or apartment, I swear, man!"

Duce thought about it for a moment, then nodded. "All right, you can live. For now." He kept his gun on the cop. "Tell your bosses that some crazed crackhead motherfucker busted off on your partner before you chased him off. I hear anything other than that story, bitch, and I'm coming for your ass." Duce ended his sentence with the exclamation point of another hard slap. By the time the man recovered enough to pull his second piece from its ankle holster, Duce was gone.

Chapter Four

Patrick navigated Northwestern Memorial Hospital's small maze of sterile-white halls, moving through the staff-only areas like he belonged there. Nurses and orderlies were certain he was a doctor on glance alone, beguiled by a trick of the mind. Arriving at the double doors of Intensive Care, Patrick went as far as the nurse's station and scanned the name tag of the nurse minding her paperwork.

"Nurse Hannover. Patient Tania Bentley—what's her condition?" Patrick asked, trying to sound appropriately doctor-like given that his sole medical reference was a crash course in prime-time television. He felt like a soap opera star, aware of the immensity of his role and swimming in a sea of knowledge to which he was barely privy. The nurse, a big blonde saddled with pregnancy fat that she'd never lost, shot Patrick an annoyed glance. She did a double take, her demeanor instantly changing into a kind of congenial deference she probably offered those physicians she liked.

"Oh, I'm sorry, doctor," she said. She slid over to the computer. "Bentley, you said?"

Patrick nodded.

"She's stable," the nurse said after a moment, then rattled off a long list of vital signs that mostly meant nothing to him. Patrick nodded again, catching small snippets of information in the dense flood of facts.

"I don't recognize you," she said, finally. "Which department are you with?"

"I'm her family physician," Patrick replied with a warming smile. "I'll be back tomorrow to check on her."

The nurse smiled back, charmed by his unnatural presence. He always felt a little guilty using his tricks on the innocent. *I can drink a person's blood, but manipulating them makes me feel like shit. How fucked up is that?*

Patrick left.

Out the emergency room door and into the cold night air, Patrick waited for a taxi to run by. He didn't notice the nearby limousine until the window rolled down, a familiar face staring back at him.

"You're not Duce," the limo passenger said, "But I suppose you'll do."

"You're lucky." Persephone stroked the leather of the limo's seat. "At least you had a name to go by."

Patrick grunted, trying not to betray any information, not to Persephone. He wasn't even sure why he was there, but thought it best not to antagonize a daughter of the Invictus until he could uncover her interest in Duce. "Didn't get her name?" Patrick asked.

"There wasn't much opportunity after I'd insulted her."

"You insulted Tania?" Patrick said, amused yet hardly surprised.

"Rather not discuss it," Persephone replied, her eyes darting away.

Patrick was impressed at Persephone's small streak of candor; her capacity for guilt. "Fair enough," he said. "But since you're being honest, here, what's your interest in Duce?"

"It's nothing to you," she said.

"Maybe," Patrick admitted, "but it's something to you. Why else would you stake out the hospital, waiting for Duce? Unless you're looking to turn him in."

"Hardly. If that's what I wanted, I'd have other people do it for me and claim the credit. No, I have a matter to discuss with Duce. As a friend."

"I'm his friend too. Tell me. I'll make sure he gets the message."

"You're his friend?" Persephone said, her expression disbelieving.

"You don't trust me? Well, you know how I feel about you, then."

"At least I'm not betraying him!"

"What the *hell* are you talking about?"

"Why have the Carthians turned their back on Duce?"

"What?"

"Oh," Persephone realized. She knocked on the limo window. The chauffeur standing outside opened the door. "Well, if you don't know then...."

Patrick reached over and shut the door, surprising the driver. "What're you going on about?" he asked.

"You don't trust me, remember, and it appears that the Carthians don't trust you either. How unfortunate."

"Damn it, stop playing games! You came to see Duce, but you don't know where he is. I do. What is it he needs to know?"

"I have information that Duce and *you* don't have. I want to help Duce, but I'll tell him when I see him. The faster you arrange that, the faster—"

"You don't think I can get that information myself?" Patrick asked.

"Unlikely. If the Carthians haven't told you what they're doing to begin with, why would they tell you now? Duce is in trouble and as his friend, so are you. Where is he?"

Patrick paused a moment. "I'm not sure," he finally conceded, "but I can find out."

The West Side projects, better known as "the jets," served as bunkers in the battlefields of local gang wars. Built on the no-frills principles of affordable housing, these high-rises of aged concrete were North America's contemporary internment camps, ones whose enclosures were economic and whose guards also served as police officers.

Anyone says different probably lives in places that are paradises just because they're not here, Duce thought. He was on foot again, this time moving between the 15-story buildings and their communal parking lots and concrete gardens. He ignored the accumulated, unattended trash that had been thrown from windows, the syringes from local junkies and the glittering mosaic of broken liquor bottles. He paid cursory heed to the addicts wedged deep in the shadows, unable to extricate themselves from their darkness, and the gang members huddled tight together, eyeing warily anyone outside their set. Duce knew he should have played it safe, but the Beast in him wouldn't rest easy until it tasted blood. Part of him *needed* a fight. Without realizing it, Duce's neck sloped slightly forward, his head swiveling like a jungle cat, the details of his environment sharpening to a lurid edge. He glided along the pavement, with an even-weighted gait that suggested he could erupt into violence between one heartbeat and the next. It was only natural. He was hunting someone…

…Law…

…but he wasn't sure where to look.

The only certainty was that wherever Law called home, the locals probably knew him. Law had always earned friends, allies and loyalty far quicker than Duce. He was a natural leader, and when they were kids, it was a source of friendly rivalry between the two boys. Duce never liked admitting he was a follower, even though Law treated him like a brother and never a subordinate. They hung together, they rode together and they killed together. That was the nature of their lives.

After they *parted ways*, which was Duce-speak for his own betrayal in the matter, Duce eventually justified the breaking of their friendship by claiming Law was good at using people by making them feel valuable and wanted. Folks offered of themselves rather than him cajoling their loyalties from them like some emotional grifter. Law made easy martyrs of others—or at least, that's what Duce made himself believe to remove the sting of his own actions.

Finding Law was potentially easy. Duce had learned a while back how to summon an acquaintance into his presence with nothing but a directed thought; he could draw Law to him rather than searching him out. The person usually felt compelled to make the trip, often dismissing the summons as a hunch rather than an urge. Law, however, was rarely without allies and guards. Where Law traveled, his heavily armed entourage followed. And, frankly, Duce wasn't sure what he wanted from the man. Law was likely involved in the drive-by shooting, but why this reaction after over a decade of nothing? Duce had waited for some fall-out from his betrayal of Law and his former gang peers, but it had never arrived. Was this finally it? Or was Duce simply reacting out of a need for revenge? Again, Duce wondered whether being vampire dictated his survival responses, or if this thought carried the cold analytical reason of will and choice. It was hard to differentiate one from the other; both were ingrained aspects of his personality, whether he wanted them to be or not. Was the urge to confront Law a mirror to his bestial nature, a reflection of survival logic that reasoned Law was likely responsible for the drive-by and thus needed "handling?" Or was it simply human pride that demanded he rage against someone, anyone, who tried to hurt him—in this case, Law being the likeliest target of opportunity?

Duce wasn't sure enough to act. And truth was, he also wanted to see Law, to settle a curious itch.

They had been best friends once.

The cell phone vibrated, the display reading *Patrick Morneau*. Now wasn't a good time, so Duce let it ring, but it buzzed again, and a third time after. Duce figured there would be three angry messages waiting for him when he got around to them later.

"He's not answering," Patrick said, closing the cell. "Stubborn motherfucker."

"Not good" Persephone said. "It'll be ten times worse if someone catches Duce."

"Is there anything you can do? Pull some strings?"

"I've already done enough to land me in hot water."

"And you'll do plenty more." Patrick said coldly.

"Are you threatening me, Patrick?" Persephone studied Patrick, gauging his body language: the way he sat, the squint of his eyes. Nothing he did seemed hostile, but then again, he was more experienced than she was. Persephone shifted in her chair, acutely aware of the confines of her limousine.

"Ain't my thing," Patrick responded. "I'm just saying you seem to have greater stakes in Duce than you're letting on. I think Duce is important to whatever schemes you got cooking."

"Whatever, Patrick. When you talk to Duce, give him this number." Persephone handed Patrick her cell phone number. "Tell him I'll see what I can do to help."

Persephone knocked on the car's window. The chauffeur opened the door and Patrick stepped out into the hospital's parking lot. The chauffeur closed the door.

Persephone watched Patrick walk away. She flipped open her cell and dialed.

"Hello, Demetria? Yes, good. You see that man walking away? Follow him, please? Let me know when he finds Duce."

With that, Persephone closed the cell and pressed the limousine's intercom button on the armrest. "Home, please, driver."

Duce watched from the shadows, night's slow river drifting past him. Into the small hours, the lights of the jets winked out one by one, though the blue glow of televisions still painted some windows. Finally, the buildings were quiet except for the occasional crack of distant gunfire or lowrider that rumbled by, eager eyes on patrol for their gang. It was a scant couple of hours before dawn, and Duce was tired of waiting around. He was stalling, indecisive. He hated being indecisive.

Closing his eyes, Duce envisioned Laurence Michaels in his mind. Brother with a soul patch, deep black eyes

lucien soulban

that women loved, and a smile that flashed like a string of pearls. Brother with a square jaw to Duce's angular features, and at least two inches on his height. Brother with skin a dark Nigerian black to Duce's lighter tones and near-Oriental features.

Focused on that image, Duce concentrated and sent out a single, directed thought to Law:

Come to me. Now.

And Duce waited. He hoped to catch Law in his sleep, off guard and away from his entourage who were hopefully back at home. Twenty minutes passed before Duce spotted activity at the main entrance to one building. Law strode out, carefully, testing the waters, looking out across the empty lots. Likely, Duce knew, the summons confused him, put him on edge. It was like being haunted by a compulsion instead of a ghost. He had to go, and he knew exactly where to go. Problem was, for Duce, the target still possessed enough wits to make certain arrangements.

In Law's case, it was bringing backup.

Four men accompanied Law, looking like rap artist roadies, and they made little effort to conceal their guns. Tek-9 and Scorpion semi-automatics. Duce didn't recognize three of the men, but he did know Charles Finley. A large man who never met a refrigerator he didn't like. Finley's expressions had two gears, mean and meaner, and he looked like the killer he was.

The ensemble of five approached Duce's position. Duce drew on the power in his veins, ready to bolt like a jackrabbit. Five humans were still five humans with guns. Law saw Duce and slowed down. He whispered something to the others; their expressions changed and went marble hard at the sight of Duce. Charles didn't look happy, but Law...

"Shit," Law said, a smile crossing his face. "Didn't figure I'd be seeing you for some time, but somehow I knew I was coming to see you."

"Want me to bounce this bitch?" Charles said, staring at Duce.

Law thought about it for a moment with a half-grin, then shook his head. "Nah. We ain't about to start up shit at this early hour, are we, dawg?" He stared at Duce, waiting for an answer, his grin lingering.

"You know why I'm here?" Duce said.

"Nah. Just pleased to see a brother. Y'know, I think I see your pops more often than you do. What's up with that?"

"None of your damn business," Duce said. He didn't intend to snarl at that old wound.

"Shit, Duce. I'm just asking. You and your pops used to be tight. But you don't see him no more."

"Fuck you, Law. I'm not here to discuss my pops with you. And I'm not here to reminisce."

"Reminisce?" Charles said. "Big word for a punk-ass bitch like you. Here's one I learned. Eviscerate. As in I'm going to fuck you up."

"Some dude beat your ass with a dictionary, Charles?" Duce asked, shooting a stare-down at the man. "'Cause I know you can't read."

Charles was about to move when Law, laughing, stopped the big man with a raised hand. "Don't pay him no mind, Charles. He's just talking smack. What d'you want, Duce?"

"I'm here about those bangers you sent to cap my ass. They missed, bitch."

"I didn't send shit, Duce," Law said, his smile never fading. "And if I did, I'd send Charles to do the deed."

"And I wouldn't miss, either," Charles said.

"Bullshit! I saw those motherfuckers, Law. They flashed your colors. Black P-Stone motherfuckers."

"You're behind the times, Duce. I don't run with the People's Nation no more, or any of their sets."

"What? They *let* you leave?" Duce said, laughing.

"We're Black Guerrilla Family, now. And the sets give us much love. We're into more important shit. No time to bang."

"You? BGF? Revolutionary? Fuck Uncle Sam and all that shit?"

lucien soulban

"We all are, motherfucker," one of Law's enforcers said. The others murmured in agreement.

"So you see," Law said, "I ain't got time to be messing with you. The BGF got bigger things on the horizon. Besides," Law said, taking a small step forward, "I wouldn't want to fuck with any of your new rules."

"Rules? What rules?"

Law smiled and started to walk away; his men backed up and kept their eyes on Duce, their guns ready. "The rules," Law said. "I believe you motherfuckers call it the Masquerade."

Chapter Five

"You sure he meant 'Masquerade'?" Patrick asked.

"What other Masquerade is there?" Duce replied, pacing at the base of the stairs. Above them, the Art Institute loomed, draped in shadows and meager lights. "He said Masquerade, as in, the laws governing your vampire asses."

"Damn. That isn't good."

"I know. I thought maybe Law knew something about the hit, but if he knows about me...we're into some higher shit now."

Patrick nodded, like he was contemplating a painting. Finally he asked, "Duce. You know I never pry into your personal shit, right?"

"Yeah. You can be a bossy motherfucker, but you keep out of my business. Why? You about to pry?" Duce asked, raising his eyebrows.

"Law and you were tight back in the day?"

Duce shrugged, a sort of noncommittal gesture for an admission. "We were—road dogs."

Patrick looked confused.

"Road dogs," Duce explained. "Best friends within our set...our gang. We did all sorts of shit together. Shit I ain't proud of."

"So if you were best friends, why's he gunning for you now?"

Duce cringed. He kept his old life six feet under and never shared this part of it with anyone. It was embarrassing, and had anyone else asked, Duce would have put them in their place. But this was Patrick, and that was all that needed saying.

"I'm not sure he is," Duce admitted. "Shit, I'm not sure of anything, but now's not the time."

Patrick's gaze was unrelenting, his expression unmoving.

"Later, then, okay?" Duce said. "Sheriff's here."

As the name implied, sheriff was a function of vampire society, an officer of the Prince's court who enforced the Masquerade. In this case, the sheriff was Benjamin Nguyen, a vampire of idiosyncratic traits whose jurisdiction covered the neighborhood where the drive-by occurred. He arrived in his signature car, a gold 69' Eldorado in near-pristine condition. The engine under the hood, however, was no longer a V-8, but some modified beast fit for street shredding; it rumbled at the barest hint of the gas pedal. Not that Nguyen was a street racer, or even looked the part of a new urban rebel. At 5'7" with a slightly portly frame, he was an unassuming man with a taciturn, yet respectful demeanor. Black hair shaved Marine style along the sides, sharp eyes and visible scars from his youth indicated he could also raise some hell. Nguyen rarely lost his temper, but he was known for judicious spurts of violence to make a point.

Flanking Nguyen were two Caucasian men, both thick in the collar and towering above the shorter sheriff by a good foot. They provided the perfect contrast to him, and often distracted people from the real threat, Nguyen himself.

"I don't have time for this," Duce whispered as Nguyen approached.

"Make the time," Patrick whispered back.

"Patrick," Nguyen said. "I'm glad to see you kept your word. Duce. I'm glad you came to us. I respect your foresight in this matter."

"Well," Duce, "truth be told, I'm not even sure why I'm here."

"To answer some questions," Nguyen said. "The incident at Rap'sody was distressing."

"To the Primogen, you mean."

"To everyone," Nguyen replied.

"Well, it wasn't a breach of the Masquerade if that's what you're worried about."

"That's what we're here to determine. But first, I'd like to hear your side of the story.

"Look, it's easy. I come out of the nightclub and some motherfuckers cruise by, busting caps. I got hit three times. And I got people bleeding all around me. So I booked," Duce said with a shrug, "or I was going to start feeding."

Nguyen stared straight into Duce's eyes, studying him for any insincerity. Duce stared straight back, unflinching, uncompromising.

"Is that the only reason you fled?"

"No. I also booked so I wouldn't have to explain why I got three holes in my chest and no heartbeat."

"Why were they after you?" Nguyen asked, again with the hard stare.

"No clue. But I ran with a fierce crew in my day. Pissed off a lot of players from different sets."

"Any idea which gang was involved?"

"Nah, man. They were too busy shooting to flash me gang colors, but look, Nguyen, this is my business. I'll settle it."

"Not the way it works. Frankly, people would love your head on this."

"Well, whoever people are, they can fuck themselves. This isn't vampire business, Nguyen. It's some stupid shit from my breathing days. Let me handle it."

"No," Nguyen said. "Prince Maxwell wants some questions answered first."

Duce shot Patrick a look: *I knew this was a bad idea.* Patrick looked guilty.

"Come with me. No arguments, Duce."

Duce sized up Nguyen, but he knew better than to challenge the short Vietnamese man, much less the two bruisers accompanying him. Nguyen was tough as nails. Easygoing, but tough enough to dispute Solomon Birch on occasion. Nguyen was also smart, and likely had some provisional plan in case Duce bolted.

Duce finally nodded.

"Good," Nguyen said. "I admire your courage. Being a vampire often makes fools or cowards of us. I'm glad neither's the case here." He turned to Patrick. "And you were wise to bring him to me first."

"Don't make me regret that decision," Patrick said.

Patrick watched the Eldorado drive off and questioned his own advice in the matter. Did he do right by his friend? Or had he just cost Duce his existence? He didn't know, and the uncertainty of it weighed on him. There was no way to determine the gravity of the situation, or if Duce was going to survive it.

Persephone's limousine pulled up alongside the curb.

"Ah, Patrick," Persephone said through the open window. "I wish you'd followed my simple instructions. I do have Duce's best interests at heart."

"Bullshit. Maybe you're trying to help, but you've never done anyone a favor that you didn't prosper from first."

"Perhaps, but tell Duce to call me. Tell him Adenauer and Fulsome are moving against him."

"Adrian? You sure?"

Persephone looked amused at the question. "Just tell him," she said.

Patrick was about to walk away when he turned around. "By the way. Call off whoever it is you got tailing me, 'cause if I catch him, I'm kicking his ass."

"*Her.* You'll kick *her* ass," Persephone said as the limousine pulled away slowly. "And I'll be sure to let her know."

Ike Barlow was an ugly lump of a vampire; he was a string of expletives when no adjective would suffice to describe him; gashes for eye slits, buckteeth ending in yellowed points and patches of hair like weeds on a desolate and cracked lawn. It looked like God had used a scalpel instead of pencils to draw Ike.

He was Nosferatu, a breed of vampire known for their inherent creepiness, physical or otherwise. Vampires also called Barlow "The Surgeon," though few who endured his questions ever revealed why. Instead, their eyes went distant and glassy, and they were *back there* again, in a room where Barlow waited for them to return.

Duce was in that room now, and truthfully, he was a little relieved to see Barlow dressed in a clean-pressed, charcoal-gray, pin-stripe suit. Barlow looked sharp and ready for an outing, despite the pin-head grotesquery that ballooned from his neck. Not exactly the outfit one chooses for torture. Of greater relief was that Duce wasn't tied down to the chair at the center of the spartan, concrete room, though the trolley sitting in one corner did worry him, as did the smell of crusted blood and the crimson-spackled blanket covering whatever devices lay on the trolley.

"Mr. Carter, please sit, you'll be more comfortable," Barlow said with the voice of a patient host.

Duce shrugged. "Nah, I'm good."

"I insist," Barlow said. "Sit."

The word rumbled in Duce's ears; his legs betrayed him. Duce sat, pushed down by the force of Barlow's will.

"There, isn't that better?" Barlow asked. "I'm so glad I insisted." Barlow moved behind Duce, and Duce struggled not to turn around, to betray his discomfort... his lack of control.

"What d'you want?" Duce said. "Why the fuck am I here? Where's Maxwell?"

"*Prince* Maxwell is currently preoccupied. He has little time to attend to the indiscretions of some street urchin."

"Fuck you, you ugly bitch!"

"*Language*, Mr. Carter."

"Fuck you. I don't even know why I'm here. I didn't do shit."

"Well, that's what we're here to determine." Barlow moved to the trolley in the corner and reached under the bloodied cloth. He removed something small and glossy black, cupping it in the center of his palm. From where Duce was sitting, it looked like the shell of some kind of bug.

"Better than sacrificing livestock, I assure you," Barlow said with an amused grin, then concentrated a moment, his mouth silently dancing over an incantation. The beetle shell lost its shiny luster, and within seconds, disintegrated into a trickle of ash. Satisfied, Barlow faced Duce again.

"Now," the Nosferatu said, "tell me about the drive-by. And I should warn you. No lies."

"I already told Nguyen what happened."

"Did you tell him everything?"

"Yeah, I fucking told him everything."

Duce shuddered as a sudden scrabbling filled his throat for purchase and rushed up into his mouth. The chair fell away; Duce pitched forward violently, suddenly on his knees and vomiting. Glossy black beetles poured past his lips and out, spilling to the floor and crawling over his face and neck. He batted the roaches from his head and backpedaled against wall spitting, cursing, screaming.

"What the *fuck*, man!"

"Mr. Carter, I warned you not to lie."

"You *fuck*!" Duce charged forward, the razor-sharp claws of the Beast raking his soul.

"Stop," Barlow said, his voice calm.

Duce fell back to floor, his body depleted of whatever initiative had propelled him forward. He was weak, his limbs robbed of their strength, his mind sluggish.

"Now," Barlow said. "What is it you didn't tell the good Sheriff?"

"None of your business," Duce said, feeling the "your" slur and drag across his tongue. He still felt the roaches in his mouth.

"I'll be the judge of that. What is it you failed to mention, Mr. Carter?"

"That I fucked your mother." Duce immediately regretted the words, his retort choked off by the rising plague in his throat.

"A witless remark," Barlow said, watching Duce vomit more beetles. "And another lie."

"Stop," Duce said, weakened, drained by the horrifying influence Barlow had over him.

"Shortly, I assure you. You could expedite this matter by speaking the truth, you know."

"I—" Duce stopped short of saying anything else. His mind raced, trying to choose the right words to avoid another purge of bugs.

"Go on."

"The drive-by," Duce said. "Had nothing to do with me as a vampire."

"But it was against you."

"Yeah, but I fucking told Nguyen that already."

"But not why."

"I told him," Duce said, pausing to wipe his mouth with the back of his hand and crush a beetle beneath the sole of his shoe. "I told him it was shit from my mortal life."

No bugs. Barlow nodded.

"Nothing to do with vampires? Our society? The Masquerade?"

"Nothing."

"Are you sure?"

Duce hesitated again. "No."

"What didn't you say, then? To Nguyen."

"Fuck you," Duce said, getting back to his feet. His strength returned in slow sips, his limbs invigorated. "Maybe I can't lie, but your bugs can't force jack-shit from me."

"Sit," Barlow said, and Duce complied through gritted teeth, despite himself. At least he possessed the wherewithal to set the chair upright before sitting.

"You are correct," Barlow said. "My pets cannot force the truth from you, but then again, neither am I without my means." Barlow walked back to the trolley and removed a small silver chain. "You're proving a most expensive task, Mr. Carter. After the beetles, most vampires are more than eager to facilitate my investigation. You, however, require the next step."

Holding the watch by the band, Barlow mouthed another observance that quickly brought ashen ruination upon his sacrifice. Duce's strength guttered like a lit candle caught in a strong wind; his head dropped against his chest.

lucien soulban

He was tired, an immortal fatigue burdening his soul. All he wanted to do was sleep.

"Feeling more compliant, now?" Barlow asked.

Duce shook his head. "Bitch," he muttered.

"Fine. Go to the trolley and pull back the cloth."

Duce complied, moving with the grace of a puppet whose strings sagged and knotted together. He pulled back the cloth and stared at the remaining watches, and the row of surgical equipment; scalpels, chest spreaders, probes and long needles, all dulled and stained through repeated play.

"Take the scalpel," Barlow instructed, "and extend your left forearm."

To Duce's horror, he complied, his left forearm exposed to the gleaming edge of the scalpel in his own hand.

"Nguyen said I'd be safe," Duce said, trying to save himself.

"Oh, Sheriff Nguyen is an honorable man. He meant his promise and, frankly, by tomorrow, you'll believe he kept his word as well. Now. Place the scalpel against your left forearm. That's good. And start cutting."

"I should have been there," Solomon Birch said. "Should have been me conducting that interrogation."

Ike Barlow tried to smile sympathetically, but his shark's grin offset the effect and his smile turned into a leer. "Well, I'm sure Prince Maxwell still has his uses for Mr. Carter. And I assure you. He suffered appropriately."

"Not appropriately enough. What did you find out?"

Barlow shrugged. "He's stubborn, I'll give him that. I would need more time with him, but Prince Maxwell wanted to see him, so I had to make Mr. Carter reasonably presentable. He is hiding something, though. Whatever it is, it's very deep and terribly personal. He won't give it up without a fight."

"So he doesn't remember what you did to him."

Barlow looked wistful. "Not one cut, I'm afraid. It's not foolproof, of course, but the mind tends to suppress traumatic experiences as a matter of course. Normally, I'd leave a memory or two intact just to give that nightmarish certainty that something foul happened. Not with Mr. Carter, however, as per your instructions."

"Not what I wanted, trust me, but the Prince moves in mysterious ways."

"You don't agree?" Barlow asked.

"I respect the Prince."

"Of course."

"But I don't believe you can control something forever... even through blood."

"Then what would you suggest?"

"Control it for as long as you think you can, then neutralize it as a threat."

"A wise course of action. Dust can't fight back."

"No," Birch said. "Destruction isn't the answer. It's rarely the answer you think it is."

"I'm surprised."

"That I feel that way?" Birch asked.

"In part, yes. I wouldn't have figured you for the voice of temperance."

"Don't get me wrong. Violence is a useful tool, but destroying a brethren isn't. Once you kill, it becomes the preferred method of dealing with your problems."

"Is that experience speaking?" Barlow asked.

Birch shot Barlow a blank, neutral look. "Don't go fishing where you can't swim."

"I'm only curious, brother Birch. You surprised me, is all. What is your plan, then? For Duce Carter, I mean."

"I'll help Prince Maxwell see the truth. That Carter is more trouble than he's worth."

"And how do you plan to accomplish that?"

Birch shook his head, his smile widening at the thought. "No, no. I don't want to say anything just yet."

"Of course," Barlow said with a bow. "Should you ever need help, however, your brothers and sisters in the Lancea Sanctum stand ready at your side."

"Actually," Birch said, "I do need help with one thing. You think your Nosferatu brethren can help?"

lucien soulban

Barlow offered a wide, broken smile in response.

"How do you feel, Terrell?"

Law studied Terrell carefully, his hands on the shorter man's shoulders, looking deep into his black eyes. Terrell, had blockish features and well-groomed corn rows. He cocked a smile, his lips thick.

"Fierce, motherfucker," Terrell said, almost bouncing as he walked into the weathered apartment. "I feel fierce."

"Cool. Didn't hurt none, did it?" Law said.

"Nah. It just felt..." Terrell hesitated. "Fuck that. Shit's like nothing I ever felt before, y'know what I'm saying?"

"No," Law said, "but it's cool."

"It's just—like I'm hungry, all the goddamn time!" Terrell said with a nervous laugh. "Feels like I'm a damn crackhead. Can you believe that shit! I need blood. Fuck, I need it now."

"Terrell. Remember why I picked you?" Law said, trying to distract Terrell from the hunger.

"Yah, man."

"I picked you 'cause you're a fierce motherfucker. I picked you 'cause I knew you could control this."

"Yeah. Yeah. I remember," Terrell said. "But I didn't know it would be like this. One minute, I'm feeling like a goddamn god. The next, I want to drink from every pussy in sight."

"Yeah, well, we got your back on that," Law said and walked over to the bedroom door. The door opened and Charles came out holding a struggling hostage—a twenty-something African-American in baggy clothing, his head covered in a burlap sack, his hands tied behind his back. Charles threw his cargo to the floor.

"But," Terrell said, "he's Afrikan."

"No," Law said, his voice firm. "He's an Amerikan bitch. Been providing the regime with intelligence about our movement!" Law sent his foot hard into the man's face, dropping him flat to the floor.

The man moaned through the burlap sack and writhed on the floor in pain. Likely his nose was broken and his teeth cracked. The front of the sack turned a dark color, wet and moist.

Terrell's nostrils flared and his eyes focused on the hostage.

"That's right, brother," Law said, nodding for Charles to make his way out of the apartment. Law was heading that way himself. "This bitch is no longer one of us. No longer protected by us. He's lunch to you," Law said. "Super-size his ass."

Law closed the door in time to hear the muffled groans as Terrell descended on the hostage. Charles looked shocked, and curious enough to want to go back inside, but Law stood in his way.

"This ain't no fucking zoo," Law said, laughing. "Let the man eat in peace."

"Man," Charles said, "that's some fucked up shit in there."

Law nodded. "Yeah. I know. Don't got much of a choice, y'know? Shit's too important to back out now."

"We all going to do this shit, dawg" Charles said.

Law nodded. "Don't worry yourself about that now. Just be ready for Joliet. You're taking Terrell with you for a test run."

Chapter Six

Sleep proved discomforting, more so than usual. Duce stirred awake, exhausted, aching and unsettled. His hunger, the blood thirst, roared in his ears, his reserves tapped thin, though he couldn't remember why. He reached for his cell phone and punched in Patrick's number. He remembered seeing Patrick last night, but his memories felt smudged by God's thumb.

"Hello," Patrick answered.

"'Sup? It's me."

"You okay?"

"Don't remember much after that shit with the Sheriff."

"Man, I'm really sorry about that."

"Time for I told you so later. I gotta feed. I'm ravenous."

"All right, but come see me after. We need to talk."

"Cool," Duce said, hanging up. He stumbled to the bathroom and stared at his reflection. Vague flashes shot through his head. He remembered speaking with Prince Maxwell last night and being pumped for answers before two goons dropped him outside Elysium. He shook his head hard, trying to wipe away that image.

Every time he went to see Maxwell, he was forced to drink the Prince's blood. He could still taste the potent vitae in his mouth, the same blood that the Prince used to keep Duce servile. It was the same trick he'd considered using on Tania, the blood oath, but Duce recognized the hypocrisy in his actions. It was slavery, forced feelings of loyalty through a strange addiction. Sure, it meant Tania would never betray his secret, but the same chains tied him to the Prince.

Not that Duce had a choice. To bring about a peaceful evolution of the city's antiquated political model, Duce had to give the Carthians some sign of progress. Otherwise they'd pursue change through revolution, and Duce knew that wasn't the answer. Instead, he sought concessions from the Prince, and the price he paid for those concessions was the blood oath. Not that the Carthians knew about it. If they did, he'd appear weak, and predators, even Carthians, rarely tolerated weakness in their ranks.

Duce's anger surged. He'd agreed to the blood oath so that the Prince would give the Carthians certain allowances and so he would feel like they weren't as threatening as their rhetoric claimed. But the Prince was slow in providing those concessions. After all, Duce was now enthralled through a bond that made him compliant to the Prince's wishes, and so Maxwell could drag his ass for as long as he wanted.

Duce struck out at the mirror, shattering it into fragments.

"Why would the Carthians be moving against Duce Carter?" Halliburton asked. He massaged his gold pinky ring with his thumb and offered a half-smile that Persephone always found lascivious. "More importantly," he said, "why should I care?"

Persephone matched Halliburton's smile, though she knew she couldn't match his looks. Vampires quipped that he'd been Embraced during a photo shoot, but truth was, he was better at keeping pace with mortal trends than most vampires. Clean-shaven with unblemished milk-white skin, black eyes that matched the timbre of his hair, and angled features, he cut a handsome if androgynous figure.

"Well," Persephone said, settling back into the living room settee, "with Duce in place, the Carthians are manageable. He keeps their noses clean and their actions respectable."

"No, no, no, no," Halliburton said with a quick, darting laugh. "Respectable Carthians are an oxymoron, like *sophomore.* I will admit that Duce does keep their noses clean, though I'd reword that particular analogy. I love your outfit, by the way," he said, suddenly shifting tack. "Did you wear that for me?"

"Like it?" Persephone asked and glanced down at her ensemble; a simple black button-up shirt with a black and red scarf draped over one shoulder, black pants that truncated at mid-calf and a wide belt with metal studs. "I was inspired by Capucine and the Beatnik look. That was the *haute couture* of your day, wasn't it?"

"It was, though I would have enjoyed the Sophia Loren or Brigitte Bardot look as well. Capucine is a nice touch, though."

"Thank you."

"Ahhh, Persephone, that's what I like about you. How many of your ilk would know to dress up to the era of their associates?"

"I couldn't say," Persephone said, smiling "but not many, I'd like to think."

"Well then, you've earned my attentions. Why should I care what happens to Duce?"

"Because as it stands, he's a stabilizing force for the Carthians. He keeps them from acting out."

"That he does."

"Whether the Primogen realizes it or not," Persephone said, "Duce actually helps maintain the status quo. With him around, the Carthians are less likely to strike against the Invictus. They'll maintain the rhetoric, but Duce doesn't believe in bloody revolutions."

"All right," Halliburton said. It was obvious he knew where the conversation was headed, but wanted to hear Persephone voice his observations.

"Bethany Adenauer is the exact opposite," she said. "She's reactionary and she's short-sighted. At least Duce understands that longevity is his leverage. Bethany doesn't, and that makes her dangerous. At best, she'll turn the Carthians into a united front with dreams of a Mao Tse-Tung style revolution. At worst, she'll shatter the Carthians into camps and give us more groups to worry about."

"So what you're saying," Halliburton said, "is that helping Duce is actually helping maintain the status quo? Interesting sell, Persephone, but I am curious about one thing."

"Ask."

"What's your interest in Duce? And spare me the 'he's good for the Invictus,' speech."

Persephone smiled. "Nothing gets past you, does it?"

"Not even flattery," Halliburton responded.

"Duce is an asset, and valuable one."

"An asset? That's all?"

"I like him, certainly—it's hard not to like that kind of passion, especially in your enemy. But he's also my trump card. I control Duce, I control the Carthians."

"Nobody controls the Carthians, dear, not even themselves. That's why they're dangerous."

"Perhaps," Persephone said, "but I only need to foster the illusion of control for the Invictus to take me seriously. To negotiate for my help."

"Ahhh, there she is. I see her now."

"Who?"

"The Ventrue in you," Halliburton said, referring to Persephone's lineage as the kingmakers of the vampire world. "But why tell me all this?"

Persephone shrugged. "Because you're horrifyingly good at reading people. And because you've already figured out most of this."

"True. I do relish the confession. Thank you for not disappointing, and thank you for not lying. So what is it you want from me, and bear in mind that my help is a one-time deal."

"Those *motherfuckers*," Duce said with a snarl. He paced around Patrick's apartment, an impressive feat given the confines of the living room and the tight passages between the simple wood furniture. Several times, Patrick had to pull in his legs from where he sat on the armchair.

lucien soulban

"They think they can take my shit from me," Duce ranted.

"Duce, man. Beth's always been trying to undermine you. That's nothing new. You gotta figure out why Adrian's with her on this. Hell, maybe Persephone doesn't have her shit straight."

"I'm planning on finding out, trust me. It's time to visit Adenauer."

"Don't think that's smart."

"Patrick, I'm not sitting on my ass and watching her take what's mine."

"First off, the Carthians don't belong to you. Second, going after Beth isn't going to solve a damn thing. She wouldn't be where she is without the backing of the Carthians. We need to talk to Fulsome. He's got the pull for this."

"But he hates that bitch as much as I do."

"Yeah. So what did you do to piss him off enough to help her?"

"Me?" Duce asked, disbelief spread wide across his face.

"Yeah, you. Maybe you don't want to hear this, Duce, but you've been pissing off Carthians since the day you were bit."

"Fuck them. I tell them the truth."

"Your truth, you mean."

"No. The truth, Patrick. Do you know why the Black Panthers were doomed to fail?"

"Boy," Patrick snapped, "don't tell me about the Black Panthers. They were my generation! The Panthers failed because of the government."

"The Black Panthers were going to fail regardless because they didn't recognize that revolution in a capitalist society needs money. Instead the Panthers looked down on all that shit, like they were too big for it. Now take motherfuckers like Tupac."

"Tupac was a thug."

"Yeah he was. He was a thug. But he was a proper thug."

"What the fuck does that mean? A *proper* thug?"

"Tupac was second generation Panther, and he knew that to lead a revolution, you gotta have the money and the power to demand the respect. Otherwise the respect you earn is nothing but a handout. You can't turn your back on a capitalist society and still hope to change it."

Patrick looked at Duce like he'd lost his mind. "And what the fuck does this shit have to do with the Carthians?"

"Everything. The Carthians don't get that you can't change the system without understanding how the system works. You can't revolutionize shit without using the system against itself. The good rap artists, the ones trying to end inequality, understand that. You take brothers like Mos Def, Tupac, all of them. They don't sport the bling-bling because they're flaunting it. They know how the system works and how to use it against itself."

"The Carthians aren't that naïve, Duce."

"They're not? Bullshit! They come in here and act like nobody's tried changing the status quo—like they're the first motherfuckers to stand up to the Invictus in centuries. Only they're not the first. All the others failed because they didn't understand the nature of their enemy—understand their tools. You come in with all the noise, and the Invictus will bounce your ass. Hard."

"So," Patrick said. "You think you're the first one to try and change the system from the inside. I guarantee you that half the Invictus you're trying to save started out like you."

"Maybe, but I'm not them. And I have one tool that men like King and Malcolm never had: Time. I got more time than both of them had, combined, to change the system. But it requires patience and subtlety, and the Carthians don't get that."

"Fine. Look, let's just speak with Adrian, all right?" Patrick said, getting up. "But I want you to think about something, and think about it carefully. No arguments. No disagreements. Just consider this. You want to change shit? Cool. But remember something. King and Malcolm never had time because they were murdered, not because they weren't vampires. They were shot, and you may be immune to aging, but you ain't immune to dying."

"I'm sorry, Duce. You fucked up," Adrian said.

Duce matched Adrian's gaze with his own unblinking stare. Patrick watched quietly from an adjoining table in the empty, dark restaurant, which had come a long way since Duce was first there six months ago.

"So you say," Duce responded.

"You know what? I admire your pride, I really do," Adrian said. "It's taken you far. But the trouble with pride is that it can also screw you up."

"Adrian, please. Don't lecture me. You stab me in the back and then play like I deserved it?"

"Deserved it? No. I'll admit you didn't. But it was coming."

"Fuck, here we go again!"

"Yeah! Here we go again. You fucked up, Duce. The Carthians are tired of waiting for the right opportunities. We've done nothing to create those opportunities, and whenever someone is enterprising enough to try, you slam them down."

Duce looked at Patrick, incredulous. "Am I the only sane person here?"

"Welby's plan was sound."

"Bullshit! That's desperation and impatience talking. Welby's plan was full of bullet holes, and we would have been too."

"You turned your back on Welby, one of your own people, and now, no one's seen him in four months."

"You know what? If Welby was dumb enough to approach Steinitz alone, then he got what he deserved. And second of all—"

Patrick groaned. Duce and Adrian turned to Patrick, annoyed and surprised at the interruption.

"Damn! Y'all love to hear yourselves talk," Patrick said. "I've heard this argument a million times. You killed it months ago. Move on!"

"Fine by me," Duce said.

"Look, the point is, the Carthians are tired of waiting. We decided to act, with or without your support."

"Only you waited till I was being dragged over the coals so I didn't notice your power play? What? Are you afraid of facing me like a man?"

Adrian laughed. "We used the opportunity to our advantage. And for your information, we're only calling for a vote of no confidence in your leadership. Let the Carthians decide who's best to lead."

Duce laughed. "Bullshit! You and Adenauer probably strong-armed everyone into a decision, and you'll probably use the no-vote to promote yourself as my successor!"

"Doesn't change the fact that we still have a problem," Patrick said, elbow resting on his thighs, his gaze at his own feet. He waited for both men's attention before continuing. "A vote of no confidence means Duce can defend himself before an arbiter and all Carthians. It's his right. Problem is, Adrian, seeing as how you're our Myrmidon, you're hardly impartial."

"I'll assign someone else."

"Someone we both agree on," Duce said.

Adrian nodded. "I'll make the necessary arrangements."

"All right," Duce said and got up to leave. "Let me ask you something, though. I assume that if you get the no-confidence through, you'll go for the position of prefect?"

Fulsome shrugged.

"And Adenauer?" Duce asked

"Myrmidon."

Duce laughed. "That bitch is never impartial. And how long do you think it'll take her before she comes after your ass?"

"She'll never get enough votes."

"She'll get enough to be a thorn in your side," Duce said, heading out the door. "Adenauer will screw you over. If you survive me, of course."

Duce and Patrick were quiet as they walked back to Duce's black SUV, both men lost in their respective thoughts and misery.

"The Carthians never agree to anything unanimously," Patrick said, finally.

"Thinking the same thing," Duce said. "There's gotta be a couple of us who don't believe the hype."

"Brown and Hoff. Maybe Lubich? No, forget Lubich. She'll support Adenauer."

"You don't know that."

"The hell I don't," Patrick said, a straight-edged smile on his lips. "They're women. They'll support one another because they're folk. Just like you and me."

"Wait, hold up. You mean to say that if I was white, we wouldn't be friends?"

Patrick shrugged. "Not racist. I like white people. But they don't get it. They can't connect. I say shit, and you get it. Right?"

"True."

"I've met few white folks who don't put on airs. They're either uncomfortable around us and watch what they say— and you won't know it until they say something foolish and can't stop apologizing for it. Or they try playing themselves off as cool and treat you like a soul brother. In which case it comes off as insulting. I just don't want to deal with that shit."

Duce shook his head, but at least, he was smiling.

"What?" Patrick said, almost indignant. "Tell me, how many whites or Asians you got as friends?"

"Now?" Duce asked and paused to think. "None. But then, you're also the only brother I'm cool with. Don't trust most other motherfuckers."

Patrick nodded slowly. "Yeah, man. Same here. But before the bite, what color was your crew?"

"That's different," Duce said. "I didn't have much of a choice in my friends. It was where I grew up that mattered."

"Yeah, and *when* was my deciding factor. I was a child when Luther marched on Birmingham. Rosa Parks, Malcolm X, Angela Davis...man, I was raised on the laps of all these cats. But white people, they were a separate species back then. Some were helpful, most were—" Patrick shrugged— "Living in separate neighborhoods and going to separate schools, might as well have been another planet."

"Yeah, well, when I left my set, I started exploring—meeting different people. I mean, I ran with Latino and some Asian gangbangers, but it wasn't the same thing. I started associating with a different class of folk."

"I remember. I pointed you out to the Carthians, remember?"

"I know. But, hey man," Duce said, suddenly realizing something. He stopped walking and interrupted Patrick's progress as well. "I never asked you this, but why is it you never bit me? I mean, don't get me wrong, I'm glad my sire was a woman, and all."

"I asked Alexandra to bite you because I knew you wouldn't be down with another man doing the deed. Also, you wouldn't get hit with the same shit I did."

"Shit? What shit?"

"You know. Being called Chocolate Milk."

"Oh right. You had a white sire. They still call you that?"

"Doesn't matter," Patrick said, and resumed walking. "I didn't want you suffering for being my childe."

Duce popped open the doors of the SUV and let it idle a moment before he gunned the engine, getting ready to pop her out of neutral and put some burn on the street.

"I haven't forgotten," Patrick said, almost quiet.

"What?" Duce asked, bringing his foot off the accelerator and the engine back to a low purr.

"I haven't forgotten," Patrick said, "that you owe me a story. About your set?"

The comment robbed Duce of his wind; his shoulders sagged. He gunned the engine again and popped the gear into a hard first, screaming out of the parking space and into the street in one fluid swipe. They were two streets over before Duce said:

"Don't like talking about that shit. Besides, I got bigger problems now with the Carthians."

"Bigger problems than someone trying to kill you?"

"Look! I don't like talking about what happened with my set."

"You said you'd tell me later—"

"And I will, all right. Just not now. I need to worry about other shit first."

"Fine," Patrick said. "Later, then." The car was silent a moment before Duce turned on the stereo and drowned the quiet beneath the heavy word beats of a rap lyricist Patrick had no hopes of ever identifying.

"Where we headed?" Patrick asked.

"You said Persephone's been trying to reach me?"

"What d'you want with Persephone? She said her piece."

"Well. Since she's the only early warning we got about the Carthians, I'm figuring we should see what she wants to talk about."

"Nothing good."

"You don't know that. But she's got contacts, and I need help."

"Help doing what?"

"Help convincing the Carthians that I'm connected to the Invictus. That I can call in favors when I need to. Favors and contacts Adrian and Adenauer don't have." Duce didn't mention his connection to the Prince because he didn't want to explore that avenue yet, not unless he was desperate. It was bad enough he was drinking Maxwell's blood.

"And why would she do that?" Patrick asked.

"Because she needs me as much as I need her."

"You sure of that?"

Duce shrugged.

"You also need the Carthians' help. They're your kin."

"I know. We'll go see them first. Brown, Hoff *and* Lubich. I think Lubich will help us. We hook up with Persephone after that."

Chapter Seven

Gimble's offered a beautiful view of the city, complemented by the breezy jazz playing over the speakers. Through the windows, the lit Wrigley Building shimmered in the darkness, adding to the bar's romantic allure. Even the clientele was quiet, talking in watercolor tones, leaning in close to hear and enjoying the intimacy their proximity provided. Business suits and evening dresses were the order of the night, though Duce still cut a dashing figure in his casual black slacks and untucked long-sleeve burgundy satin shirt. Patrick, however, looked displaced, his faded jeans and baggy white sweater distinctively outside the scope of his environment. If it bothered anyone, nobody betrayed the slightest irritation. This was the kind of place people came to be alone, and the décor included high booths to provide that privacy.

Persephone was the exception. These days she dressed for the attention. Duce wasn't sure when the change happened, but she was different from the vampire he'd first met, more self-assured. Persephone drew attention to herself with her deep red crepe evening dress and its plunging neckline that betrayed her navel with the odd bounce. A double-looped band of pearls hung from her neck, and she drew stares away from the other women.

"Duce, Patrick," Persephone said, arriving at the table. Duce stood out of courtesy. "I'm glad you made it."

"Not sure what we're doing here," Patrick said while Duce seated Persephone before sitting himself.

"Well, Patrick. I'm not surprised you're here, even though this meeting was for Duce and myself."

"Patrick's my road dog," Duce said. "He hears what you have to say."

Persephone shrugged. "Fine, but if I'm going to help you, there are times it'll have to be you and me. Alone."

"Why are you trying to help him, anyways?" Patrick asked.

"Haven't we discussed this before?" Persephone replied.

"Not with Duce around."

"All right. I think Duce and I can help each other," she said with a comfortable smile.

"How?" Duce asked.

"Well. Adenauer and Fulsome are making a play for your seat, right?"

"Actually," Duce said, "Adrian Fulsome is calling for a vote of no confidence. He's just promised that bitch a seat at his table if she supports him."

"Hm. You have to admire Fulsome's foresight. He knows Adenauer's ambitious," she said, thinking her way through the problem. "He's letting her make the high-profile moves to place her in the line of fire."

"What high-profile moves?" Patrick asked.

"Oh, I get it," Duce said. "High-profile, like letting Adenauer talk to the Primogen. She's dumb enough to think that's a good thing."

"It isn't?" Patrick asked.

"Nah," Duce said. "See, the thing about old school vamps like the Invictus and the Sanctified is that they like the way things are."

"They prefer the status quo," Persephone said, "and that includes their enemies. They know Duce, they know what to expect. He's a part of the landscape."

"So Beth's a threat because the Invictus don't know her like they know Duce?" Patrick asked.

"Pretty much," Persephone responded. "Or they know her well enough to recognize the danger signs. And

Fulsome's using Adenauer to draw the heat away from him like a good Ventrue."

"So, what?" Duce said. "Fulsome lets Adenauer grab the attention to frighten the Invictus, then steps in to look like the better candidate?"

"Possibly," Persephone said.

"Only problem is," Patrick said, "I think everyone's underestimating Beth, you two included."

"Girl's ambitious," Duce said. "No doubt."

"And flagrant," Persephone said. "I wouldn't be surprised if she also has the title of Prefect in her beady little sights."

"Yeah," Duce said. "Fulsome's playing it all coy n' shit, but Adenauer, she'll play it large and loud."

"Maybe Fulsome is counting on that?" Persephone asked. "Waiting for Beth to do something stupid? If I was him, I'd not only anticipate it, I'd try using it to my advantage."

"How?"

"I'm not sure. Maybe I'd use it to gain concessions with the First Estate," Persephone said, referring to the Invictus' unofficial name. "Recognize me and I'll keep Adenauer under control."

"Seems way too iffy," Patrick said. "Adrian can't pull that without looking like a sell-out to the Carthians. It's a bad gamble."

"Most moves in the game are," Persephone replied.

Patrick shook his head. "Man, fucking around with lives and calling it the game? I hate that shit—this mentality we all got like we're playing God."

"God? No, dawg. But I call it like I see it, and we are playing a game here. It's deadly and it's fucked up, but if you don't plan your strategies in advance, then you're dust. So I gotta know now. Are you with me? Cause I'm gonna play the game hard."

Patrick shook his head. He was angry, frustrated by the looks of it. "I hate games," he said after a moment. "And I hate that we play them."

"So? You with me?"

"Yes, motherfucker, I'm with you," Patrick said. "I got your back."

Duce nodded. "Cool."

"Now that that's out of the way," Persephone said, "what's your strategy?"

"Hold up," Duce said. "You never answered Patrick's question. What's in it for you?"

Persephone shrugged. "We can help one another," she said. "I won't lie to you. You're a valuable asset, but—"

"Only as the head of the Carthians," Duce concluded.

"Only as the head of the Carthians."

"Excuse my ignorance, but what does Duce-in-power do for you?"

"Frankly, it's a prestige thing. If Duce remains in power, then I have an 'in' with the Carthians, something no Invictus here possesses. If the Invictus wants to deal with the Carthians, they'll likelier approach me to broker that deal. I become a stronger player in the Invictus."

Duce studied Persephone in quick glances. She knew he was bonded to the Prince through the Vinculum. In fact, Duce's first contact in the First Estate was Persephone; she had brokered the deal with Prince Maxwell. So the Invictus already had an in to the Carthians through the Prince even if they didn't know it. Likelier, Maxwell was protecting his secret Vinculum and Persephone was using that to her advantage by pretending to be the only one with the inside track to Duce. After all, Maxwell couldn't dispute her without acknowledging the Vinculum's existence, and effectively undermining Duce's position in the Carthians and his sway over the covenant.

"Same works in reverse, too," Duce said. "I have an in with the powers-that-be through Persephone, and I can keep players like Fulsome off my ass."

"Look, Patrick," Persephone said, "Duce and I need one another to succeed and prosper. I can't sabotage him without sabotaging myself, and the same holds true for him. Not that I'd want to," she added as a personal afterthought.

"He knows I'm the only moderate in the Invictus willing to hear him out, and I know he's the only reason the Carthians haven't tried an open revolt."

Patrick remained silent a moment, considering the possibilities. "Y'know, I get all that," he said, finally. "I may like to keep shit simple, but I'm with you on that."

"Cool," Duce said, turning to Persephone. "Now, you know I can help you, but I can't do that if I'm gone."

"I know. You need my help."

"I need you to start introducing me to some players in the Invictus. I need to convince the Carthians that I'm making progress," Duce said. What he didn't say was: *And to weaken Maxwell's hold on me by showing him I don't need him as much as he figured I did. I got other 'ins' into the First Estate.*

"Already ahead of you on that," Persephone said with a smile.

The sandpaper whispered along the surface of the wood, gently wearing away the last imperfections along the edge of the walnut board. Solomon Birch closed his eyes and felt the grain of the expensive wood through the thin paper, vibrating up into his fingertips and through the empty place where his soul once resided. He could read the texture of the board like a map, its every bump and whorl rising and falling under his touch like the surface of a placid sea. Where he encountered resistance, he added a feather's weight of pressure and savored the feel of rough wood ground smooth according to his will. It was his world in microcosm. *I am the hand that shapes, the mind that bends Creation to my will.*

The door at the top of the basement stairs creaked open, disturbing his meditations. Birch heard David's footsteps on the old pine stairs and bit back an impatient rebuke. David had been his loyal servant for many years, and knew better than to disturb his master with trivial concerns.

Birch straightened from his work and laid the sandpaper down beside the nearly finished credenza. David approached, holding out a cordless phone. The ghoul's face was paler than usual, but the past few months had been very hard on him and his family. They were still waiting on the follow-up tests to see how far the infection had spread. Margery was HIV-positive for certain, but it was possible that Birch had inadvertently infected them all before Persephone revealed the method of her revenge. It had been an inspired counterstroke, Birch could now admit. One that deserved an appropriate response.

"The call you were expecting, sir," David said, handing the phone to Birch.

"Thank you, David," Birch replied. "That will be all." He waited for the older man to ascend the stairs and return to his family. Birch could hear the TV going in the living room and dishes clinking in the kitchen sink as the Brigmans tried to maintain appearances for Birch and the rest of the world.

"What do you want?" Birch growled into the phone. "Oh yes, one of Barlow's men. Yes, I know you. What do you have for me?"

There was a pause.

"Well, if I knew where Persephone is right now, I wouldn't damn well need your help, now would I, Kreskin? So just tell me."

Pause.

"So? She's at a bar. So what?"

Pause.

"Look! You ask one more question without saying what I want to know and I'll feed your ash to my goldfish. Stop. With. The. Questions!"

Pause. Lynch and Lott watched their master carefully.

"Duce Carter and some white-haired negro. Yes, I know who that is. Are they still there?"

Pause.

"Good. Follow them."

Pause.

"Then follow *her*."

Pause.

"What? No, I'm not interested in what you found in the dumpster." Birch hung up and turned back to the credenza. "Fucking sewer rats," he grumbled, reaching for the sandpaper and considering how to proceed.

"One last thing," Duce said, as the restaurant wound down for the night. "Fulsome's a problem, but I think we should focus on Adenauer."

"What are you thinking?" Persephone asked.

"Fulsome's calling for no confidence, which I can fight, but that can't be the only trick up his sleeve. He's got an ace, somewhere."

"Again, I'm thinking he's using Adenauer, somehow," Persephone said.

"Maybe, but that's the thing. Adenauer's still the easier target, right? If Fulsome's using her to draw fire, then it's in our best interest to steal his thunder. Use Adenauer the same way he is. If she's going solo, though, and planning to scoop the prefectship out from under Fulsome, we also have to figure out how she plans on doing it and use that in our favor as well."

"Essentially," Persephone said, "you believe Adenauer's the weak link here regardless."

"Right. My main worry about Adenauer, though, is that she's volatile, and may ruin the little progress we've made with the Invictus."

"Well, I hate to ask," Persephone said, "but do you have any support left with the Carthians?"

"Yeah," Duce said, nodding. "I got a couple of people still willing to back me, and a couple more on the fence. Fulsome didn't get all the support he wanted, but he gave folks enough doubt that many are waiting to see what happens."

"Typical," Patrick said.

"It's our nature. We're all afraid of change to some degree or another," Persephone responded. "Now if the Carthians fear certain change because of their nature as vampires, imagine how much more the Invictus are entrenched in their roles as old money and power. We can use that to our advantage, though. We can use that against Fulsome. Now, shall we?" Persephone said.

"Shall we what?" Duce asked.

"Meet with some people in the Invictus. A couple, I think, are rather curious about you."

Duce nodded. "That sounds all right. Patrick?"

"You go on. I'll see what I can do on my end of things."

Duce and Patrick knocked fists together, knuckle to knuckle, before parting company. Persephone left a generous tip for the waitress, even though they ordered one drink apiece that never touched their lips.

The parlor of the Morris House was chintzy in a faux-Victorian manner. The chairs with velvet upholstery and gold stitching, the stenciled walnut tables and the brocaded curtains clashed with the electric wall lamps and modern-looking clientele. A soft operatic aria played over hidden speakers, lending the illusion that it was being sung elsewhere in the building where life in the 1800s carried on with the blessings of Her Royal Majesty.

"Where the fuck are we?" Duce asked.

"Shh," Persephone responded, a big grin on her face. "The Invictus take their leisure quite seriously."

"Yeah, I see that," Duce said. A few patrons in the parlor stared at him, as if they knew him for an outsider to the covenant's pleasures. Duce stared back, not much caring for their kind either.

"The Morris House is one of several era-themed salons."

"Era-themed?"

"Yes. It provides an atmosphere where some of our members can relax in the environments they remember."

"Please!" Duce exclaimed, drawing a few more stares. "Nobody here remembers whenever the hell this was."

"Lower your voice, Duce," Persephone said, maintaining her practiced smile while talking, "they may not have been born to this era, but they're still older than you and me put together. That's the problem with being Carthian. You're too damned utilitarian to enjoy what you have. This place isn't about feeding anymore than a bar's about perpetuating survival. A salon is where you go to interact, unwind and—"

"Drink socially," Duce said. "I get it. Is there a seventies-era crib? I'd be cool with some funk."

"No."

"Eighties? Run DMC? Erik B. & Rakim? Big Daddy Kane? Public Enemy? Damn, I'd settle for Fresh Prince, even. Who is this bitch singing?"

"Okay, now you're being deliberately rude."

"Nah, nah. It's all good," Duce said, chuckling. "But what you're saying is that all of these salons are from eras—"

"From eras before the 1950s."

"Ah, yes. From when the world was white."

"It's not like that," Persephone said.

"Oh, it's not, is it?"

"Okay. Maybe a little. But many of the older vampires are beyond color."

"Bullshit. Some of these motherfuckers can't even change their look to match the 21st century and I'm supposed to believe they let go of their racist shit? We are the most entrenched animals on the planet. No growth, no evolution. We're stagnant."

"But we *are* capable of change."

"No. We can adapt, I'll give you that, but we got no more control over it than a skunk deciding on how it's going to protect itself. We don't change because it's natural. We change because survival demands it. Also means we only change as much as we need to."

"So what? This mean you'll always be this insufferable?" Persephone asked with a grin.

"Probably. It also means I'm black and that's never anything I'm going to forget or want to forget. I'm proud of that fact."

"Whoah," Persephone said, her eyebrows raised high. "Where the hell did that come from?"

lucien soulban

"I'm just saying that there are certain things I'll always remember, like the reason why I'm not impressed with these salons. They smack of social elitism and racial bias."

"Whatever, Duce. I really don't care one way or the other. But like it or not, you need some of these people."

"I don't know."

"Fine, then. Let Bethany and Adrian rob you of your allies. You don't need anyone, right? You don't need supporters."

"Yeah, but...Invictus?"

"We're not all bad," Persephone said. "Or was our tryst a means of currying favors with the enemy?"

"Tryst?" Duce said. "If you mean, did I sleep with you for power, the answer is no. That was all pity sex." Duce chuckled at the shocked expression Persephone shot him. She punched him in the arm.

"Nah, nah," he said laughing, "I'm fucking with you. It's all good."

"How good?" Persephone asked, drawing in closer to him.

"Real good," he said, practically whispering. "Some of the most intense and fucked up shit I've ever been in. But I thought we didn't want to go back *there*. Thought we agreed."

Persephone shrugged. "*There* wasn't so bad," she said.

"No it wasn't," he responded. "But I...uh—"

"I know," she said softly. "Now's not the time."

Persephone left Duce and walked up to one of the frilly-dressed, black-haired hostesses circulating among the small handful of clients. She spoke briefly, shooting glances back at Duce, before returning a moment later.

"Griffin's ready to see us," she said.

The taco stand on 60th had no name, but it served about the best Mexican fare on the South Side according to those folks enraptured by the romantic notion of culinary safaris. Patrick had eaten here once, when food meant something to him. Now, it was just another place he thought he'd never visit again in his diminishing circle of travels.

Patrick waited at the intersection as instructed, holding a brown paper bag whose bottom grew more translucent with grease every passing second. He was indifferent to the smell wafting up through the bag. He wanted to miss the smell, the taste of food, but he didn't. He tried to reminisce about the flavor, the textures, but it was a distant echo, barely felt against the constant pang for blood.

A beat-up Chevy Nova, green and battered brown, rolled up to the intersection. For a second, Patrick thought it might be another ganger representing his set's territory. Instead the driver leaned over and stared at Patrick through the passenger-side window. He looked like a younger, lighter-skinned Ossie Davis, with a drooping face and a black afro peppered prematurely.

"That mine?" he asked, nodding to the bag.

"I guess it is—Reggie, right?" Patrick asked and was greeted with a nod. Patrick entered the car.

Reggie took the bag with a smile. Satisfied with the contents, he placed them on the floor and pulled back out into the street. He began the slow sweep through this section of South Side.

"Tell you, brother," Reggie said, "this shit's like Krispy Kremes. Can't have just one."

"That's 'cause they double fry the shell," a voice in the backseat said.

Patrick half-turned in his seat. Reggie nodded to the young white man who reclined in the back seat, drifting in and out of sleep. "My partner," Reggie said. "Adam."

"'Sup," Adam mumbled, not bothering to open his eyes. He scratched his goatee.

"Double fried? You sure?" Reggie asked.

"Pretty sure. Like General Tso's Chicken."

"Huh. Only in America, right. We fry everything else, like candy bars and shit. Got to the point where we run out of shit to fry and got to doing them a second time."

lucien soulban

"Actually," Adam said, eyes still closed, "deep-frying candy bars started in Scotland."

"You sure?"

"Pretty sure."

"Well, then, what about fried ice cream? I only had that in Mexican restaurants. You ever had fried ice cream, Pat?"

"'Fraid not," Patrick said, mystified by the conversation.

"Not sure," Adam said. "Don't think fried ice cream's traditional Mexican, though. It could be Tex-Mex. Or a variant on the Baked Alaska."

"All right, then what about General Tso's Chicken?"

"What about it?" Adam said.

"Is it Chinese-Chinese, or American-Chinese? You know, like Tex-Mex. Because it's double-fried, right?"

"Yeah, yeah, I get you. Not sure, but I'd say it's American fusion."

"You sure?"

"What did I just say, Reggie? I'm *not* sure."

"Excuse me," Patrick said, "could we get this done?"

"Mm. That's a sad statement there, my brother," Reggie said. "Don't like talking about food? Man can't have hope if he don't like talking about food."

"Don't have the appetite I used to," Patrick said.

"Now that's a pity," Reggie said. "You'll never find yourself a good black woman that way. Black women don't trust motherfuckers without an appetite."

"That so," Adam said, half-asleep.

"Yes, it is. Black women love a man with meat on his bones. Unless you ain't into that, Patrick. You ain't gay, are you? Tell me the brother isn't gay," Reggie asked Adam.

"I don't know, man. Could have his switch on bitch, y'know?"

"I'm not gay," Patrick said, interrupting the pair. "Maurice said you had something for me?"

"You got what we want?" Reggie asked, watching the road. Patrick reached into his breast pocket and pulled out an envelope. Adam leaned forward, picked the envelope from Patrick's waiting hand, and proceeded to count the bills inside.

"All here," Adam said.

"We're good, then," Reggie said. "What is it you want to know?"

"You looked through the police records?" Patrick asked.

"We did," Reggie replied.

"And?"

"Sealed."

"What? Why?"

Reggie shrugged. "Wasn't sure at first. Thought maybe he was a minor when he ran with the Black P-Stones. Maybe he got out before he turned 18? Never got tried as an adult? But then, the numbers didn't add up. Given his date of birth, he was definitely 18 before his final arrest."

"So I just paid for nothing," Patrick said, angry.

"Now hold up," Reggie said, still smiling. "Maurice said you wanted information, and I don't like disappointing Maurice."

"So we dug deeper," Adam said. "His records may be sealed, but that doesn't include the files we kept at the Gang Crimes unit."

"What'd you find?"

"That he was a bad motherfucker in his day," Adam said. "Banged with the best of them. He was a mule for local pushers, then turned enforcer... suspected of several murders. Acquitted, from what we can tell, though he did spend time in Audy Home. Juvie hall."

"Then what happened?" Patrick asked. "Why are his files sealed?"

"Wondered that ourselves," Reggie said. "He was a rising ghetto star. According to our sources, though, on his last trip through the slammer, he copped a 35."

"A 35? What's that?"

"Adam, if you would..." Reggie said.

"Rule 35 of the Federal Rules of Criminal Procedure says that you can earn early release if you provide federal prosecutors with reliable information concerning criminal activities."

"In other words," Reggie said with a grin, "he ratted on his former gang buddies. We figure he provided federal agents with enough dirt to bust his friends."

Patrick sat in silence a moment, digesting the information. "But you don't know that for a fact."

"Our source is good," Reggie said. "And it's hard to get your record sealed as an adult without pull. Way I figure it, Duce negotiated with prosecutors. Gave himself enough to earn a Rule 35 release and to seal his records."

Patrick shook his head. "No. No, that doesn't sound like the man I know. That doesn't sound like Duce."

Reggie shrugged. "Sorry man, but the facts play out."

"All right," Patrick said. "Let's say I believe you. What happens if his set finds out what he did?"

"Dead." Adam said.

"Yeah. See, gangs got this creed. Learned it from the Aryan Brotherhood... in prison, y'know? It's called Blood In, Blood Out."

"Only most gangs don't use that term because it's Aryan."

"They call it other shit, like 'All is Family' or "Blood is Blood," or some shit like that."

"Okay," Patrick said. "I've heard that before. So Blood In, Blood Out means you...?"

"Kill to get in," Adam said.

"And you die to leave," Reggie concluded. "Nobody leaves a gang alive."

"Nobody?" Patrick said. "Bullshit."

"Okay, maybe it's an exaggeration," Reggie said, "but the fact is, gangs are hardcore enterprises. It's damned hard leaving them on good terms."

"And if they ever found out Duce fucked them over," Adam said, "they'd order his death. No question."

Birch was just beginning to apply the first coat of varnish when the phone rang again. He set the brush carefully on the can's steel lid and snatched up the handset.

"Your timing is exceptional," he snarled. "What did you find?"

Pause.

"Morris House? Who'd they meet?"

Pause.

"Well, then, find out! No, wait. I'll do it." Birch put the phone down and reluctantly capped the can of varnish, then placed the brush in a bucket of mineral spirits. "David!" he called. "Get the car ready!"

Some things just couldn't wait.

lucien soulban

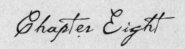

Chapter Eight

Joliet, Illinois, a so-called anchor city for Chicago, was a beautiful community still undergoing its transformation from industrial workhouse to tourist and family destination.

Andrew Keeler, a prison guard at nearby Stateville Correctional Center, was just sitting down for dinner with his wife when there was a knock at the door. Joliet was the kind of place where people opened the front door without much forethought, and Keeler found himself facing two masked men. One looked like a walking fridge and the other was shorter than his companion. Keeler was no small man either, and despite the paunch and thinning red hair, he was still strong. He tried pushing the door closed, but the short intruder shoved the door open one-handed. Keeler fell back, hitting the floor. The small intruder was fast, running into the house and charging after Keeler's screaming wife. Keeler turned and tried to get back up to save his love, but the large man walked through the door and slammed his fist into the CO's neck, snapping his spine. Keeler died instantly. He never saw the small man sink his teeth into his wife's neck and tear it open in a spray of crimson.

"Where the fuck you going?" Charles said, eyeing Terrell as he headed for the crib. Mrs. Keeler had been running for the baby when Terrell tackled her and tore her open in his lust for blood.

"Finishing the job," Terrell said, licking the blood from his lips. His dark clothes were covered in gore.

"Uh, no you ain't, bitch," Charles said, pointing his gun at Terrell. "You leaving the little shorty alone."

"Man, why you coming at me all hard?"

"You think I'm letting you go off on some baby? You out of your goddamn mind! Now get your ass back in the car," Charles said, unafraid. "We got five more houses to hit."

Terrell nodded and made his way past Charles. "All right. Best you not point that gun at me, though."

"Best you follow orders. Law will have your balls for this shit."

"Seems to me, Law ain't in charge, anymore."

Charles drew back the hammer on his gun and pointed it in Terrell's face. "Say that again, brother. Say that again."

Terrell shrugged. "I'm just talking," he said, walking away all calm and collected. "Now, don't we got five more houses to hit?"

Charles looked back at the crib and the ugliness around him. He followed Terrell out, but kept the gun in his hand just in case.

Footsteps clattered against the ugly cement floors, scattering hard echoes like buckshot. Duce had an hour to get home before dawn arched its eyebrows over the horizon and made life very uncomfortable for him. But he was almost there. Ten stories away, in fact.

Duce walked through the parking garage, eyes forward but his attention darting to shadows and potential ambush points. He thought he'd left this paranoia behind, a part of his history known as "back in the day." There was no escaping this, however. He was doomed to a life of blood and violence, but then:

Maybe I have it right.

Maybe everyone else was lying to themselves, believing they were a society of the just and equal. Duce shook his

lucien soulban

head and spiraled down into his own thoughts, still angry from the meeting with Griffin.

Fucking arrogant prick.

How could Griffin think the world was okay the way it was? Didn't he see the injustices, the inequalities; did anyone see it?

Because they don't want to, Duce realized. Because it would be admitting that existence wasn't sanitized, spotless, Lysol clean. That the disparities between different incomes, communities, races, ages—everything—were widening too fast to stitch them back together.

But did it need to be stitched together again? Could you do that without creating Frankenstein's dilemma? Life at a horrible expense. A patchwork society with no identity of its own.

Duce wasn't sure as he entered the elevator and waited for his floor to arrive. Griffin wasn't stupid. Just comfortable like most Invictus. Instead of trying to help cure society's woes by participating in its betterment, they focused on making their own existence more palatable in these modern nights. It was like stealing a truckload of medicine for just one injection to cure themselves. And screw everyone else for not thinking to steal it first.

What did I expect, though? Duce thought to himself. The Invictus traced their history back to the days of Rome, when men sodomized slaves, women and children as perks of their status as men and nobles. While the act of sodomy had changed connotations in the recent century, the practice was very much active among the Invictus.

Only, they don't need to unzip to fuck you over.

Duce stepped out the elevator door and moved down the hallway, burying himself deeper in the pit of his silent rant. He understood the Carthian frustration; the want, the need to strike out against something, anything, that would resonate. Maybe Duce was better off just letting the Carthians rage and thunder. Upend the system and start fresh. Give their childer the chance Frankenstein never gave his creation, a clean slate, a fresh beginning.

Only.

Only it wouldn't work out that way. Those who achieve power become the status quo. They'd be fools otherwise. The status quo means they remain in control. It was a game they understood. Only a few luminaries were ever strong enough to do what was right for the people and not what secured their position.

And maybe I'm not that man.

Duce inserted his key into the lock and paused at that startling realization. Maybe it was the survivor in him, or the vampire, but Duce wasn't sure he could walk away from the Carthians and their dreams of equality; even if by leaving, he preserved the covenant's integrity.

Duce unlocked the door—

But I'm a better candidate than Fulsome and Adenauer, any day.

—and turned the handle seconds before noticing the scratch marks around the lock.

The door splintered under the barrage of gunfire. Duce was already diving sideways, but it didn't save him from two bullets that tore through his torso; one bloodless bullet punched clean through him. Duce hit the ground already scrambling to his feet, trying to escape down the corridor and stay low. More shots ripped through the door and surrounding walls.

In the apartment across from his, a man screamed in shock. Others cried out in disbelief and fright.

Stray bullets weren't discriminating.

The ground continued slipping out from under Duce's legs, till he finally tripped and hit carpet again. He twisted around and backpedaled ass-wards, pulling on the grip of the Beretta nestled in the small of his back.

It snagged.

The shattered door to his apartment swung open.

Duce pulled harder, then realized.

The holster snap!

lucien soulban

Two black men strode through the apartment door, Tek-9s at the ready, ugly mad-dog sneers on their lips, shades coined Murder Ones covering their eyes.

Everything slowed; the gunmen now seemed to glide through gelid air. Duce didn't remember pushing blood through his veins to move faster, but the Beast had that covered. Duce pulled the Beretta loose, the snap popping free, and aimed.

Back in the n-hood, where Duce called home, he discovered two quick truths about himself. He wasn't a good fighter; couldn't brawl worth a damn compared to some of the other brothers. Not that it mattered. Many bangers weren't used to throwing fists either. Nobody brought fists to a gunfight.

That said, Duce's second epiphany came quickly afterward. If he wasn't any good with fists, then he'd be fearless with guns.

That worked much better for him.

The assassins shot first, raking the corridor with bucking automatic fire. Two more bullets tore into Duce, including one that barreled through his right thigh, vaporizing the femoral artery. It was potentially fatal—if he was alive. Now, it just hurt.

After that, recoil sent the other bullets in wild flight.

Duce responded. His first couple of shots missed; he fired at the guns shooting at him; that was instinct, something many folks under fire did, shooting at the source of the threat. The fourth shot punched the lead shooter in the shoulder and knocked him off his feet. The other shooter flinched and ducked under the barrage. Duce continued shooting, three more shots into the second guy, tracing a path that traveled up his waist, till the last bullet ricocheted inside the assailant's brain pan.

A moment passed. No more gunshots. From neighboring apartments, Duce heard:

Hello, 911! coupled with cries of agony, laments and *Oh God! He's bleeding!* Someone's family breakfast had been violently terminated. Duce turned his attention to the pained grunts from nearby. The first shooter, shot in the chest, was desperately trying to crawl away.

Duce stood and fired one shot into the hallway ceiling, shattering one light. The retort echoed across the floor and more screams erupted. The second shot blew out another light, plunging the hallway in darkness. That would keep the neighbors inside long enough for Duce to conclude his business and remain unseen if anyone was stupid enough to look through a peephole.

The first gunman was trying to crawl away, his fingernails digging hard grooves into the carpet, smearing a trail of blood in his wake. He was still holding his piece. Duce stepped hard on the assailant's gun hand. There was a snap and the man screamed; he let go of the Tek-9. Duce leaned down and took off the ganger's sunglasses. He looked straight into the man's wide, terrified eyes.

"Represent," Duce said.

"Nh—no. Please, man. Dh, don't—don't kill me. Please. Oh God. Don't."

"Represent," Duce said again, and brought his Beretta to the man's temple.

"Sweet Jesus. Ohjesusohjesusohjesusohjesus."

"Shut the fuck up, bitch. Represent!" Duce realized he was shouting now.

"Gangster Disciples, Dearborn Homes," the man blurted out, crying. "Folk Nation."

"Gangster Disciples? What the fuck y'all want with me?"

The man moaned in response, the gun barrel digging into his temple. "Don't kill me, please! I don't wanna die I don't wanna die. Please, God! I don't know who you is, man, I don't know who you is."

"Shut up! Shut up! Why you after me? Did Law send you to punk me?"

"I don't know no Law, I swear to God, I swear to God. Rasta told me where to find you, man. He want you dead. Not me. Please man, not me."

"Where's Rasta? How'd I find him?"

"Please, don't kill me!"

"Tell me where and I might let you live."

"West Madison. He slingin' tits, man."

"And if you're lying?"

"I ain't. I aint. Please don't kill me. I got a baby girl."

Duce pistol-whipped the man on the side of his head. "Then why you not home being her *daddy*?"

"I'm sorry. Please, Jesus. I'm sorry."

Duce said nothing. He kept the gun trained on the man's temple, considering pulling the trigger. The man continued sobbing, and precious seconds bled away. Too many thoughts rifled through Duce's brain. He wanted to pull the trigger; needed to pull it; tie up all strings, never waste an opportunity. Back in the day, he wouldn't have hesitated. That was the nature of war. Soldiers die.

But, back then, Duce didn't have a choice. None of them did, really. It was kill or be killed, stay alive at all costs and above all, protect your family. Back then, survival wasn't a choice, it was instinct, much like now. Only Duce despised being forced into decisions. He'd left that life behind, a life where options were as narrow as a forest trail. Here, he had a choice, damn the consequences.

Duce reached into the man's back pocket and pulled out his wallet. He found the driver's license. The man's name was Marcus.

"I'm keeping this, bitch. Case I need to find your punk ass and finish what I started, you get me?"

"I get you man, I get you," the shooter said through wracked tears. "Thank you, oh God thank you."

Duce took the two Tek-9s, one from the man and the other from his partner staining the carpet. "Best you bounce," Duce said and walked into his apartment. Behind him, the shooter ambled away, moaning in pain from the broken hand and shot to the shoulder.

The apartment was a mess. The two shooters, in waiting for him, felt the need to fuck up his place, slashing furniture, urinating on the wall, breaking the breakables. Stereo, television and DVD players were all unplugged and stacked near the door, ready to go for when the shooters had finished the deed. His best clothes were likewise crammed into two suitcases, one of the thieves discriminating in taste.

Duce smiled at the irony. In preparing to rob him, the shooters had effectively packed for him. They'd facilitated his getaway.

It took a minute to do a quick circuit of the apartment, changing pants and shirt to hide the gaping wounds in his body and grabbing any essentials he couldn't live without: a couple of photos and a worn copy of Malcolm X. Otherwise the apartment was free of anything Duce couldn't replace, and he realized how little he had anchoring him to the past. Everything he had was disposable or small enough to fit in a suitcase. He shook free from the thought and headed for the bedroom.

Duce produced a matchbook from his night table and screwed up the courage to light it. While sunlight and fire were the universal banes of his kind, Duce was also a Mekhet, a breed with a special affinity for darkness and a greater intolerance for flames. They were like brittle paper around fire, and it required extra effort to remain in its presence.

After lighting an entire matchbook, Duce quickly flicked it away when it flared. The thought of burning to his second death was a pulse of panic that drew a snarl to his lips. The bed burst into flames, forcing Duce to head for the living room, going over mental details before he left. He'd rented this place under an assumed name, so it was impossible to trace to him — though how anyone had found him was beyond Duce. Few neighbors ever saw him because of his nocturnal habits, so he was safe there. In effect, there was little tying him to this place. He was ready to leave.

lucien soulban

As Duce entered the living room, the wall plaster and door frame behind him exploded from five wild shots that sent Duce diving to the floor. The shooter, Marcus, had returned, fumbling with a Saturday Night Special in his off hand, his gun hand hanging limp at his side. The sixth shot went wide, followed by a series of clicks as a humiliated Marcus continued firing.

Duce roared a curse and pulled his Beretta.

He emptied the remaining clip into Marcus.

No second chances.

Both suitcases in hand, Duce headed for the elevators. He called one up, and as the door opened, he pulled the adjacent fire alarm. By the time folks dressed and headed out their doors, Duce was already in the garage. A moment later, he threw his luggage into the trunk and, by the time the police and fire trucks arrived, Duce was already heading for a distant hotel. Dawn was less than a half-hour away.

Persephone felt tired. Exhausted really. It was a strange malaise that settled into her muscles and added a hundred pounds to her soul. It was part internal lassitude and part gravity conspiring to bring her low. The fatigue itself wasn't unusual, though the fact that it was a precursor to something and not a symptom felt strange nonetheless.

Dawn approached, and with the skies growing lighter at the promise of daylight, Persephone grew more tired by imperative of her existence. All vampires slept during the day, completely unconscious and sometimes unable to roust themselves. Dawn was less than ten minutes away, and despite several feet of intervening concrete and steel, Persephone could still feel its imminent arrival.

Persephone's condo was a comfortable affair, with white furniture and more metal than wood to its touches. It was a far cry from her more humble beginnings, and endings, but it was still cold. Not for a lack of trying, Persephone tried making it her own, but missing were all the indefinable touches that gave the place a sense of history. Everything seemed trapped in the now, a reminder that Persephone had no past, or not one she considered important enough to remember. Still, she loved her small slice of privacy, her sanctuary from the world out there.

Moving through the living room on autopilot, Persephone shucked articles of clothing along the way, and entered the dark chamber of her bedroom. Dawn seemed to quicken its pace, and Persephone surrendered to her fatigue. She was nearly asleep when she slipped between the covers, enjoying the silken touch of the blankets. Her last anchors of consciousness snapped free.

Something touched Persephone's exposed foot and her leg jerked.

Persephone's eyes struggled to open, but it was difficult fighting momentum, that race downhill already in the sprinting. She fell unconscious again.

Something scrabbled across her ankle and up her thighs. Someone in an adjoining condominium screamed.

With Herculean effort, Persephone pushed herself into a sitting position and reached for the lights. The fatigue refused to surrender its grip on her, however, and she drifted toward that restless, sleepless state mortals feel after several days of hard partying. She flicked on the lamp, her eyes briefly blinded by the shock of light. Something fell on her chest... another in her hair. A third something bit her leg. The pain was sharp and brief. She batted them away and fell out of bed, scrambling away.

Her eyes adjusted to the lit room. All around her, the steady but almost imperceptible drone of clicks played at the edge of hearing. Insects, by the hundreds, covered her ceiling and fell to her bed and floor with a muted patter. Roaches, centipedes, silverfish, beetles and millipedes streamed through the ceiling vent and rained on her floor and on her. More bit her.

From the other condos, despite the well-insulated walls, Persephone heard more neighbors screaming. Running and yells from the hallways above her, below her, everywhere. Persephone scrambled up and ran out the bedroom, desperately ignoring whatever she crushed under bare feet. The living room was likewise suffering from the plague of insects. They spewed through vents and through all the little holes Persephone never knew existed. More fell on Persephone, and she batted them away. She needed to move. She needed to stay awake.

She headed for the front door, then stopped. Despite the infestation inside, Persephone's condo rested within the building's core where no window ushered in daylight. The same couldn't be said of the hallway, however, where neighbors converged and likely left their doors open. And beyond each door rested the possibility of a window; the possibility of sunlight. The risk was small, admittedly, and the fear likely trivial, but could she afford to leave? Afford the danger regardless how unnatural the events in here?

Someone pulled a fire alarm and Persephone almost cried out. Fire alarm meant the fire department would come. Fire department and this plague of insects meant the building would be evacuated—out into the street, where daylight waited.

Panic swelled in Persephone's throat. She imagined her burnt skin cracking and splitting open, her voice screaming an agonized aria drawn from lungs that needed no breath. She'd seen it before; tortured vampires in such pain that they forgot to inhale and continue screaming, their voices strangled and dry.

An almost bestial, guttural moan escaped her lips, and Persephone was strangely aware of how close the Beast was to surfacing. She had to control herself. She couldn't stay awake all day, and if she surrendered to the Beast now, she'd attract attention. Persephone focused on planning and schemes, anything that allowed the practical portions of her intellect to overrule her emotions.

The insects were the problem, and it was unlikely this was a natural phenomenon. Their numbers no longer increased, but they were scattered everywhere, driving more people into the corridor and out the building. The alarm continued its droning nag.

Persephone grabbed the nearest pair of shoes, brown heelless leathers, from the floor and slipped them on after shaking several insects loose. Moving into the kitchen, she squashed a few of the intruders along the way with a vengeance. She had to hurry. Fatigue slowly pushed her downhill again and she wasn't sure if she could resist for much longer. With a kitchen rag in hand, she batted several bugs off the door beneath the sink before opening it.

The interior of the sink cupboard was covered with bugs—a black, writhing mass that crawled everywhere; over insecticide, trashbag boxes, cleaning supplies and gleaming pipes. They spilled to the floor, but Persephone ignored them as best she could despite the constant edge of revulsion that sent shivers through her body and brought the Beast nearer to her skin's surface.

There was no choice in the matter, though. Disgust or threat of exposure to sunlight were hardly level options. The fire department would undoubtedly evacuate the building, and Persephone had no other escape route, no one to call for help. Nobody else knew about her haven; it was a secure location to protect her against ambitious vampires and needy mortals. Not even her driver knew which of the four adjoining condominium buildings she called hers, or which assumed name she'd used to purchase her property. Persephone was stuck here, and that meant she had to endure her new roommates and avoid the fire department and exterminators who would undoubtedly enter the various condos to deal with this plague.

Gritting her teeth, Persephone grabbed the trash bags and pulled free a handful from the box. The front door was next where, despite her inclinations to keep her haven secured, she unlocked the interior bolts. If whoever arrived to deal with this situation realized the door had been

lucien soulban

locked from the inside, they'd search the condo more diligently. Best they thought the place abandoned and conduct a cursory search.

Back into the bedroom, Persephone closed herself in the walk-in closet where the high carpet prevented the larger insects from slipping beneath the door's lip. Still, there were insects inside as well, but Persephone no longer cared. She had scant few seconds left before fatigue overwhelmed her.

Maneuvering against the back wall, between hanging dresses and long jackets that nearly touched the floor, Persephone opened a trash bag, kicked off her shoes and slipped inside. She knelt to the floor, using the wall for support and opened a second trashbag over her head.

Persephone fell immediately unconscious in her makeshift sleeping bag, her last thought a prayer that nobody would search the closet too carefully or poke the strange bag hidden beneath the layers of long clothing.

Chapter Nine

Home. Home was supposed to be somewhere nice, in a neighborhood of green grass and greener trees. A place filled with pleasant memories and security, where children play, people laugh easily and folks remember growing up.

This place wasn't built for those kinds of memories. The grass was overgrown and the tree looked choked by the surrounding concrete. Of the house itself, the porch's wooden railing was broken and missing spokes; the dirt-white paint had peeled in large swatches, revealing the ugly, termite-eaten wood beneath. The windows were barred, and the screen door was a thick security grate with a heavy lock. Despite all its flaws, the house wasn't unique to the block; the neighborhood was in equal disrepair.

Coming here's a bad idea, Duce thought. He thought that whenever he visited. Seeing his old home like this, his entire neighborhood overgrown by poverty, was more disheartening with each visit. His home was no longer his own, the 'hood a stranger to him. Well, mostly. Duce recognized a few locals. Mothers trying to raise their children and grandchildren despite the environment; an addict or two strung out on crack.

Walking past his broken home, Duce reached the stoop of a more respectable neighboring house clothed in pale greens. He rang the doorbell and smiled at the familiar strangled/drowning buzz.

"Who's there?" a woman's voice asked a moment later.

"It's me. Duce."

The door opened and a white-haired, thin woman of generous years pulled Duce into her embrace. Duce was careful in the strength of his hug, but hers was fierce, like she was embracing her own son.

"Child, how are you?" she said.

"Auntie Fina,' Duce said, settling into the small woman's arms, "I'm good."

"Come in," she said, but she was already pulling Duce inside by the elbow and looking outside before shutting the door.

Fina's home was sanctuary from the violence outside. Cloth doilies covered the tables and chairs, Christ stared down from the walls in various media — paintings, sculptures, crucifixes, macaroni even — as did framed embroidered sayings: "God Bless this Home" and "Blessed is the Child." Duce remembered spending nights here when his Pops was busy working.

"Sit down," she said, and headed for the kitchen.

"Auntie Fina," Duce said, "please, I'm good. Nothing for me."

"Nonsense. You used to love my lemonade." She vanished into the kitchen, leaving Duce to study the room and pick out the new additions.

A young girl, six maybe, with pigtails and wearing a checkered dress, poked her head out from the hallway corridor. She ducked back into the darkness as soon as Duce smiled at her.

Fina returned with two perspiration-beaded glasses of lemonade, the bottoms wrapped in napkins. She handed one to Duce and sat across from him in a rocking chair.

"Still caring for us strays," Duce said, nodding toward the corridor with a smile.

"You saw Bettina, did you?" she asked.

"That's *Bettina*?" Duce said. "How old is she?"

"She's six, but she's got the sass of a teenager."

"Like her mother," Duce said. "Where's Latisha? She around?"

Fina gave a Duce a look, one that said *you know better than to ask*. Duce nodded. "Sorry." His gaze wandered over to a shelf; Latisha's childhood pictures were still up, but there were none of her as a teenager.

"Nothing to be sorry about. My granddaughter made her choices."

Duce nodded and played with his glass.

"What are you waiting for, child?" Fina said. "Drink."

It wasn't that Duce couldn't drink. It was just, he wasn't sure he could stomach the overly sweetened lemonade. He brought the cup to his lips, before he remembered something to save him. "Did you get the money I sent?" Duce asked.

Fina hesitated. "I did, but Duce, it's too much!" she said, emphasizing the point by patting her knees with both hands.

"It's the least I can do. But, you haven't cashed it yet."

"Well, Duce, honey. I wanted to talk to you before I did."

"What about?"

"Where're you getting this money from?" she said, studying him. "I'm not living off bad money."

"C'mon Auntie. I wouldn't do you like that."

"Duce, I taught you to speak better than that."

"You're right," Duce said with a soft smile. "The money's clean. I wouldn't do that to you."

"That's better," she responded, then changed her demeanor. "But I still have to ask. Where are you getting all this money to throw around?"

"I'm not throwing it around," Duce said. "I'm spending it on people I care for, like you—"

"And your father," Fina said, raising an eyebrow. "Now don't tell me you've been visiting him, because I know better."

"I know, I know," Duce said. "Please. Can we talk about something else right now?"

"All right," Fina said. "We'll talk about something else. Like where this money's coming from."

"I did some consulting for a book," Duce said. "Y'know, about gangs and the streets. The publisher liked me enough

lucien soulban

that she hired me as a consultant and fact-checker. To help writers get their facts straight. I do it for a few T.V. shows now, and even a couple of movies."

"You never told me that," Fina said, a generous, proud smile spreading across her face. "Which books did you help with?"

"Don't go troubling yourself," Duce said. "I have copies. I'll bring you a couple, but my name's not even in them."

"How come?"

"Because I don't want people knowing me as the ex-gangbanger," Duce said, which was partially true. He also didn't want people prying into his past.

"But look at you. Every time I see you, I can't help but praise the Good Lord you turned out all right. You should be proud!"

"Thank you, Auntie. But you know, you had a lot to do with that."

"Duce Carter," Fina said, shocked. "What's the matter with you?"

"What? I'm just saying you helped me along. What's wrong with that?"

"Just... I never heard you give compliments."

"Pff. I'm not that bad."

"I'm just teasing you. Though you know, it would be nice to see more of you around here. Some of the local boys could learn something from you."

"I—I don't know, Auntie. I'm not role model material."

"Sure you are. Look at how you turned out. Folks around here could do with a little hope."

"They have you," Duce said.

Fina blushed. "It's boys like you that give me hope. And— I think it's time you saw your father," she said, getting up.

"Auntie, I—"

Fina leaned down and kissed Duce on the forehead. "He's got much to be proud of, honey. But only if you give him that opportunity."

Griffin was an addict; weak by his tastes. At least that's what Birch figured. For one thing, he preferred feeding on men. Probably tapped into some unresolved latent homosexual issues he'd never explored in his breathing days. So instead of sucking dick, Birch assumed Griffin satisfied his urge on the neck of a pretty boy. That way, he didn't seem gay for it. Of course, Birch surmised this thanks to his connections at the Morris House, which the Invictus owned and operated. While there was nothing as crude as hidden cameras or double mirrors on the premises, word about someone's preferred tastes always wormed its way out of the apple. Rather than being gossips, however, the Invictus knew how to stockpile information for their use.

In this case, Birch found little he could use to his advantage. Few vampires cared enough about gender to feed from one or the other exclusively, and Griffin hid inside that gray truth with the conviction of a truly skilled liar—the ones who deceive themselves better than they do others.

Birch had another approach, however, simpler than blackmail. He waited in the building that housed the blood parlor. It was nearing midnight when Birch received the call from his contact at Morris House. Griffin had just entered the penthouse elevator, garage-bound.

The elevator doors opened and Griffin nearly ran into Birch's chest. He wasn't paying attention to the floor; he was nowhere near the garage, but then, the elevator wasn't supposed to stop anywhere else. At 5'8" with the bone mass of a bird, Griffin was easily outclassed by Birch in every physical asset. Griffin inadvertently backed up into the elevator, momentarily caught by surprise. Birch placed his hand against the door, preventing it from closing.

"Bishop Birch," Griffin said, trying to recover. "What's going on?"

"I think we should talk," Birch said, and indicated that Griffin should exit the elevator with a nod of his head.

"And if I refuse?"

"Then you deprive yourself of valuable information, and you're not the sort of man who misses those kinds of opportunities."

Griffin thought about it for a moment, but Birch knew he was soaking up those valuable seconds to compose himself.

"All right," Griffin said, flipping open his cell phone. "Driver, I'll be a little late. I'm meeting with Solomon Birch." Griffin hung up and then walked out of the elevator.

"Y'know," Birch said, "if I intended to kill you, then your driver would be a quick detour."

"Possibly," Griffin said, following Birch down the corridor. "But you're assuming that was actually my driver."

"You're right, I am." Birch reached an office with heavy wooden double doors and opened it. He entered a conference room clad in the deep, somber colors one expected of big business and dropped into a leather chair. "But like I said, I'm here to discuss business."

Griffin sat opposite Birch with a bemused expression that curled one side of his lips. "I'm listening," he said.

"Let's cut to the chase. I know you met with Persephone and Duce Carter."

"And? You know I'm not going to discuss the peculiarities of their visit."

"Wouldn't expect you to," Birch replied. "But I'm figuring they approached you with a deal and you agreed to the meeting if only to stay current on matters, am I right?"

Griffin allowed a half-shrug and a nod.

"Let's talk, then…."

The deep shadows of the unlit bike alley running between the chain-link fences and hedge maples of suburban homes provided Duce with all the cover he needed. He moved through the alley, knowing which houses had motion-sensor lights that lit when someone ventured too close to their fences. It was an invisible obstacle course down a narrow path, memorized a hundred times in the making.

Without tripping any of the lights, Duce finally arrived at one stretch of fence lining the backyard of a National-style home with its utilitarian look, side-gabled roof and one-room deep interior. It was a comfortable affair for bachelors (widower in this case), and relatively cheap. Duce knew that for certain, because he'd bought the place.

Through the slanted window blinds, the blue-static wash of a television set flickered.

Pop's home Duce thought, *probably watching Jeopardy for the second time.* He always watched Jeopardy twice; made him feel good to know all the answers the second time around.

Twenty feet was all that separated Duce from walking across the bump of the back porch and up to the sliding door. Twenty feet away from knocking on the glass and saying, "Hey Pops, how you doin'?" Twenty feet from re-acquainting himself with the man he hadn't seen since he'd bought him the house in a quiet, safe neighborhood. And it was twenty feet he couldn't make, for the real distance here was time. Nearly five years since his last face-to-face; that's a lot of twenty feets.

How do you apologize for five years? I've been busy for five years? Been away? Been dead....

So Duce did what he always did when he came here. He watched the light flicker and tried not to think of his Pops sitting there all alone, spending his twilight years waiting for that final tap on the shoulder.

The kitchen light came on, startling Duce. He rarely saw lights on anywhere in the house, and so he waited to see a rare glimpse of his father. Instead an elderly woman shuffled into view, all white hair, smiles and a bathrobe. She called back to the living room, and Duce heard his father's voice. She returned with two iced teas in hand.

Duce smiled. *You go, Pops,* he thought, and walked away feeling less burdened. His Pops wasn't alone. Not anymore.

The smell of pesticides was strong. That was the first of her nocturnal senses to awaken. Claustrophobia came next;

lucien soulban

like being caught in the roped bedsheet during delirium-drenched sleep. There was a shell around her, encasing her, suffocation for that which could not breathe. She pushed out, breaching the plastic membrane and tearing the trash bag.

Persephone snarled in the darkness and fought to drive the rising panic back into its stable. A moment passed, followed by another. She was safe; alone.

The apartment was in shambles. A thin carpet of dead bugs covered the floor and the stench of pesticides was overwhelming. Someone had sent the bugs after her. Someone was trying to scare her... intimidate her, though she wasn't sure who.

Duce sat in the car a few moments longer, thinking about his father, before popping his cell open. He dialed and waited for Patrick to respond.

"Yo, Pat. My crib's gone."

Pause.

"No, I'm all right. I got another place, but look, we gotta meet. Discuss strategy."

Pause.

"Yeah, I know the place. One hour? Cool."

Navy Pier was lively, bustling with teens enjoying the evening, lovers looking for that romantic fall-time footnote to their dinner date, and parents with their children waiting in line for that last ride on the Ferris wheel before everything shut down for the night.

Duce walked through the crowd, taking in each face with his gaze. He was too paranoid to enjoy himself, too bundled up in nostalgia to forget his summer escapes here. Navy Pier was his retreat from the blood-stained concrete of home, where rides on the Ferris wheel brought him high into the air and the black jewel of Lake Michigan sparkled at night.

In front of the twin-towered Chicago Children's Museum, near its speckled, black fountain, Duce found Patrick sitting at a bench and staring at the children with their parents. There was a sad twist in Patrick's eyes, and Duce knew it was for the son or daughter he could never have. The only progeny that would come to him now were through acts of such violence that the terms "made," "created," and "bit" were more appropriate to his offspring. More appropriate for their artificial mockery of the real act.

Patrick never talked about it, however, and Duce never asked. That was the nature of their relationship.

Most of the time.

"'Sup," Duce said, sitting down.

"What's up?" Patrick said. "What the fuck happened to your crib?"

"Some motherfuckers tried to fill me with holes, so I booked."

"Who? Gangbangers again?"

"Look man, I'm tired. Can we get into this shit later?"

"No, Duce, we can't. You owe me a story, and I'm not doing anything until you come clean. What happened with you and Law? Why are folks coming after you so hard?"

"Man," Duce said, "why you on about this again? I said I'll tell you."

"Then do it, Duce. You said I was your road dog? Then talk to me."

Duce sighed and leaned forward, his elbows resting on his knees. "I—this isn't something I like talking about. Not something I'm proud of."

"Lord knows we've all been there."

"Not like this, man."

Patrick leaned forward as well. "All right. Then how about I start?"

"You?"

"Yeah me. You don't become who you are in this world without some shame in your back pocket."

"I'm listening."

Patrick paused a moment before beginning. "After I got bit, I thought I could live in both worlds. Y'know? Be a vampire and still hang with all the brothers and sisters."

"Yeah. You told me this shit already. Realized you couldn't exist in both worlds so you chose this one."

"I didn't tell you everything. Like why I left."

"I thought it was preemptive, to stop before you did something bad."

"I did do something bad. I left because I fucked up. That's why I've been telling you to leave your mortal life behind. You'll only bring pain to folks."

"Man, I've already left my mortal life behind. Just some of it won't let me go."

"And your dad? Your auntie? You still visiting them?"

"Yeah, I forgot. You know about that," Duce said with a chuckle.

"Well?"

"Yeah. I still see my Pops, and auntie. I...." Duce drifted off.

"You what?"

"I felt bad. About leaving Pops behind. After my mom died, he was all alone, y'know? Never had many friends. Then I get arrested. Get thrown in jail. And suddenly he's visiting me twice a week. He never did that before. It was always my mom who visited me in jail. When he started showing up, I figured it was because he had nothing better to do, or he was keeping a promise he made to Mom."

"Be careful, Duce. I understand the need to see family. See the place where you grew up. But you'll bring misery on them if you're not careful, whether you realize it not. Accidents are never premeditated. They just happen, and they happen all of a sudden, too fast for us to stop."

Duce looked at Patrick and gave him an upturned nod. "What'd you do?"

"I got mad," Patrick said and fixed Duce with a chilling gaze. "I got *real* mad. Some fool boy tried to rob me. First time I'd ever been shot. I mauled him. Just tore him up."

"You knew the boy?"

"No, but my uncle did. Saw the mother at church a few times. Knew her son when he was a snot-faced little boy. He couldn't have been more than fifteen when he pulled the gun on me."

"He shouldn't have shot you."

"He didn't know better. I did, though. I knew better than to be there, with mortals. I murdered a member of the community, and you know what the ties there are like."

"Yeah, I get it."

"Nobody knew it was me, but they asked for my help. Asked me to help them hunt down the monster that did that to Bobby."

"Did you?"

"Yeah. I helped them organize patrols, but when the police seemed more interested in chasing down folks who killed white people, I watched members of the community drift away from the neighborhood watch programs. Their spirits were crushed. And I helped. I made them realize how insignificant their lives were."

"That must have been harsh, man."

"Harsh? I felt bad for killing the boy, but just to rub salt in the wound, I got to see the community I loved disintegrate. Evaporate."

"So you left."

"So I left."

Duce and Patrick sat a while, staring out across the thinning crowds on the pier, neither of them saying anything. Cold was settling into the air as temperatures dipped toward the late fall. It felt like it would snow soon.

"It was a drug bust," Duce said, finally breaking the silence. "Law n' me were caught in a DEA bust that was trying score some major players. We were small time."

Patrick said nothing.

"Problem was, we shot at the DEA and they had enough shit on us to lock us up and forget we ever existed. I—I was sure I was looking at life. Or long enough that it might as well have been life. So I copped a deal with the lawyers. Didn't testify or nothing, but I told them where to go and

lucien soulban

who to go after. It wasn't enough to pull my ass into court and testify. But, my information led to some big-news arrests, like a fucking snowball. They let me slip through the system. Looked the other way. They told me they'd seal my files, to protect the cases they got going on, and they called me in whenever they needed some new shit."

"Why they do that?"

"They said I wasn't a credible witness. On the stand, y' know? So they kept me hidden so nobody knew about my involvement. Made for a stronger case without the defense calling my life into question or even knowing about me. Seems they had plenty of other snitches."

"After they let me go, I was sure I was dead," Duce said, continuing. "But the only homie who knew I'd been sprung was Law. I was sure he'd tell the brothers what I did."

"He never said anything?" Patrick asked, his eyebrows riding high.

"Not that I know of. The People Nation never came after my ass. I circulated word that the F.B.I. and C.P.D.'s Gang Crimes Unit had me under constant surveillance," Duce said with a small chuckle. "So they let me drift away so I didn't jeopardize their drug trade operations. I just vanished. I made a clean break and slipped away. Man...I was just tired of their meaningless shit. Started getting involved in other communities, reading about brothers like Malcolm, King, Cleaver... shit, even Che Guevara. I tried reading the Koran, finding faith, but Allah never stuck as a concept."

"No, man, I get it. You mostly dug biographies or autobiographies, am I right?"

"How'd you know?"

"Someone comes from the streets the way you did, all the posturing in the world doesn't make a lick of difference. That's all history and philosophy. Someone else's interpretation. Someone who never saw the shit you did. Biographies and autobiographies... that's *struggle*. That's experience talking there. And the experiences are honest because someone with a face lived them."

"Y'know, that's it," Duce said, straightening. "I never put my finger on it, but I think that's the problem with the Carthians. It's all posturing. Few of them have the experience to draw from. They get their rhetoric from other folks. They haven't seen the injustices in this world. They haven't seen the shit minorities got to struggle with every day."

"They haven't seen the failure first hand," Patrick said, smiling. "They only read about the successes."

"Right, because nobody really writes about the losers," Duce replied, "unless they were bastards like Hitler."

Patrick patted Duce on the shoulder. "Man, Fulsome and Adenauer don't get that. For them, this is a power struggle on their way to becoming the next Marx or Lenin. You can't let them lead the Carthians down that road."

"I know," Duce said, getting up and pacing slowly. "Have they found a Myrmidon yet?"

"Yeah. Fulsome called me earlier. He's suggesting Annie."

"Kenneths?" Duce said, his face scrunched. "Really?"

"I didn't figure her for Myrmidon material, either, but Fulsome's got a point. She sits on the fence a lot, and she's been staying neutral in all this. I asked Brown."

"All right. Then call Fulsome back. I want to meet with Kenneths before I agree to her. I want to get this problem settled and behind me fast."

"Yeah, Duce, but face it. You don't have shit in order to swing opinion back in your favor."

"I don't need shit."

"The hell you don't. Right now the Carthians are dissatisfied with the way things've been happening. You're not giving them any reason to change their tune if you don't bring anything to the table."

"This isn't a negotiation. This is about why I'm a better choice for them."

"This is like an election, but unlike elections, you need to make promises you can keep."

"Like what, Patrick? Right now, I don't even have my crib," Duce said, continuing to pace.

lucien soulban

"Well, who told you to burn down your apartment?"

"How'd you know I burned my crib?"

"Because I'm not stupid and I listen to the news. Shootout last night in an apartment building, followed by arson. Tenant was black and is currently missing…man, you better hope Sheriff Nguyen doesn't put that shit together."

"No reason for him to," Duce said, "and you haven't answered my question. What am I supposed to show the Carthians?"

"I don't know," Patrick replied, "though I'm beginning to think that maybe getting Persephone's help isn't such a bad thing."

"This you saying this?" Duce asked, laughing. "Since when you trust Persephone?"

"Trust her?" Patrick looked indignant. "Motherfucker, *never* trust her. And I started thinking this way when you torched your apartment. Haven't you heard about burning bridges?"

"Yeah, well, as soon as I'm done with this Carthian bullshit, I'll take care of my problem with Law."

Patrick bit his lower lip and shook his head.

"What?" Duce asked.

"Duce, you sure this isn't all tied together?"

"What? Law and Fulsome and Adenauer? You're being paranoid, man! Not everything's a conspiracy."

"You only get to say that if you're human," Patrick replied. "But the drive-bys and all this shit coming back to haunt you at the same time Fulsome and Adenauer come after you doesn't seem a little like conspiracy?"

Duce stopped pacing. "What? That Fulsome's engineered this to fuck me over?" Duce tried shaking his head, like he was dismissing the idea, but he stopped. The idea wasn't easy to dismiss.

"Not to fuck you over," Patrick said. "To distract you. He's using your past against you so you'll never see him sweeping the rug out from under your feet."

Duce shoulder sagged. "Fuck, man. If it's true….why didn't I see that?"

"Tunnel vision. You know what you want, and that's good. But you don't see what's around you, and that's what's getting you in trouble."

"Motherfucker. Nobody plays me like that."

"What do you want to do, Duce? I can tell you what I think you should do, but it's your call."

Duce remained quiet, considering his options. He couldn't afford to act impetuously here. Now wasn't the time.

Not that it helped.

Anger wasn't a reasonable listener. Somebody was trying to play him by using his past against him; all the shit he'd endured to their benefit; his identity, his secrets their plaything.

Duce couldn't see past the biting fury that built and struck discordant notes through his skull, tap-dancing on his naked brain. It took him a moment to realize his jaw ached. He was clenching his teeth hard enough to crack walnuts. His temper was slipping, the Beast crashing against his ribs, trying to get out. He wanted to say something, anything, but open his mouth and the rage might find voice.

Duce walked away. Without a word or sound, Duce walked away.

Thankfully, Patrick let him go. He understood the anger enough to stay out of its way.

The room was quiet. Griffin stared at Birch over steepled fingers. Not that it bothered Birch; his gaze was marble, his expression stone. No indicators to betray his hand in the negotiations here.

"If you can promise me a private audience with Prince Maxwell, we've got a deal," Griffin said.

Birch allowed a smile and shook his head. "No. I'm not staking my reputation on whatever pyramid schemes you got cooking."

"Then we're at an impasse."

lucien soulban

"Nonsense," Birch said. "The private audience with Prince Maxwell is pure vanity, admit it."

Griffin shrugged.

"You want people wondering how you scored the Prince's ear," Birch said, "but you already got two concessions here that make this deal worth your while."

"I'm not sure," Griffin said, teasing each word with a deliberate roll of the tongue.

"The hell you aren't. This is a good deal. And frankly, you have more to lose if I walk away than I do if *you* leave."

"Then why approach me at all?"

"Because me negotiating with you is a courtesy. I could do this without you, but frankly, you're not my problem, and I'm trying to make sure it stays that way."

"Hm."

"Take it or leave it. I'm not begging. In fact," Birch said standing up. "I've got somewhere else to be. And my offer dies the minute I leave," he said, nodding to the door.

"I wouldn't bother with intimidation tactics, Birch. They rarely move me."

"It isn't a tactic, Griffin. It's fact. And you should know well enough that I don't play games. In or out, your choice." Birch moved for the door.

"Fine, I'm in." Griffin said. "You have yourself a deal."

Birch nodded. "Good. You know what to do, then," he said, then walked out the door into the empty office building.

Chapter Ten

Duce's jaw no longer hurt, but he was still angry. The point of flesh between his eyebrows contorted into a concerned knot, his nostrils flared and his eyes were slits. A cool patter of rain chilled the night, but it soothed Duce's face.

The storm rolled across the sky, and Duce watched from a roof ledge, waiting for the anger to bleed away. The rain was his meditation, its touch heavenly distraction. Nothing else mattered in this moment, only the need for calm.

That Fulsome was plotting against him was one thing, but if Duce's present dilemma was tied into his past, then everything he'd worked for and built was about to spiral out of control. Wasn't death supposed to wash away the past? Wasn't he supposed to be above mortal concerns now?

Well, he wasn't.

Regardless of whether the drive-bys and the coup were tied together, one thing was certain. Duce's past was still a part of him. It had no intention of letting go.

So Duce considered his options. He couldn't go after Fulsome without tipping an already weak hand and alienating the Carthians forever, or for however long it took them to come after his ass. Being the leader of the Carthians was no longer about holding power or changing vampire society for the better. It was about self-preservation. Because the moment Fulsome and Adenauer assumed control, then every grievance against him would come back to haunt him. He'd be unprotected, easy pickings and, in short, ash.

The other avenue was confronting Law, but Duce wasn't certain what that would net, especially when he wasn't sure of Law's role in this.

Then there was Rasta, the man who'd hired the two punks to kill Duce in his own apartment. He'd have information Duce needed, like how they found him.

Duce smiled. That was a lead he would enjoy pursuing.

"Hello," Persephone said into the intercom, dropping the wet suitcase at her feet. Prince Maxwell's brownstone haven loomed above her.

"Who is it?" a voice asked, crackling with speaker static.

"It's, uhm, Persephone. Is that you, Samuel?"

"Yes."

"It's Persephone."

"Yes, you said that already."

Persephone looked back at the curb. Her driver was still waiting by the limousine, hiding under his umbrella and waiting to be released for the night. "Is Maxwell or Robert there?" she asked.

A pause. A long, uncomfortable pause.

"Why do you want to know?"

"I need to speak with them. I can't go back home. I really need somewhere safe to stay. Can I talk to them? Robert's not answering his phone."

Another pause.

"I'm afraid they're occupied. Perhaps if you returned later."

"Well—can I at least speak with Robert? Please?"

Silence except for the patter of rain.

"Samuel, please. I have nowhere else to go." Her voice cracked at the last part.

"I'm sorry, Persephone. Good night."

Persephone's arm dropped to her side, and she stood a moment, staring at the speaker box. She turned to the camera watching over the front door and could feel her sire watching her back. The limo driver placed the umbrella over her head and took the suitcase.

"A hotel?" he asked.

Persephone nodded. "Sure. A hotel," she murmured through numb lips. A few steps from the limo, she turned to look up at the dark windows of the building. She understood what was happening. Robert had warned her not to help Duce or get involved. She'd ignored the advice, and was now paying the price for the prince's displeasure.

The heavens cried curtains of rain that choked visibility down to inches; thick ropes of runoff coursed down graffiti-tagged concrete walls while collecting water poured down the gullets of storm drains. Duce moved through the downpour, heading toward a West Side apartment building. He kept to the street's dark corners, past shot-out lampposts, unlit alleys and boarded-up windows of not-quite abandoned structures. Relatively new pairs of sneakers hung from wires above his head; ghetto tinsel, but they also announced what Duce already knew—a drug dealer worked the local corner.

The age-scarred building was eight stories of brownstone, the exterior a testament to its age and solid construction, the interior likely cancer-rotted and littered with debris and human waste. Still, it wouldn't stop the dealers from operating here until such a time in the distant future when the highly active Chicago Historical Society and the City agreed on the building's status and made efforts to clear everyone out.

The building's basement rose halfway out of the concrete, the basement windows at street level and ground-story windows well above people's heads. Wooden boards covered everything. The front door waited at the head of a wide stoop, but Duce knew there was no entrance there either. Likelier, the transients and crack addicts slipped through from another location near the building's rear. And if this was Rasta's crackhouse as Duce's sources

lucien soulban

claimed, then the wood-covered doors and windows hid reinforced steel plates and thick bars designed to deter police raids. If that didn't work, than the arsenal of weapons inside would.

Fortunately for Duce, crackhouses relied on street sentries with cells to provide early warning, sentries who were either staying dry and warm at home tonight, or were too blinded by the rain to be effective. Duce orbited the building, unmolested except for one moment when he almost tripped over the body of a crackhead lying in the trash-encrusted alley. Whether the man was dead or unconscious, Duce neither knew nor cared. He couldn't fathom anyone who surrendered himself to such addictions. Or rather, he couldn't until he found himself staring at the man's exposed jugular.

Duce fought the urge to check the man's pulse with his teeth, and continued onward.

The circuit of the building's periphery told Duce all he needed to know. Everything was sealed up on the ground floor, with gun-slits in the window boards and one entrance into the place. The fire escape was also inaccessible from the third floor down. Not that it mattered to Duce.

His body temperature spiked, almost to discomfort; the vital fluids in Duce's veins turned to a sanguine vapor and suffused his muscle fibers. The rush was intoxicating, euphoric even. Duce scaled the drain pipe deftly. Once at the third floor, he jumped to the adjoining fire escape. His sudden weight drew a loud, groaning screech from his perch that cut through the rain and announced his presence. At least the windows up here were open. Duce quickly slipped through one window.

It was doubtful the apartments themselves ever remembered a time when they were beautiful. Folks had stripped stretches of wood floor to warm their winters, while the walls were peeled like grapes and covered with stains. Festering mounds of dark matter littered the room's corners, adding a gut-retching stink to the interior. Duce didn't need to breathe, and was glad for that.

Instead, he moved swiftly from the room, pressed onward by approaching footsteps that raced down the stairs to investigate the noise from the fire escape. Duce darted into the hallway and into an adjoining apartment where filth-stained junkies on stained mattresses rested on the floor. Most were too far gone to notice Duce. The others didn't care.

Through a hole in the wall, Duce entered another apartment, and then stopped. Footsteps in the stairwell reached his floor. Duce moved quietly into a bedroom, slipped behind a door and waited. Snippets of angry voices filtered through the walls and there were more footsteps nearby. The floorboards creaked; someone was trying to move quietly, but their weight betrayed them. A nearby door squeaked open, Duce realized, maybe in the next room.

Floors creaked again. Someone approached Duce's bedroom door, likely with a gun in hand. Duce pushed himself into the dark niche, flush against the wall. Someone was behind his door now, two inches of wood separating him from them. The door moved toward Duce, slow, the groan of rusted hinges drawn out. It stopped inches from Duce's face.

Silence.

Then there were more creaks, and steps walking away to join the voices in the hallways. Footsteps heading back upstairs. They were checking the other floors.

Duce allowed the minutes to pass until the footsteps vanished, and a few more to go by before he moved from his spot. He knew where they were now—the dealers—and moved for the stairwell with sure, quiet steps.

Up the first flight of stairs, Duce heard not one peep from above. Up the second, he went, past one near-oblivious crackhead in the corridor fucking an unconscious woman with oozing needlemarks in the cradles of her elbows. Duce continued moving, ignoring the violent smells of human decrepitude, living decay of bodies and souls.

On the sixth floor, Duce heard the artificial timbre of television voices coming from above. A quick glance up the empty dark stairs told him no sentries tonight. The heavy rainfall outside made it obvious why. Duce moved up slowly, gritting his teeth against every creak and groan that protested his weight. He paused, but there was no response to his heavy-footed creeping. Up he continued, until he could see into the immediate corridor.

The passageway was dark, except from one door where the bluish cast of a television flickered and danced along the wall. There were guffaws from the thugs watching the program and the grating laugh track of whatever comedy played. Two living voices that Duce could hear, but he had no idea how many fools were in the building. Duce continued scouting.

Up the last flight of stairs, Duce came to a reinforced metal door with a lock and sliding slat. Likely, this was where they sold and distributed whatever poisons were popular these days: Crystal meth, crack, black heroin. Duce doubted this was a drug lab; it was probably a distribution node for sharks like Rasta. Still, if Duce wanted in, he'd have to knock and let himself get captured, or draw them outside, or...use a key.

A thin smile stretched Duce's lips; he went back downstairs. The two sentries he'd bypassed would likely have keys. Only Duce couldn't rush in there and attack the two, despite his speed. That would raise the kind of holy shit he was trying to avoid.

Instead, Duce waited until he could ambush one of the two when they left.

Law was trying to read the latest online article from gangster-turned-activist Sanyika Shakur, but it was hard to ignore Charles, who seemed to be in his constant orbit, waiting for something.

"Something on your mind, dog?" Law asked, never looking up from the words on the pages he'd printed up.

"Uhm—yeah. Yeah, there is." Charles said, waiting.

With a smile, Law put down the papers and motioned with an open hand to the kitchen seat across from his. Grabbing a Coke from the fridge, Charles popped it open, relishing a swig.

"I love Coke," Charles said, swallowing a mouthful; he sat down and placed the drink on the table. "But I can live without it."

"I know, brother."

"Now I got no problem taking the bite, y'know?"

"But?"

"But, I seen Terrell in there, Law, and I got to wonder. If he's acting like a crackhead with this blood shit, are you sure it ain't another ploy to keep us Afrikans down? A trick to fuck us over, yet again. Like crack and all this other shit."

Law leaned back with a huge grin on his face. "Man," he said, "I'd hate to be the motherfucker who underestimates you, brother. But I wondered that myself."

"And?" Charles asked, leaning in.

"The hunger's harsh, true, but you saw the shit they could do—all that strength, speed, the ways they could fuck you up with their mind?"

"Yeah," Charles said with a smile, obviously hungry for a taste of it himself.

"I mean, look at Duce, making me come see him."

Charles's smile vanished. "Man. Reconsider that shit with Duce. I don't think it's a good idea—"

"Drop it, Charles. I told you how it was going to be. And it's gotta be no other way."

The big man bit his tongue, but nodded. "All right, man," he finally said. "I don't like it, but I got your back."

"I know you do. But look. Duce don't matter in the end. What matters is getting bit. Yeah, it means we'll probably suffer, but if the cause is good...."

"I know, I know. Just making sure it ain't a trick."

"You know what," Law said, "it probably is, but as long as we're ready for it, that's all that matters."

Charles took another swig of Coke, downing the entire can. "Listen, man," he said. "When it's my turn to get bit. I want you to do the deed."

"No doubt," Law said and lightly punched fists with Charles. "No doubt. Before I can do that, though, I think it's time."

"You mean with Duce?"

"No time like the present. He already knows I'm here. I think it's time to deal with this shit."

Charles nodded and straightened up in his chair. He watched as Law punched some numbers on his cell phone.

"What up?" Law said into the cell. "Yeah, it's me. This shit with Duce. We gotta do it. Tomorrow."

Two hours passed for Duce; two hours of mind-numbing boredom, listening to snippets of some bad comedy line-up. Finally, from the room:

"Yo, man. Dion late. I'm bugging out of here."

"Motherfucker always late, you know that."

"Yeah, well, bitch late for his shit. Ain't my problem. Later."

Duce moved down the stairwell, as quietly as quick would allow, hoping the sentry would walk his way. He was one floor below when the sentry walked down the stairs; another floor lower and Duce would have some distance between the two sentries, enough to quietly ambush one of them.

Halfway down, Duce heard someone walking *up* the stairs below him. Duce hissed; he was trapped on the stairwell between two people and about to be discovered. No time for civility. More Vitae boiled from Duce's veins, lubricating his thoughts with its oil-slick touch. The world slowed to a trickle, and Duce moved with lightning's grace, down the stairs and up into the face of a young ganger who was eighteen at best. The animal took over, instinct overriding reason just short of celebrating the wild Beast.

The young blood didn't have time to open his mouth. Duce punched him in the throat, hard. And somewhere deep inside, Duce was shocked at the speed of his own brutality, the ease with which it surfaced. He collapsed the boy's trachea, strangling off any cries for help, a sad apology in his thoughts at ending this life so quickly. Before the boy could suffocate, though, Duce clamped down on his neck. Hot blood laced with adrenaline burst into his mouth and dribbled from the corners of his lips. He imagined the eyes rolling into the back of his prey's head, the eyelids fluttering like panicked butterflies.

The boy's heartbeat slowed, a lifetime relived in each panicked beat. Slower still, till the seconds between beats were too long to sustain. Then he died, his heart hitting a brick wall; his last moment a descent into darkness through excruciating ecstasy.

"What the *fuck*!" a voice said.

Duce had miscalculated. The sentry, a black bandanna-wearing gangbanger with a beard, was downstairs quicker than he anticipated.

Spinning, Duce threw the boy's corpse into the sentry in one smooth motion. Both hit the ground hard, the sentry stunned by the force of the blow. Before he could say a word, Duce pulled the corpse off him and clamped his fist around the sentry's jaws, fingernails digging into dark cheeks. Hands flailed and grabbed Duce's wrists, trying to pull the gag off, but the sentry couldn't overpower the inhuman strength keeping him down.

The sentry's eyes finally focused, then went wide. Duce could only imagine how he appeared; face encrusted with blood, two long fangs visible from under his upper lip, a callous inhumanity in his gaze. The sentry struggled harder, but Duce was stronger and fueled with fresh blood. A few moments passed, the struggle equally furious and futile, before the sentry tired, his grip slipping.

"Rasta," Duce said. "Where he at?"

The sentry's eyes darted up toward the stairs.

"How do I get past the door? You got the key?"

The sentry nodded as best he could despite the hand clamped over his jaw.

"How many of your crew still up there? Scream and I do you like I did him." Duce nodded to the dead boy, then relaxed his grip a little.

"Four—" the sentry said, before Duce clamped his mouth again.

"The key. Slowly."

The sentry struggled to reach into his pocket before pulling out a single key.

Duce nodded in appreciation. "You get to live," he told the sentry. Then his gaze fell on the dead boy next to him, and it all felt so suddenly arbitrary. One dies, one lives. No reason to it all. No rhyme. Just a minute between two reactions: Primal and rational. This moment deserved more than what Duce could offer—not for the boy he'd killed, but for himself, to justify taking someone's life.

Duce turned on the nasty charm, the one that held mortals like rabbits before a snake. The sentry's eyes widened at the majesty of his captor and he struggled as Duce leaned in close to his ear. Probably thought Duce was going to bite him. Then again, Duce wasn't sure he wasn't going to anyway.

"You get to live, but you're the only motherfucker in this building who gets to say that. The rest I'm leaving for the rats."

The sentry was shaking violently.

"But I'll be looking for you now. I'll keep coming back to find you. In your crib. With your peeps. In all the nasty shit-holes you stick your dick in... I'll find you. And if you ever say a word about what happened here, or I don't like the shit I see, brother, I'll peel you like a grape and wear your face for Halloween."

Tears poured from the sentry's eyes and rolled down Duce's fingers in fat droplets.

"Only God can save you now," Duce whispered, and stood.

The sentry scrambled to the stairs, crying, before he looked back at Duce.

"It's too late for Rasta," Duce said, looking up the stairs, his fangs visible and his face fierce with unholy horror. "Is it too late for you?"

The sentry, still crying, shook his head and scrambled down the stairs on all fours, vanishing from sight.

Please don't come back, Duce thought. *Please, God. I don't want to kill another boy.*

Duce waited a few minutes, composing himself, then realized the crack addict he'd seen earlier in the hallway was tucked into one of the corner shadows, watching him and whimpering. His "partner" was still unconscious, her skirt still pulled up to her stomach, her legs open and glistening. Duce locked eyes with the man, searching for some sign of humanity, some recognition of intelligence. All he saw was a frightened animal, waiting for the danger to pass.

Duce walked up the stairs.

Sadness was worse than fury. Fury blinded. Fury allowed vampires to lose control. Sadness, however, bore the curse of clarity. Every action in its most vivid, heart-wrenching detail.

Duce knew death, and he knew murder. He wanted neither of them, but he was kin to both.

The solitary guard watching television proved easy to overwhelm. Duce was on top of him in an instant, choking off his startled cry as he plunged his fangs into the man's neck. He drank the guard nearly dry, fueling the raging furnace inside him, then slid the still-bleeding body to the floor.

Everything after that was a matter of speed. Everything after that seemed to happen in slow motion.

Duce slipped the key into the metal door. The door opened, revealing a corridor with hallways branching off to the sides

lucien soulban

and a table with a lockbox and a pile of white packets. A gun-man in the corridor, an ex-linebacker with an Uzi, looked surprised, his mouth opening slowly to yell a warning to some-one in a room behind him. That was all Duce needed to see.

He raced past the gunman—muscle fibers pulled steel-wire taut and stitched against his skin—and clotheslined the man under the chin. Bones snapped like brittle twigs. He turned to see the man hitting the ground, the pain only just registering on his face.

Duce raced to the open door in the corridor, where the vacant glow of a television emanated. One man, nothing Rastafarian about his Vietnamese expression, was stand-ing up from a rocking chair, pulling an Ithaca shotgun. A terrified expression flowed like molasses across his face.

Between one heartbeat and the next Duce was at the chair, grabbing the man by the front of his shirt. One push sent him flying backwards into the bedroom wall. Before the ganger could hit the floor, Duce grabbed him again and rebounded him into the wall a second time for good measure, leaving a deep dent in the sheet rock and a trail of blood as the body slid to the floor.

"Uh-uh, bitch…"

Duce turned toward the voice—

"…this is my house."

—and found himself looking at a well-built, shirtless man with light black skin, gang tats covering his arms, a full beard and natty dreads spilling out over a black headband. The Skorpion submachine gun in the man's hands erupted in a staccato roar, punching a line of bullet holes across Duce's chest and right shoulder.

People can count on two things in a fight:

First, animals may look graceful in motion, but when they collide, it's a down and dirty affair. Essentially, 90 percent of all skirmishes end up on the ground.

Second, Duce didn't know enough techniques to keep the brawl off the floor. And they hit the floor pretty fast.

Rasta moved with the speed of a vampire, but the Beast inside Duce didn't react to him as a fellow Kindred. *He's a ghoul!* Duce realized, a human who fed on vampire blood and was invested with some of their ability. He managed to tackle Rasta, braving the blistering fire that tore through his chest, and fought for control of the gun.

Rasta reached around and placed Duce's neck in a chokehold with his forearm. It was a natural mistake, human instinct taking over in the heat of the fight, but little good against someone who didn't need to breathe.

Duce pulled the forearm off his neck. He was stronger, but Rasta was still armed. Duce bit into his foe's arm, his teeth scraping bone. A roar of pain exploded in his ear, followed by point-blank gunfire into his kidneys. Duce screamed and fought down a fit of panic as the muzzle flash of the weapon seared his flesh. Desperate, he tried pulling Rasta off his back, but only succeeded in unbalancing himself.

Both men hit the floor and rolled around in a struggle for leverage. It was a brutal wrestling match, a flurry of knees, elbows and fists. Duce landed several jabs to Rasta's face, but it was like punching stone; the man was naturally tough. Rasta swung with his Skorpion, catching Duce in the temple and cracking his skull.

Duce tried rolling off Rasta, but his opponent knew better than to let go. More fumbling grabs trying to pin the other until Duce managed to get on top. He wrapped his fingers around Rasta's neck in a stranglehold. Rasta opened fire again with the Skorpion that remained in his tenacious grip, punching large holes in Duce's stomach and larger exit wounds in his back.

After a blinding flash of agony, Duce reacted, the Beast clawing through in a moment of pain-borne cruelty. He didn't even consider his action, merely the moment. Duce's stranglehold turned into twin thumb jabs with both digits shoved into the soft meat under Rasta's lower jaw. Duce's thumbs slipped into the flesh with a sickening rip. Rasta tried to scream, but Duce held his mouth shut, a cruel scowl twisting his expression. Rasta was now pulling at Duce's wrists in pure panic, throwing away his smoking gun.

Probing the two bloody wounds, Duce secured a grip on inside of the jawbones. He pushed out in opposite directions, to snap the wishbone of Rasta's lower jaw. Rasta let out an inhuman howl that echoed through the building. The soft underside of his jaw split open, tissue and muscle tearing, blood pouring out in a crimson river. Duce snapped Rasta's jaws in half, unhinging them with an audible double pop.

In a furious, final spasm, Rasta threw Duce backwards and scrambled away. His fractured jawbones hung loose in the dangling pouch of skin that had once been his lower jaw. Duce stumbled back as well, stunned by his own brutality, suddenly aware of himself, of his situation. He stared at Rasta, his eyes wide in horror; in horror of Rasta who now flailed on the ground; in horror of himself.

Rasta was no longer a threat. He cried and gibbered, leaving ripped fingernails in the floor. The pain and shock of it all was unbearable. Duce staggered to his feet as Rasta thrashed and moaned on the grimy floor, lost in a world of unending pain.

Duce couldn't bear it any longer. There was no choice in this moment, no easy decision through which Duce could seek escape. He'd come here seeking answers, and instead killed three men in as many minutes, and now a fourth was to follow.

Vitae seethed through his body, sealing shut most of his terrible wounds. Duce grabbed the Ithaca shotgun lying next to the unconscious Asian gangbanger, and pointed it at Rasta's head.

He fired two blasts at point-blank range.

Rasta slumped to the floor, his head a red and grey pulp. Duce stumbled back out into the night.

Chapter Eleven

Persephone had received the call about a half-hour ago. She'd hesitated, but she needed this about as much as he needed to see someone. She gave him her room number at the Hotel Inter-Continental Chicago, North Tower. He was confused.

"My condo's being fumigated," she responded.

He knocked on her door a half-hour later.

Duce knocked on the door, the interior frame supporting his exhausted body. He'd changed clothing. No bloody, ripped apparel to betray the violence of the evening. His eyes, however, betrayed the night's cost.

Persephone opened the door. She didn't hide her shock at the broken look in his eyes, but then, Duce thought she looked tired, too. Neither of them said anything. Their pain was private, but their suffering didn't have to be. Duce slipped into the lavish hotel suite and into Persephone's arms. They held one another, part surrendering into the embrace, part supporting the other for some perceived need for comfort.

They said nothing; there was nothing that needed saying.

They'd agreed not to be intimate again, but that promise was years ago. Might as well have been ages. Now they played games around one another, trying to see who'd break first.

Tonight, they both did.

lucien soulban

The bedroom was dark, anonymous. It was easy to get lost in the shadows; in the act. They slipped over and around one another, their cold flesh welcome comfort, their limbs intertwined, shifting from one fluid knot to the other. Underneath it all, however, was the anticipation; the paused breath before the bite and consummation unraveled them both.

They explored one another with their mouths and hands, each minute a different sensation. Finally, Duce kneeled on the bed and opened Persephone's legs at the knee. He hesitated; she waited. They both knew what came next, and next after that. After this, there was no returning from their decision not to be intimate. After this, they'd be back to three years ago; or was it four?

It didn't matter.

Persephone answered his uncertainty by moving into him. Duce fell into her and they both gasped at the warm familiarity of the moment.

But with each thrust, the façade of comfort sex fell away. With each thrust, the animal gained momentum. It started with soft grunts and whimpers, but slowly turned into urgent hisses. They were building to a different climax, and they both knew it. No Hollywood instant where they fell into each other's arms, panting, sweating. This was not that kind of moment. Duce hissed, his fangs exposed. Persephone grunted, her sharp teeth glistening in the dark. The passion turned aggressive, fingernails tearing away shallow curls of skin, mouths clamping down on flesh and drawing blood in the hard pinch of teeth. Persephone and Duce fell into each other, but not in the way mortals did. There was no moment of unity, just two animals clawing each other for purchase. They drank deeply, parched by a desert they couldn't see, some heat they couldn't feel.

It was all part of their game, that ride along the sword's edge, the game they all played.

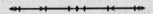

Patrick moved through the throng of naked and half-naked bodies. Women reached out to caress his crotch and pull him into their orgies, but he drifted past them; past the grunts and groans of human intercourse, past the false intimacy.

Some people carried flashlights to navigate the orgy rooms or highlight the action, but most people steered by touch. Patrick needed neither. He saw the world through a collage of colors, living lights of the people around him. He saw through eyes that amplified the ambient light and saw the unseen thanks to his unique vampiric sight. That a few auras Patrick spotted were pale and several years beyond death was hardly surprising.

Patrick walked past the soap dispensers containing lubrication; past the bowls filled with condoms and ceiling slings cradling men and women getting fucked. This was Club Dionysus, the new Rome for orgies and debauchery, where sex had become safari and spectacle. Straight men accepted head from gay men; straight women tasted pussy for the first time; all to combat some worldly ennui.

None of this mattered to Patrick. He branched away from the main orgy rooms into the maze of hallways and dark fuck niches with their doors, vinyl-covered couches and small clothing lockers. Inside were willing slaves who waited in unlocked rooms. On their stomach meant they wanted to get fucked. On their back and they'd be good for giving or receiving head. Patrick opened and closed doors. Some occupants didn't bother looking up; others waved him off; a few looked disappointed he didn't walk in.

Patrick finally found a naked woman, her skin a lightly tanned brown and sprinkled with a white floral tattoo that covered the side of one leg. Her hair was black and long, pulled into a ponytail that curled against the middle of her back. She lay on her stomach.

Patrick stepped into the room and closed the door. He watched her.

"I don't fuck kind," she said, sensing another vampire in the room. She turned around and looked at Patrick with a cocked eyebrow. "Oh, you," she said.

"Do I know you?" Patrick said.

"Sorry. I meant I'd seen you around before." Her accent was Greek.

"Not here for that," Patrick said. "You're Demetria, right? I heard you're for hire."

"Depends on the job."

"Some folks are fucking with a friend of mine. I want them stopped."

"I'm not cheap."

"And I wouldn't be here if I cared."

"Destruction?"

"Not yet. I need you to tell me whatever you find out first. I'll decide after that."

Demetria nodded. "Give me twenty minutes."

Patrick turned to leave. He stopped. "You're a pretty girl. Why you doing this?"

Demetria smiled. "Beauty has nothing to do with this. I enjoy the duplicity."

Demetria's face wavered, and for a moment, Patrick saw a fence of yellow teeth on burn-curled lips, beady eyes, swatches of hair and a misshapen head. The image was gone. Patrick was staring at the beautiful Demetria again. She looked Nosferatu.

Patrick hesitated a moment. "Are you the woman Persephone had tailing me? 'Cause you're acting like you know me."

"Twenty minutes," she repeated.

"Here we are again," Duce said, stroking Persephone's hair. He remained seated, leaning against the backboard.

"Welcome back," she said with a giggle and snuggled against Duce's chest.

"What. You saying you never left?"

"Not really. I guess part of me's always been here with you."

"Yeah," Duce said. It sounded about right to him.

"So? Where does this put us?"

"I don't know. Everything's unraveling. Like the world's spinning faster."

"There's too much happening at the same time for all of it to be coincidence."

"That's what Patrick said. I got to agree. Just got to figure out where all the connections are." Duce was quiet for a moment before a thought occurred to him. "Say... just what are you doing here, anyway?"

"Excuse me?" Persephone said, raising her head from Duce's washboard abs.

"No, no. Not with me. I mean in this hotel. What happened to your place?"

Persephone scrunched her nose in disgust as she remembered the ordeal. "Bugs started raining down from the ceiling. There were thousands of them. I had to—"

A violent shiver shot through Duce that startled them both.

"What the hell?" Duce said, shocked at his own involuntary shudder.

"Did you just shiver?"

"Yeah. The thought of the bugs—" Duce shook again. A discomforting feeling nestled itself deep in his stomach like he was on the verge of being sick. It didn't budge, but Duce didn't feel queasy, though it felt like he should be.

"Since when do bugs creep you out? Hey! Since when do dead guys shiver?"

"Never liked bugs in the first place. It's weird, though. I can't stop thinking about them."

"Trust me. I know how you feel," Persephone said, sinking back down into Duce's arms. "I don't know if I can go back there. I hid in the closet. By the time I woke up, the fumigators had gone through the building."

"Building? It wasn't just your apartment?"

"No. They were everywhere. I'm pretty sure management evacuated everyone. It happened at dawn and I barely managed to stay awake. I don't want to think what would have happened if it was during the day."

"Maybe they were already spraying the sewers, or something, and herded the bugs into your building."

"Maybe. But *right* at dawn, just before the sun rose? Seems like good timing to me."

"True. If someone wanted to stay awake to summon the bugs, it would have to be before the sun rose."

Persephone sighed.

"Since when do dead girls sigh?" Duce asked.

"They sigh when they know they're being played."

"Being played? Listen to you, getting all urban on me."

Persephone smiled. "It's just—I don't like being played. Damn it. I don't even know who to blame."

"You think it's linked to my problem?"

"Maybe. I don't know. I just don't believe in convenient coincidences."

"Like the shit happening to us."

"Yeah. Like what's happening to us." Persephone shifted position and straddled Duce's lap. She rested both hands on his shoulders, leaning against him. "Your turn," she said. "What happened to you tonight? Why the sudden need to see me?"

Duce closed his eyes a moment before answering. "I don't want to go there yet," he said.

"Don't start avoiding the problem, not now. If everything is interconnected, I need to figure out why and how. I can't do it if you're withholding information."

"Man," Duce said, shaking his head with a small smile. "You and Patrick...."

"Personally, I prefer just me," Persephone said. "But at least Patrick's looking out for you."

"Yeah. He's good people."

"What happened tonight?"

"All right. I'll tell you, but I gotta ask something first."

"What?"

"Are we back to where we were? Y'know, years ago?"

"I don't know," Persephone admitted. "I liked where we were."

"Same here. It was intense. It's just... is this the right time to be doing this? With everything happening to us?"

"Probably not. But when isn't something happening to us? Or to you? Or to me? There's never going to be a perfect time."

"It's different," Duce said. "There's a lot more stuff going on."

"You're right. But you know what? We're already in this together. If someone is engineering all this, it means we're stronger together than apart."

"I'm not disputing that. I'm not sure we can afford to start getting into each other again. Is this going to distract us?"

"Duce," Persephone said, kissing him on the lips and whispering into his mouth. "It's already a distraction not being with you. It'll be worse if we deny each other. We'll be thinking about nothing else."

"True," Duce said, brushing her lips with his whispers. "At least we could get this out of the way and worry about other things."

"True," Persephone said with a smile. She fell to the side and Duce rolled atop her.

"You still owe me a story," Persephone said.

"After," Duce replied.

They kissed, soft and casual, both of them knowing it wouldn't end that way.

It never ended softly.

Part Two:

Blood Out

"Revolutions are born in the blood of innocents."
—Patrick Morneau

Chapter Twelve

"Thanks for meeting me," Duce said. He looked around the bar, studying the locals, all of them white. Two guys at a table playing pool, some old barfly drowning her sorrows at the jukebox with songs from her better days and a barkeep handing out beers in frosted bottles were all the sights to be had here. Not the kind of place he normally frequented.

Annie Kenneths shrugged, her perpetual frown unchanged on her thin, pale face. Her long black hair rested flat against her scalp. "It's not a problem, Duce. Adrian said you wanted to meet with me. Decide if I was the right woman for the job? So, what'd you want to know?"

"Never figured you for Myrmidon," Duce said. "Never expressed an interest one way or another."

"Wasn't sure it *would* interest me."

"So what's with the change of heart?"

"The covenant needs someone to step up to the plate, and frankly, I'm the only one not embroiled in this crap."

"True, but you never really ran with the rest of us. You been avoiding us?"

Annie shrugged again, obviously uncomfortable with someone poking around her private affairs. "I don't really agree with most of you."

"What do you mean?"

"Well. I don't follow your philosophies. I think most of you have it wrong."

"That so," Duce said with a laugh. "Then why you hanging with us?"

"I'm agnostic," she said, "so all the religious shit the other covenants are feeding us doesn't wash with me. And the Invictus...don't trust the man in power."

"So, if you don't trust the man in power, how you gonna trust this man in power?"

"Look, Duce. I may disagree with what most Carthians think, but I'm with the covenant because I believe in the *process*. The fact that you can defend yourself against a no confidence vote is far more than the Invictus allows."

"What do you believe in?" Duce asked.

"Is that really relevant to my role as arbiter?"

"For me it is. You've been with the Carthians for, what, a few years now? And I still don't know shit about you. Now you step forward to act as arbiter, and I'm not sure why. So yeah, if you're asking me to trust you, I think what you believe is relevant."

"Fine. I'm a Libertarian."

"Ah. Individual liberty, personal responsibility."

Annie laughed, her frown lines fading for a moment. "You read our website."

"Something like that. I get what your party is trying to do. I don't agree with some of it, though."

"This your idea of getting on my good side?" Annie asked.

"Individual liberty, remember?" Duce said with a grin.

"All right. Point is, I believe everyone should have the right to liberty."

"And the Carthians are the closest thing to that philosophy."

"Actually, no. The Gangrel are the true Libertarians of our species," Annie said, referring to nomadic and feral vampires who spent their nights on the roads. "Only, I'm not Gangrel."

"Does that make a difference?"

"If you want to survive in the wilds it does."

"Good point."

"The Carthians are the closest thing to a choice I have."

"All right. Then if you don't agree with what Fulsome or me got to say, how can you be neutral?"

"Exactly because I won't be swayed by either of your rhetoric."

"So why trust either of us in power?"

"Because it's not your policies that are at stake. I think the real question is whether you make a good leader. This isn't an election. It's a call for a no confidence. You have the right, however, to address the Carthians before they make their decision. And frankly...." Annie hesitated. The expression on her face suggested she was considering her response.

"Frankly?"

"The thing is, I can't tell the Carthians how to think. They've got to make up their own minds. I can, however, give you and Fulsome equal opportunity to be heard and to present your arguments to any attending Carthians. Let them make their choices, but let them understand where both of you are coming from. I think that's why I really want to do this."

"But do you really think the voting booth is the place where we should be making our speeches?"

"I thought about that," Annie said, "but as Myrmidon, the only way I can guarantee you both equal time is to put you in the same room. That way, everyone hears what you two have to say. Anyone who skips out on the speech will also lose their right to vote in the matter. It seems only fair. Otherwise, my role in this is perfunctory."

Duce thought about it for a moment, but he was already nodding. It was exactly what he wanted, the chance to regain the other Carthians' trust. "All right. I'm good with you as Myrmidon. When do we do this? I want this done quickly."

"Sure," Annie said. "Fulsome said any time, so I'm setting the no confidence vote for this Tuesday, ten o'clock."

"Tomorrow. I want to get the ball rolling on this," Duce said.

"I'm doing you a favor. Fulsome's probably been planning this for a while. So whatever you do, you better come prepared. You have till Tuesday. I'll call Fulsome myself to make the arrangements. And anyone who isn't there from the beginning forfeits their right to vote."

"Make this quick," Birch said into the phone. He listened to the voice on the other end.

"Hotel Inter-Continental Chicago?" Birch said. "The girl lives beyond her means. Good to know." Birch closed the phone before his Nosferatu informant could chatter his ear off again.

Tapping his phone against his chin, Birch considered his options. He knew what to do next, but he needed help. He dialed a number from memory.

"Barlow, it's me."

Pause.

"Persephone's staying at the Inter-Continental. Know anyone with contacts there you can trust?"

Pause.

"Good. Here's what I want you to do."

Patrick opened the door, inviting Duce into his apartment. Duce clapped Patrick on the arm and dropped into his regular spot, the comfortable brown armchair.

"You're in a good mood," Patrick said, his eyes narrowing.

"Better," Duce said. Being with Persephone last night had helped his frame of mind, though the memories of his fight with Rasta lingered.

Patrick studied Duce. "You get laid or something?"

Duce shrugged with a smile.

"Christ. Not Persephone?" Patrick said, his shoulders slumped.

"Whatever, man. Don't need your approval."

"Two words: Jungle Fever."

"Oh, don't even play that shit with me. You fed from plenty of white girls and from sisters. Enough to know it ain't about the skin color. It goes deeper than that."

"Right, right. It's all about the red."

"Man. Something about Persephone's blood that I can't get enough of. Last night, we were—"

"Whoa! No no no no. Don't be telling me about your shit! It's bad enough you're sipping from her cup. And not because she's white. She's Invictus, Duce. Are you nuts? You're just an asset to her."

"I know. Politically, we both need something from each other. But it's more than that. There's something...furious about us."

"Furious?"

"I don't know. Can't really call it anything else. It isn't primal. Smacks too much of the JF. It's more like—" Duce stopped himself, his smile wavering, but the intensity still lingering in the glint of his eyes.

"Stop leaving me hanging," Patrick said. "Like what?"

"Like—we want to tear into each other's flesh. Taking fucking *bites* out of each other. Like we want to see the red beneath. We want to see each other bleed."

"Now that's fucked up," Patrick said. "Remember, next time, to keep this to yourself."

"What?" Duce said, laughing. "You never felt that way for someone else?"

"Never," Patrick said.

"Whatever, man," Duce said. "It's not why I'm here."

"What is?"

"I—killed two men last night."

"What?" Patrick said, almost shouting.

Duce gritted his teeth. "Sorry, man. When I found those gangbangers in my crib, I got a name from one of them. Some motherfucker, a dealer named Rasta, sent them after me. Only, it turns out Rasta's a ghoul."

"Are you serious? Where is he now?" Patrick asked.

"Dead. Him and most of his crew. I—reacted. Before I could stop myself... four more men dead."

"Christ, Duce. Can anyone place you there?"

"Only the player who survived, and he sure as hell ain't talking to the police, much less reporting it. And by now

lucien soulban

the rats will have been at the bodies, so nobody is going to worry about any bite marks."

"Except whoever made this Rasta a ghoul," Patrick said. He fell silent a moment, considering the matter with furrowed brows. "Duce...you can't leave a trail of dead bodies and not expect someone to trace them back to you."

"I know, I know," Duce said, pressing the palms of his hands into his eyes. "But I gotta figure out who's gunning for my ass. And how they tie into Fulsome."

"If they tie in."

"Shit...if...." Duce said, trying not to contemplate the thought that these might be two different events colliding perfectly with one another.

"How you feeling?" Patrick asked. Normally, it wouldn't be a question he'd ask, but Duce understood the concern. When vampires killed, it had a habit of wearing down their souls and bringing them closer to the Beast.

"Hey, don't blind yourself, Patrick," Duce said, feeling strangely drained and apathetic. "I killed people in my day before I was bit. Not proud of it, because I know I can do it again."

"Yeah. Only now, it's different. You didn't have this devil riding on your shoulders, pushing you to fall over the edge."

"Sure I did," Duce said. "The Devil was always with me. The only difference now is that I can hear his footsteps more clearly. I know he's there."

"I don't think you do, but—" Patrick said, raising his hand to stop Duce's protests, "I said I'd watch your back, and I will. Somebody's got to protect you from yourself."

"All right then," Duce said.

Patrick's phone rang. He checked the display, his mouth dropping open enough to let Duce know it was trouble.

"It's Sheriff Nguyen," Patrick said.

A numbing cold shot through Duce's stomach and settled deep in his guts....

The knock on the door was persistent, strong. It wasn't housekeeping's knock—certainly not this late at night, and it wasn't room service since Persephone never ordered anything.

A quick glance through the peephole showed a nervous-looking hotel manager with a balding scalp and generous midsection, and two thick-necked goons behind him. All three sported nametags and the hotel's crest on their black jackets.

Not good, Persephone thought, and steadied her bearing to prepare for whatever was to come. She willed blood to flow into her cheeks to give herself a rosy cast, and she "pushed out," her term for enrapturing others with her beauty. She felt glib and relaxed, comfortable with her sexuality and looks. Such was the nature of her ability to entrance others, partly the ability to sway people's judgment, mostly a sense of unshakable self-confidence that mortals would be hard-pressed to unsettle.

Persephone opened the door, and for a moment, the manager and his two aides were speechless.

To his credit, the supervisor managed to fumble out a sentence.

"Miss—uhm, Persephone Moore?" he asked, uncertain.

"Yes. Is there a problem?" Persephone asked, her casual confidence and easy sexuality battering the three men. One of the goons looked away, obviously embarrassed and uncomfortable for whatever their errand demanded of this beautiful woman. Persephone couldn't help but smile.

Good, she thought. Let's make them as uncomfortable as possible.

"I'm sorry—ah—to have disturbed you, but I—uh. I'm afraid I have, uhm, bad news."

"Don't tell me there's a problem with my credit card," Persephone said, wearing a coy smile that actually drew a nasal sigh from a goon.

"Oh, no, no," the manager replied. "Your credit card was fine. It's just, uhm, I'm afraid you, uh, can't stay at the Hotel Intercontinental, I am so sorry," he said, blurting out the last bit.

"What?" Persephone said, genuinely surprised.

That look of astonishment hit the three men hard. Obviously, they didn't want to disappoint her.

"Why?"

"I'm very sorry," the manager repeated. "It wasn't our choice. But, ah, we've been asked to escort you. Out. I mean, after you pack of course. We'd be glad to help you. I'm just, uhm, really sorry about this. I don't know what to say."

Persephone forced a sad smile to her lips, trying to batter the three visitors into submission with her vulnerability. "Well, who would ask you to do such a thing?" Persephone asked, her eyes growing wide. "I mean, what could I have done?"

"I really don't know," the manager said, his voice pained by the nature of his duty. "I really wish I could say. I'm just a night manager here. It's the hotel manager who told me to do this. And he said something about one of the owners making the request."

"Really? Who? Maybe if I spoke to him?" Persephone said, trying to determine who was orchestrating this.

"I, ah. He didn't say who. Just told me to, you know, escort you out. No charge, of course. The hotel won't charge you for your stay here."

"Of course," Persephone said, her mind reeling, twisting as she examined the possible reasons for what was happening. She found no motive for her eviction, however; at least nothing beyond pure harassment.

"Well," Persephone said, trying to bargain for more time. "Couldn't you let me stay a while longer? Until I find a place to go?"

The manager squirmed under Persephone's best doe-eyed look; he looked like a child who had to pee. "I really can't," he said, his face a knot of anguish. "I wish I could, but the owners already called the police. They'll be here any minute."

"Police," Persephone said, taken off guard. "Are they coming to arrest me?"

"No, no. They're just coming to, ah, to escort you from the hotel. I'm so sorry. Can I help you with anything?"

Persephone was in shock now. The police en route and her with no place to go. She'd given her driver the two nights off, so there was no way to reach him.

"Miss Moore? Can we help you with anything?"

"Yes," Persephone said, still distracted by events. "If you could arrange for a taxi?"

"Certainly. I'll get right on it. These two gentleman will help you with your luggage," the manager said, indicating the two mountains of muscle at his shoulders. Both men were trying hard to look elsewhere as the manager scurried down the hallway.

Persephone closed the door and wandered about her suite in a daze, collecting everything with the grace of an automaton. Finally, she picked up the phone. She dialed Duce's number.

Duce hung up, looking at Patrick with a confused expression on his face.

"What was that about?" Patrick asked.

"I'm not sure," Duce said. "Series of attacks out in Joliet. Six prison guards from Stateville, and some of their family, murdered. Some of the bodies had their throats torn open. The Sheriffs are se*riously* pissed."

"What's that got to do with you?" Patrick asked.

"Not sure. Nguyen said he and the other Sheriffs are contacting all the covenants, but he did say witnesses saw two black men at one location, driving a stolen car that they traced back here in Chicago. He was probing to see if I knew something about it."

"Why?" Patrick said indignantly. "Because the perpetrators were black? That's profiling!"

"I know, but there's some strange shit going on. I just hope—"

Duce's phone rang, startling the two men. Duce looked at the call display, and then relaxed. "Persephone," he said, flipping the phone open.

It didn't take a moment before the two of them were heading out the door, fast.

Chapter Thirteen

"Did you see any cops?" Duce asked, loading Persephone's suitcase in the rear of his SUV.

"No," she admitted. "But I didn't want to take that chance."

"Smart choice," Patrick said, holding open the door for Persephone.

She got in, with a tired but grateful smile to Patrick for the small courtesy. Duce slipped behind the wheel, a few thoughts orbiting his head.

"Where to?" he asked, pulling into the street traffic, but he already knew the answers.

"I don't know. I don't know where to go."

"Stay with me," Duce said, knowing Patrick wouldn't approve. "It's cool."

"Are you sure?" Persephone asked.

"Yeah," Patrick said. "Are you sure?"

"What's that supposed to mean?" Persephone said, anger darkening her face.

"Yo, stop." Duce said. "It's my choice here, and it's to protect y'all."

"Protect us?" Persephone asked.

"Someone's following you."

"I figured," Persephone said. "But who and how?"

"Don't know, but I was telling Patrick it's time to go on the offensive. I'm tired of being hit by shit. I want to throw some of it back in their face."

"Fine by me," she replied. "What are you suggesting?"

"The Carthians are casting the no confidence vote on Tuesday. That means I need to know what Fulsome and Adenauer are planning and how Law fits into this."

"Fine," Persephone said. "I'll see if I can't nail down Griffin's support. With Halliburton and Griffin in your court, it'd make your case much stronger."

"What about me?" Patrick said.

"Your choice, brother," Duce said. "Maybe find out who the hell's on our tail and why?"

"All right," Patrick, "but it'll be hard. I didn't even know Persephone had Demetria following me."

Persephone looked shocked and Duce could see Patrick in the rearview mirror, smiling.

"How'd you—" Persephone began.

"You had Patrick followed?" Duce asked, interrupting Persephone.

"Yes," she said with a snap. "I needed to reach you urgently and I didn't think Patrick would help. He wasn't being cooperative."

"Yeah, well, here we are," Patrick said.

"Look, I'm sorry. But timing was crucial and I didn't have the luxury of winning your trust. So I opted for the heavy-handed route."

Nobody replied. The car fell into silence except for some light jazz on the radio; Thelonious Monk on piano, his fingers dancing across the keyboard like rain on a quiet night.

Finally, Patrick spoke. "You seeing Law? Don't know if that's smart."

"Gotta do it. If Law's wrapped up in this shit, I gotta figure out how and if Fulsome's using him to bait me."

"You need back-up?" Patrick asked.

"I'm good," Duce said. "Right now, I really need you to find whoever is on Persephone's ass."

"Other than you," Patrick said, then immediately held up his hands. "Shit, sorry, didn't mean that. It slipped out, man."

"I'm letting that one slide," Duce said. "But it seems to be happening a lot. Casual, nasty shit just has a habit of

lucien soulban

finding play when you don't mean it to." Duce thought about his fight with Rasta and his men; punching one in the throat; shooting two others; fingers slipping into the soft skin under Rasta's jawbone....

"What about your ass?" Patrick asked. "Who's watching it?"

"Law," Duce said. "But this shit they're pulling on Persephone is different. It's all harassment. Means it's probably someone else. Think you can put your differences aside and help her out?"

"Hey man, I wasn't the one who had *her* followed."

"Yeah," Duce said, shooting a quick glance over at Persephone who was staying quiet and uncharacteristically small. "I ain't happy about that."

"Spare me," Persephone muttered. She no longer seemed small.

"Excuse me?" Duce responded.

"You heard me, Duce," Persephone said. "Both of you. I will not be talked down to. I am sorry for what I did, but I don't regret it. I'm trying to help you here, and I'm taking great risks doing so. And so far, instead of thanks, I've lost my haven and I was driven out of my hotel like some common criminal. I'm sorry that I don't appeal to your sense of fair play or that my experiences don't match your misadventures, but frankly, I'm not going to handicap myself here. Are you?" she said to Duce.

"No," Duce said.

"Fine. I needed to find Duce and I did what was necessary. Otherwise, Patrick, you would have kept me far from him. Now that's behind us, right?"

Silence a moment before Patrick spoke up. "I'm willing to let it go."

"Yeah," Duce said. "Sorry. Just got a lot of shit on my mind. But it's cool."

"Good," Persephone said, staring out the window. "But I have to ask," she added a short pause later. "How'd you know it was Demetria?"

Patrick shrugged, smiling with the cat-who-caught-the-canary smirk. "It's a thing," he said.

Duce's cell rang. He answered and exchanged a couple of words, bringing the SUV to a stop at a red light. He quickly cupped the mouth-piece with his thumb.

"It's Adenauer!" he said, throwing a questioning look at the others. Sort of a "what the fuck" kind of glance.

"She wants to meet me... alone."

It's a trap, man.

Duce parked his SUV across the street from the Blue Dog Note, a low-key blues bar on Harrison. The clientele was clean-cut and mixed, but the smoky glass façade revealed nothing of the interior.

I don't think so. Why go in for some heavy shit like trying to whack me?

Duce let the engine idle and considered the sanity of his actions. None of this made sense. Why would Adenauer call a meeting?

Duce, love, are you sure it was Bethany Adenauer on the phone? Nosferatu are good at disguising their voices.

The engine guttered dead and Duce pocketed the keys as he closed the door and locked them remotely. He waited for a car to pass before darting across the road.

Persephone's right. Maybe it wasn't her on the phone. Somebody's already tried capping your ass twice. Maybe they're tired of chasing after you. Maybe they're making you come to them.

Duce opened the door to the Blue Dog Note, and was hit by the pungent waft of cigar smoke and the light instrumentals of improvisational jazz. He headed for the coat check to his right; there was a dark stairwell on the left going up.

I can't take that chance. If Adenauer wants to meet, I got to see what she's up to.

The coat-check girl with milk chocolate skin and cork-screw braids in her hair took Duce's leather jacket; her smile was generous, her eyes never drifting away from Duce for more than the second it took to hang his jacket. He felt

lucien soulban

polite, so he smiled back. She slipped him the claim chit with her phone number on the back.

Maybe, Duce, but something 'bout this doesn't ring right.

It took a moment to make a circuit of the ground floor. None of the faces registered as vampire, and everyone seemed pretty relaxed—perfectly natural given the environment. He went back to the coat check and the stairwell.

Yeah, man. I know. But I don't think it's a trap. Too public, too obvious.

Duce took the stairs to the club's half-floor overlooking the blues stage. A few booths were taken, but it was a light night and the crowd small and low key. Everybody had that gel cool to their groove as they soaked up the vibe. None of the folk here registered as Kindred...

Besides, I warned Adenauer that people knew I'd be there. She'd be foolish to attack me, and if I don't see her there, and see her alone, I bounce.

...except for Adenauer. She sat at a table along the balcony's railing, overlooking the stage. She seemed to be enjoying the music, though Duce would never have figured her for a blues woman. Even her customary sneer was subdued.

Shit, I wish I wasn't about to say this. But, Duce? What if this was what Adrian was planning. The big thing he was going to nail Beth with—if we're right about him. What if it's something to do with you and all this shit happening?

It took Adenauer a moment to notice Duce, but when she did, her sneer crept into view again. She flicked her long black hair over her shoulder and motioned to the chair across from hers.

Shit. You're right, Pat. I wish you hadn't said that either...

"Sit," she said, like she was doing him a favor.

...But I gotta do this.

"Fuck you," Duce said, his calm mien unbroken. "I'm not your dog to 'sit.' And second," he said, taking the chair right next to hers, "I'm not sitting with my back to the stairs."

"Don't blame you," Beth said, her attention split between Duce and the stage.

"What do you want, Adenauer?"

"You know," she said, turning to stare Duce in the face, "that's part of your problem. You refer to people by their last name, like some punch-clock tyrant, and then expect people to be your friend."

"I don't want friends," Duce said. "I'm trying to help the Carthians achieve focus, and the only way I can do that is to be their leader, not their friend."

Bethany shrugged. "And has it worked, for you? Oh wait! No, it hasn't."

"Yeah, well, it doesn't help when you and Fulsome are sabotaging everything I do."

"It's not sabotage. We're protecting the Carthians. That's part of the democratic process. And if you remember correctly, I fully supported you at the beginning."

"Whatever. You were helping yourself."

"Don't flatter yourself," Beth said. "And we're Carthians, not Invictus. We aren't into the centuries-long games."

"Maybe that's your problem," Duce said. "Spontaneity is good, but we're too shortsighted! You'd have us running around trying to change shit we don't even understand."

"What's to understand? That the Invictus is a dying regime. We're here to replace it with something better."

"Just like that, right?"

"Sometimes things are just that simple."

"Maybe, if this was television or you're George Bush Jr. In the real world, shit ain't that simple, and the Invictus isn't just going to go away. They plan on staying, and the harder you push, the harder they'll push back."

"Aw, what's the matter, Duce? Afraid of a little bloody nose?"

"You know what? Fuck you," Duce said, getting up, drawing attention to the table. "I didn't come here to be ragged on by some suburban cracker-ass bitch who never suffered a day in her life. I fought for what I got. And nearly died, too. Doubt you could say the same, huh?"

People on the second floor tried turning back to listen to the music, but most were focused on the conversation.

"Y'know," Beth said, standing as well, though she came well short of Duce's eye-level, "that shit gets really old, really fast. What? I'm supposed to apologize for having rich parents? I'm supposed to feel sorry for you because of where you grew up?"

"What would you know about where I lived?"

"Oh, a fair deal," Beth said with a smirk. "And it's funny you should ask since that's why I asked you here. An old acquaintance wants to meet with you." Beth nodded to someone over Duce's shoulder.

Duce turned, instantly regretting having turned his back to the stairs. He knew the face walking his way, knew it like his own.

Law.

"He wanted to talk to you, so I arranged the meeting," Beth said before leaning in close and whispering: "And if you want to save your ass, you'll listen to what he has to say."

"You going to say something?" Law asked, seated across from Duce. "Or you just going to stare at me like these fool crackheads?" he said, thumbing the few customers paying attention to them. Most went back to the show.

Silence. Duce continued staring at him and Adenauer before he finally responded. "What the fuck you doing here?"

"Thought it was time we talked."

"We talked last week."

"No. You came in and treated me like your bitch. Wanted to make sure we cleared that shit out the way before...."

"Before what?"

"Before he joined the Carthians," Adenauer said.

"Bullshit!" Duce hissed, struggling to keep his voice down. He wasn't sure what to expect, but it sure wasn't this.

"No way in hell he's becoming a Carthian, much less getting bit." Duce fumbled for coherence, trying to pull a string of words from the knots in his thoughts. Law? A vampire? Suddenly his pond was shrinking, the life he'd left rushing up on his rear fender. He felt trapped, infringed, the life he'd created a lie in the light of his ex-friend who bore the banner of his "real" days.

"They know I can put you back on track," Law said. "Redeem you. I told them all about you, back in the day."

"Back on track? Motherfucker, they're trying to hit me with a vote of no confidence. They're trying to kick my ass out of the Carthians."

"Only if you don't help us," Beth said with a smile.

"But it won't come to that, right, Duce?" Law asked.

"Help you?" Duce said.

"We want you to Embrace Law."

"*Excuse* me?" Duce said. "Now I know y'all are bugging. Go fuck yourselves!"

"I told Adrian you wouldn't agree," Adenauer said with a grin.

"Yo," Law said to Adenauer. "Let me talk to my boy here. I'll straighten it out."

"All right," she said, looking uncertain. Law leaned in to kiss her cheek, but Bethany stood suddenly. Duce realized she was embarrassed. She looked at Duce to see if he noticed anything, and hurried off when she realized he did. Duce nodded to himself... Law had feelings for Adenauer, but they weren't reciprocal.

Is Law under a Vinculum? Duce wondered.

"What you nodding at?" Law said.

"I get it," Duce replied. "I get it even if you don't understand the shit you stepped in."

"What you on about?"

"You think they're giving you a chance to redeem me? Truth is, asking me to give you the bite is a way to fuck me over."

"Man, they said you'd see it that way."

"They also tell you that me giving you the Kiss weakens me up here?" Duce asked, tapping his head. "Makes me more pliant? No? Or that once you're Embraced, I become fully responsible for you? You screw up, it's my ass. They control me through you. And if they think I'm that blind or desperate enough to stay in power, they're fucked in the head."

"I'd do it for you," Law said.

"Not if you understood what it really meant to be one of us."

"Man, Duce," Law said, shaking his head, "what the fuck happened to you?"

"Me? I got out, that's what happened."

"You ran. You punked out and you ran like a motherfucker."

"What the fuck was I supposed to do? Spend thirty years in jail? Get shot again? Shanked? Dead by 20?"

"You're dead now."

"Not the same thing," Duce said.

"Yeah, I can see that."

"And what about you? You left the Black P-Stones, right? Or so you say."

"I did, motherfucker. BGF now," he said, revealing the inks on his forearm: A dragon encircling a prison guard tower... the banner of the Black Guerilla Family. "New Afrikan all the way."

Suddenly, another piece of the puzzle fell into place: The prison guards murdered in Joliet. The Black Guerilla Family was a prison gang started by Black Panther George Jackson for the purpose of maintaining dignity for incarcerated African-Americans. They hated correctional officers, the chief enforcers of their abuse and misery, and targeted them whenever they could. He kept that realization to himself, however, and continued with the conversation. If Law was involved with the attacks, Duce needed to know how and why.

"So why you tripping over shit I did when you were following in my footsteps," Duce said, easily slipping back into slang. He had to concentrate not to fall into those old, familiar rotes.

"I don't give a shit about Black P. If I did, I would have told them what you did."

"Bullshit. You didn't tell them I punked them out?" Duce said, almost laughing.

"No I didn't." Law said, fixing Duce with a stare. "I never told them you were the leak. Then I hear shit about you being under F.B.I. surveillance, and how you *volunteered* to step away to protect the set. You were a goddamn hero, and I still didn't say shit then, either."

"What?" Duce said. "Why? I betrayed the code."

"Because I had your back, motherfucker. We were road dogs. Fuck that... we were brothers. I had your back, and I thought you had mine."

"I couldn't—" Duce said before he stopped himself, stuffing the words back in his mouth and fighting hard to keep them down. Always felt like he was justifying himself to Law when they were younger. Not anymore. But if Law was telling the truth, then Duce was operating off very erroneous assumptions, assumptions that took him in completely different directions in life and in death.

Was Law lying, though? Duce hoped he was; hoped this was some petty-ass attempt at revenge. The only problem with that was, Law was direct. He never played these kinds of games, and he rarely lied about the important things.

"You couldn't what?" Law asked.

"Nothing," Duce replied. It was a lie they both recognized, but Duce wasn't about to tell Law that he couldn't face his friend after having turned evidence against his own set. As far as Duce was concerned, at the time, his actions rendered him *persona non grata* with the people he'd once called friends. Duce had assumed he was an exile and under a death threat, because it was far easier to *believe* you were right than be *proven* you were right.

"All right, nothing then. But you still haven't said. What happened to you?"

"I just told you, I—"

"I ain't talking about that shit. I know why you left the set. Shit, man. You were too much of a dreamer to hang with us forever. I knew that."

"Then what're you asking?" Duce said, the ﹍
building again.

"Remember, when we were young?" Law asked, lean﹍
in close. "When we used to talk about if we had the magic
gun."

Duce hesitated at the memory, a forgotten bit of history
splashing cold water on his face. "Shit. The magic gun. I
remember that."

"Right. What would you do to change your life if you
had a magic gun? Shoot bullets that could do anything you
wanted, like kill every soldier-cop."

"Or kill poverty. Yeah I remember," Duce said, almost
comfortable in those childhood memories.

"You wanted to change the world, dog. So what happened to you?"

"Fuck, Law. I grew up. Ain't no magic gun gonna solve
the world's problems. And if I remember right, we always
talked about that shit after smoking cigarettes dipped in
PCP!"

"Shit," Law said, laughing. "Those were *good*. But I'm
not talking about that. You got the magic gun floating in
your veins. A pair of bullets in your mouth. I've seen the
shit your set can do. Why haven't you used those blood-
sucking powers to help the community? Change the world
like we talked about?"

"Because shit ain't that simple," Duce said, suddenly
entrenched in what seemed like the world's oldest argument. "There're too many checks and balances to go
fucking with them. And the people with the power can do
what I can, and more. They got the years, and they got the
experience. What I want to do will take decades, centuries
maybe. I don't know. Only, nobody's willing to do what's
necessary. Take the time to understand their enemy and
how to use their tools against them."

"Understand the Man?" Law said, raising an eyebrow.
"Sound just like an Uncle Tom."

"And I hear the same shit from every one of you short-
sighted motherfuckers. You want revolution, but you want

it in blood. That shit won't work, especially here where blood's a dangerous thing."

"D, there's no such 'n such as a safe revolution. You got to spill blood, or it won't mean shit."

"I got no problems spilling blood. I got a problem with wasting it."

Law shrugged. "That's the problem, man. Sometimes sacrifice is necessary to get what you want. Maybe that's why the Carthians want me to help set you straight."

"And who makes the sacrifice?" Duce asked. "You? Never seen you do jack when someone was willing to do it for you."

"Being a good leader is knowing how to delegate shit."

"No. Being a good leader means never asking someone to do anything you aren't willing to do yourself."

"Look at the Carthians, Duce. They're willing to make the sacrifices and fight for what's theirs. They need a strong hand."

"I know that, Law. But what they want is suicide! And I'm not letting you, or Adenauer or Fulsome fuck them over for your own glory."

Law shrugged and stood up. "Not glory. And it may not be up to you, brother. Whether you do the deed or not, me and my crew are getting bit, and we're joining the Carthians. You can either get behind that, or get stepped on. It's up to you. The revolution ain't gonna wait."

Chapter Fourteen

Persephone sat in the waiting room, growing more impatient with each passing minute. While she understood Griffin's predilections, this behavior was excessive, even for him. He was at the Morris House, approaching on daily, virtually unwilling to meet anywhere else. His passion remained ensconced within the comforts of the salon, and he refused to interact with people outside of these safe environs if he could help it. How he gained sway among night's hierarchy of players was puzzling at first blush. Griffin's influence was simple enough, however. He drank at the watering holes of the local predators, and he was good at ingratiating himself with them. It was as simple as that. Certainly, he possessed some pull in mortal circles, but the fact was, his network far exceeded his actual worth. Persephone knew this, and knew that by holding Griffin's ear, she also held the attention of his closest confederates who frequented the salon. It was a variant on the old boys' network, and if Duce thought it was segregation of the worst sort, then he had no inkling of Persephone's struggles as a relative "pup" to her covenant. This, and this alone, allowed her to overlook the hours-long delays through which Griffin forced her for an audience.

If she had one comfort, it was that clusters of minutes, three and five at a time, vanished in moments of daydreaming. She remembered Duce between her legs, remembered the taste of his blood after she tore into his flesh. The memories were visceral, relived with a frightening clarity. Persephone flexed her thigh muscles and felt a small surge of pleasure pulsate through her. She shook her head and extricated herself from her erotic thoughts. They were a comfortable place to dwell...too comfortable, actually. It was too easy to get lost in them; too easy to get lost in Duce.

Persephone focused her attention on her surroundings again as a pair of vampires walked by her. They were members of the Invictus, and they eyed her closely. She stared back, trying to analyze the reason for their scrutiny. They seemed cautious, and a little too casually belligerent in their gaze. It was like they had nothing to lose by acting brazen toward her. Persephone straightened in her seat and quickly studied the room. Thinking about it, she had been receiving looks for the entire two hours she'd been here. Something was wrong.

A hostess, a petite blond with short-cropped hair, looked surprised when Persephone marched straight up to her and pulled her into a small, discreet corridor.

"Mr. Griffin isn't ready to see you yet," the woman said quickly.

"Why's everybody staring at me?"

"I'm not sure what you mean, Miss Moore," she replied, trying hard to maintain her courteous bearing.

"Don't lie," Persephone said, squeezing her arm hard with barely a casual thought.

"I've worked here long enough to have endured worse," the young woman said, looking at her arm. Worry remained in her eyes, but she wasn't cowed.

"You're right," Persephone said, releasing her grip and feeling embarrassed for her casual expression of cruelty. "I'm sorry. But you're not leaving till I have an answer. Why are people staring?"

The woman huffed and glanced down the corridor, ensuring they were alone. "Mr. Griffin isn't actually here," she said, her voice a whisper.

"What?"

"I shouldn't be telling you this."

"I won't tell anyone, I promise."

"He instructed us to keep you here for as long as possible."

"Why?" Persephone asked, trying to glean the answer herself. Was this another game to him? She wasn't sure.

"I think he wants you humiliated."

"Humiliated? For what?"

"Look, Miss Moore," the woman said. "I don't want to get in trouble here."

"And you won't. Now please, tell me. Why are people staring?"

The woman wrestled with some inner dilemma a moment, biting her lower lip in the process. Persephone recognized the look, the one all vampires wear when they're weighing their options... the one humans learn to monkey when playing among the undead.

"Okay, I'll tell you," the woman said. "But you'll owe me, right?"

"Owe you what?" Persephone said. "Be more specific."

The hostess chewed on her lip again. "I'm tired of being a blood bag. I want to be turned."

"I'm not going to Embrace you," Persephone said.

"Then sponsor me. Please. I've been fed on so much, I—I'm tired of being victimized. The last time someone fed on me, they nearly killed me. I can't walk away. They won't let me. I've seen too much. Find someone else to bite me. I don't care who. I don't want to be human anymore," she said, her eyes focusing on some fresh memory, "not after what I've seen."

"You don't know what you're asking," Persephone said. "The Embrace isn't escape. It's a smaller cage." Persephone was about to walk away when the woman grabbed her arm with tears in her eyes.

"Please! Here, I'll tell you, on good faith. Mr. Griffin says you betrayed the Invictus. That you're planning on joining some people called the Carthites?"

"Carthians?"

"I think so. He's saying you turned your back on your own covenant."

"What?" Persephone said, shocked by the accusation.

"I think he asked you to meet him here so everyone else could get a look at you. Know who you are by face."

"He said *that*?" Persephone steadied herself against the wall. It felt like someone had punched her in the ribs, hard.

"That's what people are saying."

Persephone stood there, absorbing what she just learned. If this was true, then she was in trouble. Nobody would want to deal with her anymore. Griffin was exiling her.

But why? Had he been playing with her from the beginning, when he met with Duce? *Or is this all a misunderstanding?*

"See, I told you, Miss Moore. Please, I know being a vampire isn't easy for your kind, but I'd prefer being the monster than being eaten by him...."

The hostess blanched when Persephone shot her an annoyed look.

"I'm sorry," the woman said, almost in tears. "I didn't mean to call you a monster. I'm sorry, I'm sorry."

"When is Griffin showing up?" Persephone demanded.

The hostess hesitated.

"Look," Persephone said. "I'll see what I can arrange, but I'm not making that kind of promise. I can't do even that much, however, if I don't settle this fast. I lose my contacts and you'll be lucky if I can find a Chihuahua to bite you. When's Griffin's next appointment?"

"Around 3:30 this morning, I think."

"And how far has this gone? Griffin's claims? Is it only here that people know?"

"I don't think so," the hostess said. "I think he's talking to anyone who'll listen...."

Patrick moved through the quiet corridors with their diamond checkerboard floors, past exhibits of ancient medical tools, bulky pre-1950s apparatus and an apothecary shop recreated with impeccable detail. Other vampires, their faces painted like somber harlequins and their

lucien soulban

bodies clad in assorted black mesh, vinyl, straps, plaids, chains, lace and rivets moved past him, paying him neither regard nor disregard. A couple nodded to him, acknowledging his presence. He was welcome among them, though truthfully, Patrick wasn't sure he understood them.

Patrick left them to their strange reverence, and moved up to the 4th floor of the International Museum of Surgical Science—the art gallery.

The vampires here, while belonging to no covenant, shared a loose bond. They were modern children of the Embrace with a penchant for neo-Victorian modes of dress and behavior, and little interest in the existing factions. They were the unbound, and distrusted by most camps because they owed fealty to no one but each other. A few fell into covenants, and just as easily fell back out. The covenant of mystics known as the Circle of the Crone provided some with the magical crafts they craved, while others came to the Carthians when their frustration with the Lancea Sanctum or the Invictus reached a breaking point.

In the end, though, they drifted away, Patrick realized, because they were a part of Kindred society the factions ignored or discounted. He recognized something of himself in them, the desire for individual expression. The covenants offered too rigid a framework to allow for much personal articulation. Once someone joined a covenant, they followed its operating procedure, much like any religion or cult. Only, religions like Catholicism were losing ground in North America because people were gleaning their own truths from the world around them. A little Zen here to contend with daily struggles, a little paganism there to connect to the world spirit, and a little prayer to God just to be safe. The unbound were much like those seekers born into the modern world, their faith a pastiche of the world's best.

Patrick looked at the faces of the vampires around him and wondered if they didn't have it right. He respected them for traveling the road less trod and he envied them for their place outside the established courts, outside the strictures of "The Game."

He was jealous of them because they were outsiders by choice, not because someone had thrust that decision upon them. And with events among the Carthians moving the way they were, Patrick wasn't sure he wouldn't eventually become unbound, even if Duce remained in power. The politics bothered him and by leaving, he'd at least achieve some measure of autonomy and peace. But for how long could he stay away? How long before he'd crave companionship or friendship, and find himself involved with some covenant, embroiled in the very same arguments and underhanded dealings?

Patrick shelved those thoughts when he saw Demetria, examining an oil-painting of a skull through the green-tinted lens of x-rays. She was touching the canvas, caressing it.

"Should you be doing that?" Patrick asked, standing next to her.

"As vampires, we don't exude any oily secretions responsible for damaging these pictures. It's like I was wearing a glove. Here," Demetria said, grabbing Patrick by the wrist.

"What are you—"

"Shh," she said, and brought his hand up to the painting. She used his fingers to brush the canvas. "You're too tense. Loosen up."

"This is not why—"

"—you're here?" she said, interrupting him. "Actually, we're nothing without touch. We can't understand the human condition without touching or being touched. Life shouldn't be a sterile laboratory, all distant and remote. I don't believe in artificial boundaries."

Patrick allowed Demetria to paint with his hand, but he was focusing on hers, trying to see past the unblemished skin to the true layers beneath. And he caught a glimpse of it, a quick flash of rubber-like skin, flesh braided and scarred hard by fire. He pulled away inadvertently, and quickly wished he'd stayed within the illusion of her mind

lucien soulban

tricks. Demetria cocked an eyebrow. "Not used to being touched?" she asked. "Or not used to being touched by my kind?"

"Sorry," Patrick said, unable to meet her gaze.

She offered a wistful smile. "I'm a good liar," she said. "I can make people see the way I once looked, but I can never see the face I remember. I can't look in a mirror and enjoy the fantasy. Only the reality stares back at me. So look at me when you talk to me. Bad enough I see the monster through my own eyes. I don't need to see it through yours."

"I'm sorry," Patrick said again, embarrassed...until he realized Demetria was smiling. "You're fucking with me."

"Sorry," she said, laughing. "I couldn't resist. I don't need to see my own reflection if I don't want to. Besides, I enjoy the macabre and twisted, even if it is in me. If it requires more effort to dig for that bit of beauty, then it's more rewarding finding it. I abhor common beauty found with barely a glance. Where's the challenge in that?"

Patrick shook his head. While the conversation was...interesting, he had things to do and places to be. "Look, did you find anything?"

"Not yet. Your friend Duce met with Bethany Adenauer, but I didn't involve myself with that. I stayed nearby to see if he was being followed. Nothing to report."

"Okay, keep at it. I want to ask you something else, though. I have a friend and we think someone's following her, too."

"Who is it?"

"Persephone Moore, and don't pretend you don't know her. She hired you to tail me, I know that."

"All right," Demetria responded with a grin. "I'm just surprised you're friends with her."

"Long fucking story. What I need, though, is who's on her tail?"

"Sure thing, boss," Demetria said. "Just tell me where she is, and I'll start from there."

"Stick around Duce," Patrick said, leaving, "and you'll eventually find her."

"Ah. I see," Demetria said, laughing and turning back to the oil painting. "You learn the most interesting things on this job."

The same stares seemed to follow her, and Persephone did her best to ignore the pale faces that watched her from among the mortal throngs. The few responses she received were curt, but enough to find Sebastian Garin, the prince's Herald, as he made his rounds through the Safe Harbor Lounge.

Safe Harbor was a sanctuary for young Invictus and Longinus members, and like all such watering holes, would probably fold in a few months. All it took was one elder to disapprove of his ward's haunt, one elder to flex his bureaucratic muscles, to close down the bar. It happened all the time.

Not that Persephone cared. She rarely frequented these places, except when she needed to, like now. Sebastian was speaking with a pair of Kindred, likely newly bitten, when Persephone grabbed his arm and pulled him from the conversation. His eyes went wide in shock, darting around the room, seeing who was watching them. The crush was gone, replaced by fear.

"Persephone," Sebastian said, fumbling over his words. "Now's not a good time—"

"I don't care," Persephone said. "What are people saying about me?"

"I don't know. I haven't heard anything."

"Like hell you haven't, Sebastian. I know Griffin's talking about me, and I want to know what he said. The faster you answer, the faster this is over."

Sebastian looked around again and shrugged, almost apologetically. "He says you've turned Carthian. That you're in league with them and conspiring against the Invictus."

lucien soulban

"And people believe him?"

"Of course they do, Persephone. Everyone's seen you and Duce around town, acting all chummy."

"What I'm doing, I'm doing for the Invictus," she whispered. "You have to tell people that. Make them believe."

Sebastian backed away. "I'm sorry, Persephone. I can't do that. I can't get involved here." He vanished into the crowd.

Persephone watched him leave. More faces stared at her, whispered into each other's ears and singled her out with darting eyes or an upturned nod. She wanted to tell them the truth, convince them, but they didn't care. What mattered wasn't her or her role in events; what mattered was the nature of the gossip—of the accusations. This assembly didn't deserve to see her grovel and beg. Instead, she left, challenging each gaze with a fierce one of her own. This was not over.

"Look, Duce, this is getting stranger and stranger," Patrick said, settling back into his sofa.

Duce plopped into the chair with a growl. "Embrace Law. That shit's never happening."

"Well, it's smart. If you agreed to it, it'd weaken your position. Sap some of that stubbornness of yours and bind you to Beth through your responsibility to your childe. Hell, maybe Adrian's planning on turning you and Beth in for embracing Law out of turn."

"Shit. If Fulsome knows me, then he knows he can't force me to Embrace anyone."

"But what if you don't have a choice? What if he figures your desire to stay in power will make you agree to anything?"

Duce thought about it a moment before he shook his head. "Nah, man. Nah. Sorry, Pat, but that's too risky to work. It leaves too many variables outside Fulsome's control even if I agree to the Embrace, and he wouldn't go for that. Thing is, I got my integrity and I got my pride. I won't be pushed into shit and Fulsome knows that."

"Then how about this. Adrian knows you'll reject Law, which gives him more ammunition against you."

"How so?"

"Simple, man. If Beth and Adrian convince the Carthians that Law could help them achieve their goals and then you refuse to Embrace Law, you look petty and jealous. You're no longer fit to lead because you're putting personal interests above the covenant's needs."

"All right," Duce said. "I can see that. That does sound subtle enough for Fulsome to try, but Adenauer...I know her. She'll go for something more direct."

Patrick smirked and quickly leaned forward to look at his feet.

"What?" Duce asked. "Why you smiling?"

"I just realized. You used to call Fulsome by his first name. Now that Adrian's moving against you, you switched. Started calling him by his last name."

"Did I? I didn't notice. But the motherfucker is trying to bum rush my ass."

"I'm just saying. No criticisms, but it is funny. You're lucky, though."

"How's that?" Duce asked, cocking an eyebrow, almost challenging Patrick to justify that statement.

"You're lucky that the Carthians are impatient. I think it's forced Adrian to move faster than he wants. Rather than taking his time screwing you over, Adrian's got to seize the moment."

"Well, he looks pretty strong to me."

"Not strong enough, man."

"Whatever. I can't worry about that now. I need to know what he's got planned."

"Maybe you should talk to Law some more. Figure out if Adrian let anything slip around him."

"No, fuck it. I'm done talking to Law. He's nothing but a puppet in all this, and he doesn't care."

"Doesn't care, or doesn't know."

"Law's smart, man. He knows he's being used, but it doesn't matter... especially if he's been enthralled with Beth's blood."

"That's a dangerous game he's playing."

"Problem is, I don't know who's more screwed. Him or Fulsome and Adenauer."

"How so?" Patrick asked.

"Fulsome thinks he's getting a 'yessuh, masta,' kind of vampire. He doesn't know Law. Law's tight with the community. He's a reactionary and thinks in mortal terms and a mortal sense of progress. No Traditions, no Prince, no Primogen. Law won't give a shit about those things. And Law... Law doesn't know what kind of games we play. This Danse Macabre shit. He thinks he can better the community. Make us stronger as Afrikans."

"You mean African-Americans?"

"No, Afrikans. With a 'k.' It's a political movement that separates Afrikans from white America or 'Amerikans.' Sometimes they spell that KKK."

"Yeah, yeah, I heard about them," Patrick said, then stopped. He sat back, looking dazed, shaking his head. "Ain't that a bitch," he said.

"What?"

"I just said: *I heard about them*. Like they're no longer a part of my world. Like the community is no longer in my blood. Since when do I not know what's happening with my people?"

"Isn't that what you been telling me, though? Stay away from the community for their own good."

"Yeah, man, but...I never stopped being black. Never stopped caring."

"Now you know what I'm dealing with. How can you be African-American and not be part of a greater community. That's why this 'older vampires are above color,' shit doesn't fly with me."

"Who said that?"

"Persephone."

"Duce, I get that you care for the girl, and hell if I know why, but she's white."

"Not this shit again."

"No, no. It isn't a tirade against white folks. It's a simple fact that most vampires are white, so no matter where they are, they're still among their own kind. They've always been the haves, the majority, unless they're gay or Jewish or some other submerged minority. And until they're segregated from their peers, they don't know nothing about isolation or loneliness. So Persephone can afford to say that kind of shit, because to her, it's true. It isn't about color to her because she's never been faced with the alternative. "

"Now *that* I'm willing to accept. Doesn't make her or any of them bad."

"Didn't say it did. But that's the problem. They Embrace us and tell us to steer clear of our communities. Now that's easy to say when everyone you know and remember is dead and gone."

"I know man, I know. Law's all up with the BGF. He's going to be bringing their agenda into play, not knowing—"

"Or caring."

"Or caring, you're right, that his philosophy and the Carthians won't mix."

"Well maybe," Patrick said. "Maybe *that's* what Beth's planning. Fulsome going all coy and subtle with the no confidence vote, but I can see Beth getting swept up in the notion of a black rebel. She's always romanticized intellectual revolutionaries like Che and Marx. Hell, she had a thing for you when you first came on the scene."

"*What?* Get the fuck out of here!"

"No, I'm serious," Patrick said, laughing. "But that's not the point. Maybe Law's going along with Beth because Beth is getting swept up in whatever scheme Law has planned."

Duce leaned forward, resting on his knees. "Man...that's not a bad theory. I think you got something there."

"Thank you," Patrick said with a small bow. "But do you still think Law's responsible for the drive-by?"

"Not any more. I did, but, why try and cap my ass when he wants me to Embrace him? Something doesn't add right."

"True. But at least we have a handle on Beth and Adrian."

"Hopefully. Looks like our work is cut out for us. You still on Persephone's little problem?"

"Yeah, I'm on it."

"Cool. I got things to manage. I'll catch you later," Duce said, standing up and heading for the door.

"Duce?" Patrick said, getting up as well. "What's Law's last name?"

"Michaels."

"So, how come you don't call him by his last name? Like you do Adrian and Beth?"

Duce shrugged, casual. "Old habits die hard, I guess. Why?"

"Because maybe you don't want to talk to Law, but damn if you don't got shit to resolve with him."

"Yeah, well, whatever issues Law and me got, they don't involve the Carthians. They shouldn't have brought him in in the first place."

"I hear you," Patrick said, escorting Duce to the door. "You sure you aren't up to talking to him?"

"Yeah, man, I'm sure."

They embraced each other with a firm pat on the shoulders before parting ways.

Patrick sat by the phone, considering his next course of action. In his hands, he played with an address book, skimming through pages slowly, contemplating matters. He flipped it open and found the page he needed. He thumbed the page a few times, lost in thought, before he finally dialed the number.

"Hello, Bethany," Patrick said. "It's Patrick. I need to ask you a favor."

Chapter Fifteen

Persephone studied the living room while waiting for Halliburton to arrive. The furniture consisted of fine antiques predominantly in the Rococo vein, which included exotic woods and ornate carvings just shy of Baroque; brass trimmings, large mirrors and rich upholstery complemented the ensemble. While Halliburton's stead was rich in its touches, it certainly wasn't his sleeping haven. This was his entertainment estate, where he met guests over social affairs and housed visitors staying for the day. Halliburton slept elsewhere. He'd be a fool not to.

A few moments later, a valet with a striking resemblance to James Stewart walked in and announced Halliburton's impending arrival. Persephone afforded herself a small smile. Halliburton's staff all bore vague similarities to former stars or starlets from the 1950s: Doris Day, Grace Kelly, Brigitte Bardot, Marilyn Monroe, Elizabeth Taylor, Rock Hudson. Thankfully, Halliburton didn't require them to act like their counterparts.

Halliburton was good at entrances. He swept into the room with a smile, as though expecting to meet a throng of waiting admirers. He kissed Persephone on both cheeks without pause and quickly studied her ensemble; simple black slacks and a business shirt cuffed up with the top two buttons undone. He himself wore wool straight-cut trousers and a golf shirt, both brown.

"And what are we calling this look?" Halliburton asked.

"I call it the *Pulp Fiction* collection."

"A Tarantino movie," he said, bathing Persephone in an uncertain eye and raised brow.

"Don't think Tarantino. Think Uma Thurman."

"Ah. She has a look that might have worked well in my era. But I'm surprised you didn't come here dressed like Audrey Hepburn, given your last performance as Capucine."

"Please, dear. Once was amusing. More than that, and I'm pandering. Besides, I doubt I could carry off an Audrey Hepburn. I don't have the hair for it."

"True," Halliburton said, guiding Persephone to the sofa before sitting down himself. "Tarantino's films tend to have an undercoating of violence, don't they?"

"More like an overcoating," Persephone said, immediately sensing an unusual twist to the conversation. Halliburton wasn't talking for the sake of hearing his voice. He was getting at something. She could tell by the casual air in his gestures that were contrary to the focus in his green eyes.

"I will admit that I enjoyed *Reservoir Dogs*. I own a copy."

"I remember the movie," Persephone replied.

"You should see it again. I think you'd appreciate it. It deals with betrayal and honor among thieves."

And there it is, Persephone thought.

"I am curious, though," Halliburton said, continuing, "who did you like in *Reservoir Dogs*?"

"I'm not sure I sympathized with any of them. They were all villains, weren't they?"

"Except for the undercover police officer. But I'm surprised, Persephone. You, more than anyone, should realize there are no good guys or bad guys here. There's only ambition."

"That depends. Are we talking about the movie? Or something else?"

"Indulge me," Halliburton said. "Who did you like?"

"Maybe Tim Roth's character."

"Mr. Orange."

"I suppose. He was caught in circumstances he disliked, for what he believed to be the greater good."

"But he shot a woman. Hardly heroic."

"She shot first, and as you said, there are no heroes here. He killed on panicked impulse. It was instinct."

"Hm. I'm not sure. Mr. Orange was too much a victim in all this. A victim of circumstance and a victim of his duty. Swept along for the ride, as it were. What about Mr. White?"

"Harvey something?"

"Keitel."

"What about him?"

"Tell me what you make of him," Halliburton said, leaning back with his arm draped over the chair.

"Well," Persephone said, trying to piece together Halliburton's intent, "Mr. White was lethal, but he wasn't ruled by any blood thirst. He was compassionate, loyal and reasonable, but true to his criminal nature while remaining true to his friends."

"Yes, but his loyalty was blind. He was betrayed repeatedly and allowed too many things to slip. Mr. Pink was the true professional of the mix. He snared the diamonds, maintained objectivity and figured out matters the quickest."

"Well then, let me redirect your question back to you."

"Who do I like?"

"No, no. Nothing that simple," Persephone said with a smile. "It's all too easy to pick characters when you're mining them for traits. Who did you like in relation to the others?"

"Ah. I'm not sure," Halliburton said with a widening grin. "I liked Mr. Blond."

"The psychopath?"

"Well, that would depend on the relationship. If you were Nice Guy Eddie, then Mr. Blond was a trusted friend and a loyal ally. If you were Mr. Orange, let's say, then yes, he was very dangerous."

"Are you dangerous?"

"It depends on who you are," Halliburton said. "Who are you, if I was Mr. Blond?"

Persephone shook her head and abandoned the playful façade. "You've heard the rumors, I suppose."

"Very troubling, especially if they're true."

"They're not."

"How can I be sure? You do seem chummy with Mr. Carter, more so than political incest allows for. And now these allegations...."

"What are people saying?"

"Does it really matter? Suffice to say, my dear, that I must regretfully withdraw my support in the matter."

"I haven't betrayed the Invictus!" Persephone said. She knew this was coming, but she was hoping to forestall it.

"It doesn't matter whether you have or haven't. All that matters is the perception of your actions."

"The perceptions are wrong."

"The perceptions are what they are."

"Please," Persephone said. "I still need your help. Everybody's turning their back on me, but I'm still a member of the First Estate."

"I'm sorry, Persephone," Halliburton said, standing. "You play the game remarkably well, but despite your Eliza Doolittle transformation from street urchin, you didn't play your hand well enough."

"Wait," Persephone said, standing as well. She was desperate to sway Halliburton. Without a single ally, she was on her way to losing everything she'd gained since Solomon Birch attacked her. She wasn't about to squander all she'd struggled to achieve. "Don't discount me yet."

"Do you have anything to offer me that might sway my opinion?" Halliburton asked, almost shrugging as if to say *I doubt you do.*

Persephone's thoughts were racing, a wasp's nest fractured open, the wasps inside scattering beyond her means to contain them in one cohesive cluster. Her ambition, her existence, her place in the world, forever shattered and spread thin on the four winds. Certainly, she had the benefit of long years—the ability to recover in the immediate decades—but then, maybe that was part of the vampire's curse: A Biblical capacity for age, but a human capacity for patience. She didn't want to wait years to recoup what she was losing now. She didn't want to start over again and be toppled by casual effort.

That thought made it slip through again—the Beast. Most Kindred thought of the Beast as a raging thing that killed and destroyed carelessly. It was a wild creature caged within their ribs and skulls, escaping only in rare, horrible moments. But the truth was, the Beast escaped a little every day; the casual slip of the tongue; the careless thought or word meant to hurt the other person. It had slipped through on that night Persephone insulted Duce's date at the nightclub. And it was about to happen again.

Only, this time, Persephone was going to let it happen, damn the consequences.

Survival 101: Survival isn't only about saving one's existence… it's about saving one's position.

Persephone smiled and squashed what remained of her fragile conscience into silence.

"*Do* you have anything to offer?" Halliburton asked, seeing the thin, confident smile creep across Persephone's lips.

By the curious twist of his mouth, it was obvious to Persephone that he was intrigued. He felt the confidence swell her demeanor and stature to full height and she knew, despite his proclivities, he found her attractive in that moment.

Persephone said nothing. Instead, she walked back to the couch and sat down. Halliburton sat down as well on a comfortable chair, one leg tucked beneath the other, his smile still evident.

"What is it you think you have, dear?" Halliburton asked. "And please don't disappoint me with some heavy-handed attempt at leverage."

lucien soulban

"Since when have I relied on such tactics?" Persephone asked.

Halliburton shrugged and settled his chin into the cradle of his palm. He was waiting.

"Do I still have your support?" Persephone asked.

"Depends on what you have up your sleeve."

"I have the reason why Prince Maxwell will never move against Duce Carter. I know why he'll back Duce over any contender."

"Hopefully the reason has a solid foundation."

"Oh," Persephone said, "it's legitimate."

"So? How does this change the allegations against you?"

"Because once you know what I know, you'll understand why I would never leave the Invictus for the Carthians. You'll realize how absurd the rumors actually are."

"I'm listening. If what you say proves your innocence, I'll back you against Griffin any day."

Persephone leaned forward, ready to pull her trump card. Somewhere in the back of her head, a voice begged her to shut up, begged her to stay quiet. She ignored it. "The reason Prince Maxwell won't move against Duce, if he can help it, is because..." Persephone said, drawing Halliburton over the coals with anticipation.

"Yes, what? Enough drama here, woman!"

"Maxwell forces Duce to drink his blood. Regularly."

"Are you saying the Prince has Carter under the thumb of a Vinculum?" Halliburton said, his face lit in delighted, scandalized shock.

"Every month."

"How do you know about this?" Halliburton asked. "It's obvious the Prince keeps you, his little accident, at arm's length."

"So you know my Embrace was accidental? Well, let's just say that I was responsible for introducing Duce Carter to Prince Maxwell."

"How so?" Halliburton asked, his elbows on his knees with a mock childlike exuberance; he was eager for the gossip.

"Do we have a deal, then?" Persephone asked.

"Oh, dear," Halliburton said. "If your story is half as interesting as it sounds, you most certainly have yourself a deal."

"Fine," Persephone said, suddenly feeling heavy; a lead weight spread though her chest and settled there. She shook away the feeling and continued. "But this information stays with you."

"Of course, my dear," Halliburton said. "You've given me a rare glimpse into one of the most significant alliances of our city. That one covenant essentially has the other, its enemy, on a *leash*! If anyone else found out, my insight wouldn't be worth a damn and the nature of the secret itself would be compromised. No, the power here is in keeping the secret a secret... so to speak."

"Okay. Now, Duce Carter is a good man," Persephone said, trying to alleviate her guilt at betraying his secret, "but he was having problems with the Carthians from the moment he assumed the reins. They wanted change and progress, but Duce wasn't willing to spill blood to accomplish that. He approached me, to make inroads with the Invictus—"

"Is that when you two were first lovers?"

"That, my dear, is not part of the bargain."

"My mistake," Halliburton said, his good mood never wavering. "Please, continue."

"Duce thought that if he could prove progress was possible through non-violent means, he could sway the Carthians to his way of thinking."

"And did he?" Halliburton asked.

"Within reason. I introduced Duce to the people I knew, including Prince Maxwell."

"And what happened?"

"They hated each other," Persephone said, almost laughing. "Despised one another for what the other represented."

"All right," Halliburton said; it was obvious he was trying to piece together events himself, but with little success.

"But Prince Maxwell saw a unique opportunity to control the Carthians through Duce."

"So he subjected him to the Vinculum."

"Yes," Persephone said, "but not without making a concession or two himself. You see, Maxwell's smart. He knows a Vinculum made without someone's complete assent is inviting eventual disaster."

"Certainly, we've heard the parables of our ancient nights... children feeling their love betrayed so they rise up in anger."

"Exactly. So, instead of forcing Duce to take his blood, he offered it as part of the bargain."

"What bargain?"

"That the Prince would allow the Carthians some concessions, slowly, so as not to arouse the Primogen's suspicions, if Duce agreed to the Vinculum."

"Those terms seem a little vague," Halliburton said with no small measure of suspicion.

"I don't know all the specifics, but I do know he gave the Carthians the right to assemble unmolested, among other privileges their ilk elsewhere don't enjoy."

"But it's not enough," Halliburton said, piecing together some of the issues. "The Carthians want more, and Duce can't help them commit violence, even if he wanted to."

"Trust me, he doesn't want to. Besides, Prince Maxwell only delivered certain promises slowly, if at all."

"So tell me something. If the Prince is eager to keep Duce in power, why isn't he making the necessary concessions to the Carthians? To keep them mollified."

"Truthfully, I think he took Duce's position for granted. He thought Duce was safely in his pocket. He didn't think he'd have to deliver on his promises."

"And now, he can't afford to with some members of the Primogen demanding Duce's head," Halliburton concluded. "He painted himself into a corner."

"He painted all of us into a corner, but we can save the situation and come out stronger for it."

"What are you thinking?"

"Right now, Prince Maxwell is afraid to act on behalf of the Carthians or Duce because people are calling for his head or staying neutral in the matter. Nobody wants to risk siding with him just yet."

"True. They're waiting for someone else to take that first step."

"But if you approach Prince Maxwell and say something like," Persephone said, acting Halliburton's part of the conversation: "Sire, I think we must support Duce Carter. He's kept the Carthians stable, and without his strong hand, they'll surely devolve into a troublesome rabble."

"Troublesome rabble, I like that," Halliburton said, already memorizing his lines and imagining his performance.

"I'm glad to hear it. By giving the Prince his voice back, you seem like a forward-thinking vampire—"

"I am a forward-thinking vampire," Halliburton said, touching his chest in mock indignation.

"Of course you are," Persephone said. "But now, the Prince knows it as well. You act as the Prince's proxy in this, saving him face in the matter. Now, he'll be able to act in Duce's favor without seeming involved."

"As a favor to me," Halliburton said, sighing, "which means he'll even pretend that I owe *him* a boon for him 'acting on my behalf'."

"It's a small price to pay for ingratiating yourself into Prince Maxwell's service, don't you think? He'll remember you as his salvation in the matter and the city will look upon you as a mover and a shaker. The Carthians may even come to see you as a hero."

"I suppose. But before we do this, it might be best if we considered all the angles."

"Of course," Persephone said. She settled in for a long chat with Halliburton, going over details, while in the back of her mind, she fought to drown out the voice that whispered: *Traitor.* She couldn't even justify her intentions in the matter. This had nothing to do with saving Duce and everything to do with protecting her position in the

First Estate. Now, because of her, Duce's greatest secret and shame was revealed. The fact that he was a puppet to the Prince's blood would have huge implications for the dynamics of local politics. If the remaining Invictus found out, they would use Duce to try to defang the Carthians completely. If the Carthains found out, they'd brand Duce a traitor and rage against the Invictus. Either scenario would draw its share of blood.

Persephone prayed that Halliburton knew enough to keep his mouth shut.

"What's he want?" Charles asked, pacing around the kitchen, coke in hand.

"I don't know," Law said, "but we'll know when he gets here." Law was doing his best to read a tattered copy of *Soul on Ice* despite Charles' incessant need to feel in control. Whenever something was going to happen that they knew nothing about, Charles asked questions. A lot of them. It wasn't that he was afraid or a fool; he was gauging the situation and trying to prepare for whatever was coming.

"Yo," Charles said, switching in mid-thought, "Beth said you stay the same when you get bit, right?"

"Right. You're stuck," Law said, reading still. "Don't age. Everything caught, like in a Polaroid picture."

"So, you thinking I should go on one of them crash diets before I get bit? You know, lose weight? I can't bounce back up, right? I'll be skinny forever."

"If you lose weight that fast," Law said, smiling from behind his book, "your skin's gonna get all loose and shit. You want that forever? Skin all hanging limp off your raggedy-ass bones."

"Seriously?"

"Yeah, man," Law said, putting the book down. He limp-flexed his arm and grabbed the imaginary waddle hanging a foot down from his tricep, pretending it was jiggling free. "Have all this shit swinging low and free like grandma's titties."

"Damn," Charles said, laughing, "that's *nasty.*"

"Have to call your ass 'Mr. Beach Blanket'," Law said, grinning.

"Shit, alright. Alright," Charles said, laughing so hard he was almost crying.

Law just shook his head with a grin, "You're fine as is, brother. I'd rather have Mr. Beach Ball than Mr. Beach Blanket any ol' day."

"Yeah," Charles said, sitting down at the kitchen table. "But I'll get me a shine before the bite," he said, running his hands through his curls.

"Nah, nah. Get yourself some activator. Get that Jerry Curl shit happening," Law said, tussling his own hair.

"Shut the fuck up, bitch," Charles said, chuckling.

"That shit's bound to come back in flavor. Ohh, you'll be the shit then!"

A knock on the door was enough to drain the smiles from both men. Their moment of levity was gone. Charles stared at the door, then back at Law.

"Let's see," Law said with a shrug. He stood and headed for the front door.

Charles pulled into step behind him, sporting a gun in the wide waistband of his pants. Law knew Charles well enough to know he had Law's back.

A quick peek through the peephole cover and Law opened the door for the white-haired brother waiting outside.

"Patrick, right?" Law asked. "Welcome, brother."

Duce pressed the intercom button next to the heavy, unmarked steel door three times, waited to the count of two, then pressed four times. Still waiting, he checked the length of the surprisingly clean alley again to make sure he was alone. The intercom speaker crackled.

"May I help you?" a woman's voice asked.

lucien soulban

lucien soulban

"I'm here to see Daurice," Duce said, staring at the camera above him.

"Who is this?" she said, more a demand than a question.

"Carter."

"I'm afraid I don't know a Mr. Carter," the woman said.

"Well, I'm not here to see you, am I?" Duce said. This stalling tactic was always tiring. A direct security feed wasn't enough to protect someone against an invisible vampire's mind voodoo, but a recording did the job. Whoever was inside was likely rewinding and watching Duce on tape to make sure he was alone and to verify his identity.

"Yo, Duce," a man's voice said, "come on in."

The door buzzed and Duce walked into a small corridor filled with one wide bouncer in a black suit. Ghoul with murder-ones covering his eyes and a face as broad and as dark as Chicago's home-grown Michael Clark Duncan. He patted Duce down with a metal wand and motioned him through the next door.

Two more goons were standing just inside the door, facing the interior of a large, two-story room filled with roulette wheels and poker, craps and blackjack tables. The red carpet covering the floor and the mural oil paintings on the wall couldn't hide the temporary nature of the establishment.

This place could vanish in under an hour.

As far as the clientele was concerned, the only color that mattered here was green; everyone dressed well, with a few suits, a few long dresses and plenty of gold, diamonds and pearls making the rounds at the tables. The rich didn't use the back door like Duce. They went through the underground parking entrance where the limos dropped them off. They, however, were on "The List."

The appeal of Melbourne's underground casino, or Mel's, wasn't gambling *per se*. Legitimate games could be had at above-board establishments like Harrah's East Chicago hotel and casino outside of town. No, the draw here was the thrill and danger of gambling elbow to elbow with

Chicago's underworld elite and bad boys. No telling when one might be throwing dice with a Cosa Nostra bagman or trying to bluff a drug kingpin. In one famous incident, a rich socialite and his wife walked away with two porno starlets for the night after their producer put them up in a high-stakes poker game. Melbourne was known in most elite circles as redefining the meaning of "no-limits" gambling.

Duce watched the crowd a moment, in turn earning the attention of a few people who wondered about his story. He made his way to the back bar, where hostesses in short black skirts and fishnets placed a steady stream of drink orders. Behind the mahogany bar, with its brass trimmings, was a one-way mirror. Adjacent to it was a heavy door guarded by two more goons. A white bodyguard patted Duce down before opening the door for him.

Daurice's office was better furnished than the exterior, but then, he liked living large: Heavy desk, upholstered couch and chairs, three elegant wall murals to hide the patchwork paintjob, a large safe on wheels that they could transport quickly and another door leading to the adjoining security room that monitored the table action. The room was also dark—real dark.

Duce stopped the bouncer from closing the door completely to keep some light streaming through.

"Daurice!" Duce said, holding the door open despite the bouncer's attempts to push it closed. "Turn some goddamn lights on in here!"

"Damn, Duce," Daurice Melbourne said from behind the desk. "Learn to see in the dark."

"Do I look like Ray Charles, motherfucker? I can see in the dark but I prefer the damn lights on!"

Daurice chuckled and raised the overhead track lights to dim. He was African-American, portly, near Duce's height (take an inch) with a mustache, goatee and skull stubble. Putting his remote down, Daurice made his way around the desk. Duce removed his hand from the door and ignored the bouncer's ugly, hard looks as he closed it.

Both vampires clasped hands, but stayed out of biting reach of each other's necks.

"What's up?" Daurice asked.

"Why so dark in here?"

"Prefer it. Gives me an advantage," he said, winking. "You haven't seen these new digs. Want the tour?"

"Sure," Duce said.

The conversation was light and breezy as Daurice guided Duce past the tables and wheels. They bantered about some of the faces in the crowd and the nature of attracting the right customers to keep the place hopping. Both men skirted the issue that had brought the Carthian prefect here, until Duce finally broached the subject. They walked along the outside wall, away from the loud tables and cheering clientele.

"How come you didn't warn me Fulsome was undermining me?"

"Ain't my style to tattle," Daurice said with a shrug.

"And this has got nothing to do with you backing him?"

"My choice, Duce."

"Why Fulsome?" Duce said.

"Man has initiative."

"Does the man have something on you?"

"Now why the hell you assuming that?"

"Because business is good," Duce said, looking at the tables. "And you like living large, I've seen you. Changing the status quo will fuck with the peace and it'll fuck with your livelihood."

"Yeah, man, but I'm still Carthian. I still believe in the struggle and this joint helps me bankroll the covenant. You know me. I'm not a fighter. If this is how I can help, cool."

"The minute the Carthians start spilling blood like Adenauer's promising, all this shit vanishes. The Invictus won't care if you're a non-combatant. You're a Carthian resource and that means carpet-bombing your ass."

"I'm willing to take that risk."

"No doubt," Duce said.

"See, Duce. You keep talking about the status quo, which we're fighting against, and then wonder why folks are moving against you. The Carthians are getting tired of waiting for you to act, man."

"That's the problem. People think that because I talk about the status quo, I support it. Bullshit. I'm reminding people it exists because it's a big-ass rock in our way."

"So, we roll it out of the way."

"And how many men does it take to move that rock, huh?"

"Well, if we work together—"

"But we're not working together. Since I took over as prefect, every one of y'all has been fighting me, telling me what I should be doing and thinking."

"We're not working together, Duce? Or is it that you're butting heads with everyone else?"

"I'm trying to work with you, but y'all want to rush into shit blind. How many men you need to move that rock, Daurice?"

"As many as it takes."

"So now, the Carthians waste their resources throwing a bunch of brothers and sisters against that rock until it budges. But all they needed was a couple of strong backs and leverage. Now you tell me, being a businessman 'n all. Which is more economical? Wasting manpower by throwing it against the rock? Or waiting for the right leverage to roll it out of the way with one or two people?"

Daurice nodded. "I see your point, but there's a small problem with your argument."

"What's that?"

"Maybe we do only need one or two people to move that rock, but what about everyone else who wants to contribute? You gonna leave them grabbing their Johnsons?"

"No. Each person has a part to play, but people aren't willing to listen. Everyone wants to play the martyr. Everyone wants to show their battle scars."

"It's better than watching from the sidelines."

Duce stopped and watched a poker game on a nearby table as he worked over some thoughts. He hadn't considered certain matters; hadn't looked at the root of the Carthian dissatisfaction. He didn't agree with everything they had to say, that much was certain, but maybe he was being too critical. Maybe he was ignoring the important issues, letting Fulsome capitalize on them.

"Have I been treating this like a one-man show?" Duce asked.

Daurice shrugged. "You're a smart man, Duce," he said. "But smart men don't often make for good leaders. You've been doing everything yourself. Doesn't leave much room for the rest of us."

"Then help me," Duce said. "You understand how to run a business, think in the long term, run a team—"

"Yo, whoa, whoa. Maybe you forgot, but I'm helping Fulsome."

"To do what?" Duce asked, trying to challenge Daurice into thinking.

"Help make the Carthians into a force of reckoning."

"How?"

"What?"

"How?" Duce asked, smiling. "Did Fulsome say how he was planning on helping the Carthians? Did he share anything?"

"No, man. Right now, we're just calling for a vote of no confidence."

Duce waited patiently.

"Well, he did say—" Daurice started before interrupting himself.

"What?" Duce asked. "That he wasn't me? That he imagined great things for the Carthians?"

"Yeah, something like that," Daurice responded.

"Guess what. I know exactly what Fulsome's planning. He's been letting Adenauer make all the fiery speeches, right? Letting her talk shit about revolution and preparing for war?"

"What're you saying?"

"I'm saying, Fulsome and Adenauer are about to collide over some nasty shit."

"You're grabbing at straws."

"Nope," Duce said, smiling even wider. "See, Fulsome's using Adenauer for the brimstone and rhetoric, right? He's using her to distract the Invictus. Only Adenauer isn't sitting on her ass. She's bringing in a mortal named Law, who both Fulsome and Adenauer want me to Embrace."

"So?"

"Fulsome is using Law to get at me. Make me look selfish for not Embracing him to help the Carthians."

"Why? Why's Law so important?"

"Because he's a smart man, and because he was my road dog, back in the day. That's why Adenauer is using Law. Because he's motivated and fearless... a good person to start and plan revolutions, especially since he has the weapons and the contacts. Problem being, Law is Black Guerilla Family, and he isn't just coming in to the Carthians to help us. He'll bring in BGF politics—mortal politics—into the mix."

"Can you prove it? Or are you talking out of school?"

"The six prison guards out in Joliet sound familiar? That's BGF, man."

"Wait...that doesn't make sense," Daurice said. "Why would Bethany help with that?"

"Because she thinks she has a handle on Law, but she don't understand shit about how far the BGF is willing to go."

"You saying the BGF knows we exist?"

"Nah. I don't think Adenauer is that stupid. I do think, though, that this was a test run—Adenauer flexing her muscles to scare folks."

"Fulsome wouldn't go for that shit."

"No? Listen, Daurice, either Fulsome has y'all fooled and is going to use Law and his well-armed soldiers to fight his war once I'm gone, or Adenauer's keeping this shit hidden from Fulsome until she's ready to seize power."

lucien soulban

"Man. That's some serious accusation. You best be able to back that up with some proof."

"Give me a couple of days. I'll see what I can do."

"Even if what you're saying is true, it's still not enough to swing my vote."

"I know," Duce said. "Look, I'm not trying to win your trust by badmouthing Adenauer and Fulsome. You need to see progress, I get that. You need to feel involved, I get that too. At least give me a chance to prove it to you."

Daurice thought about it a moment. "All right. I can do that."

"Thanks, Daurice."

"Anytime," Daurice said, clapping Duce on the shoulder "But remember. Two days."

The basement church was well-kept despite the hardened dirt floor and soot-blackened brick walls. A rare survivor from Chicago's infamous blaze that devastated the city, the basement was built over, thanks to the Longinus survivors of the age who hid there during the fire. Now it served as a communal shrine for the covenant, the walls left untouched except for the inset stained-glass panels backlit by the soft, flickering light of red candle lamps. Pews and an altar covered by a blood-stained satin sheet filled the small space.

During the Mass, while Birch officiated and sermonized, he noticed Ike Barlow studying him carefully from the rear pews. After offering the final blessing, he nodded with distracted impatience to the few comments thrown his way during the assembly. Most vampires realized they weren't welcome at that moment, and left quickly. Eventually, only Birch and Barlow remained.

"Is there something I can do for you, Mr. Barlow?" Birch asked, putting away the relics of his station.

"I was hoping you'd trust me enough to share your plans with me," Barlow said.

"Trust you? What on earth would give you such an idea?"

"Well, I know what you've been doing to Persephone Moore, for starters. And while I don't like the girl any more than you do, this harassment seems beneath you."

"What? You think I'm acting like a schoolyard bully?"

"On the surface, perhaps. But you're a smart man. I'm wondering what I'm missing."

Birch laughed. "Well. You and your boys have been very helpful, so you earned an answer. I'm bullying her majesty."

Barlow raised an eyebrow and struggled hard not to appear surprised. "To what end?"

"I knock her down. Put the fear of God into her with this unknown assailant act, right? Rob her of allies. Invade her haven...what's she going to do?"

"Seek help?"

"From who?"

"Her sire."

"Only Prince Maxwell doesn't want much to do with her thanks to her liaisons with Carter. So I know she can't run to him for help. Where does she go after that?"

Barlow smiled. "Of course. Duce Carter."

"Duce Carter, who isn't in favorable standing these days."

"You're turning Persephone into an outcast."

"More than that," Birch said, pleased with himself. "I'm turning her and Carter into pariahs."

"How long have you been planning this?" Barlow said.

"I've wanted her destroyed ever since the Prince Embraced her. But planning? I'll tell you something. I'm making this up as I go along."

"How very...impulsive of you."

"I saw a situation developing and knew how I could turn it to my advantage."

"The situation being?"

"The drive-by on Carter, and Persephone running to his rescue. I already figured I could use Persephone's indiscretions against her, but I couldn't have planned for all this if I tried."

"So the drive-by on Duce?"

"Not me, but I'd shake the hand of whoever ordered the hit."

"You know Persephone's trying to rally support on Duce's behalf."

"I'm taking care of that."

"I can understand your grievance against Persephone, but why Carter?"

"I thought you would have figured that one out. I want Adenauer and Fulsome in power. Duce's been keeping the Carthians' noses clean. I *want* them to cross the line. I *want* the Prince giving us sanction to handle them, once and for all."

"I'm impressed," Barlow said.

"Yeah?"

"Yes. You're far more ambitious than I gave you credit for."

"What can I say? I see an opening and I go for the jugular."

"Indeed," Barlow replied, slowly walking around the room. "So what's the next step?"

"We make sure Persephone gets the message that she isn't welcome. Make sure it's a message she can't ignore."

"I'm surprised you'd be advocating this," Barlow said. "Aren't you required to protect prince and progeny through your...bond to Prince Maxwell?"

"Yes, I am," Birch said, drawing to full height as though to shake off the shackles of his Vinculum, the one instituted after he'd hurt Persephone. "But I can't very well control what some independent-minded vampire might try of his own volition."

"I see," Barlow said.

"Make sure that you do," Birch said. He touched Barlow's forehead with his thumb and muttered a prayer. Barlow dipped his head low in reverence and whispered his thanks for the Bishop's blessing.

Chapter Sixteen

They spoke in the kitchen, Law with a cold longneck in his hand, Patrick seated across from him and Charles near the sink, grip firm on the gun tucked into his waistband.

"Mm," Law said, taking a drink. "No more of this shit after, huh?" He indicated the bottle.

"How many of your people know about our kind?" Patrick asked.

"Shit, man," Charles said, "what's with these questions, bitch? Who knows about us? Why you fucking with Duce? What d'you want with us? Better keep your nose out our business."

Law raised his hands, stopping Charles. "You're scared," he told Patrick. "Scared we're gonna fuck with this Masquerade shit, right?"

"Don't really give a shit. You break the Masquerade, though, the Invictus will break you."

"Let the motherfuckers try!" Charles snapped, stepping forward.

Law was on his feet, in between Charles and Patrick, stopping the big man with his presence alone. "Go watch television," Law said.

"But—"

"None of that, now. Go on. He ain't gonna start shit up in my home, am I right?" Law said, directing the question to Patrick.

"Just here to talk."

"You cool with that?" Law said, turning back to Charles.

Charles nodded. "I'll be in there." He nodded to the living room. "Just say when you want this punk bounced."

Law waited till Charles left before sitting down again.

"Bad temper," Patrick said. "Not good for a vampire."

"He's just looking out for me. Like me and Duce used to for each other. Like you're doing for Duce, now," Law said, downing a swallow of beer.

"About that. You know anything about the attacks against him?"

"The drive-by? That's some fucked-up shit, but nah, ain't my thing any more. I don't believe in hurting other Afrikans. Against my creed."

"All right. Any idea who would?"

Law shook his head. "Not sure, man, but what Duce did...that shit was bound to come back and bite his ass."

"You think it's your old set?"

"Sorry, cuz. Don't know shit about it, but I appreciate the fact you up front with me an' all. I heard you played it legit."

"You seem to know a lot about me," Patrick said, feeling territorial.

"Beth told me about you. Said you're an outsider. Big community player once, but now... you only hang with Duce. She said they also call you Chocolate Milk."

"Oh, what? You're gonna try and dig into me, now? Get under my skin?"

"No, no, cuz," Law said, raising his hand in apology. "Not like that at all. I personally think that shit's disgraceful. Nobody should be calling you Chocolate Milk. Problem is, we've been under the boot for so long that we've lost a common respect for each other. That's all I'm saying."

"Like you give a shit."

Law took another swig of beer. "Like you know me? Like Duce does, if that's where you're getting your shit from? But you, cuz, you should know better. The Carthians bit you because you were tight with your community," he said, intertwining two fingers. "I respect that. That's why the Carthians want me too. I'm all up in the community."

"Yeah," Patrick said. "I noticed the guns. Just what the community needs."

"Fuck that," Law said. "Malcolm X said we have a right to defend ourselves, and I agree. I'm just playing the game they started."

"They? They who?"

"The Amerikans. The government. They lock us up in these ghetto prisons and use soldier-cops as prison guards. And the bitch of it is, they open all these gun stores in our n-hoods where we raise our kids, so we kill ourselves off. Spare them the sweat of genocide."

"So what're you planning?" Patrick asked, laughing. "A prison break?"

The question was met in silence; Law continued drinking and downed the contents of his bottle.

"What the hell are you planning?" Patrick asked, a chill moving over him.

"Sorry," Law said, smiling. "Just talking out of school, y'know?"

"No, I don't," Patrick said. "And I don't think you know the shit you're getting into here. This isn't a game."

"Amen, brother, preach it. But preach it elsewhere, cause I'm not playing at shit."

"Maybe you're not, but I can tell you, someone's playing you. They're using your expectations against you to get to Duce."

"I'm not about that shit either. I don't fuck over other Afrikans, especially my peeps. I want Duce with me and my crew. I respect him. He's a proper thug."

"Duce ain't a thug," Patrick said, annoyed.

"No cuz, you don't get it. Duce *is* a thug. It doesn't mean he's a perpetrator. It means he looks out for himself. He's a fierce motherfucker who won't take shit from anybody. Always respected that in him."

"You do know that thug comes from the Thuggee. Worshipers of Kali who *murdered* travelers in India."

"I know that," Law said, laughing. "What you don't get is that the Thuggee did right by their beliefs. They had faith in the shit they did, and did it because it was necessary, like all proper thugs."

Law laid the empty bottle down on the table and spun it slowly. Patrick could see he was mulling matters over, but what those thoughts entailed, he had no clue. Already, this wasn't the meeting or the man Patrick had envisioned. The man sitting across from him acted respectful towards others even though he didn't back down. Patrick understood how, under any other circumstance, Duce respected Law and vice-versa. Both men were forthright and both men possessed strong moral convictions, even if society didn't agree with their moralities.

Only, now, Patrick had to wonder about the accuracy of Duce's assessment of Law. Was Duce right in thinking that his old friend was a potential threat and an incorrigible scoundrel? Or was Duce feeling guilty over betraying Law and coping with it by convincing himself that Law was a dangerous man? Patrick wasn't sure anymore. He trusted Duce, but even he realized that Law, while dangerous, maybe wasn't as blind or as great a danger as Duce painted him.

"You know what?" Law said, bringing the bottle to a stop. "I know Beth's fucking with Duce."

"Then why you going along with her?"

"Hold up, hear me out. I know that shit, but I couldn't let this opportunity slip on by."

"You have no idea what you're getting into here. Are you drinking Beth's blood?"

"Yeah, man, that's some sweet shit. But how else am I going to become a vampire, right?"

"Sweet Jesus," Patrick said. "Is that what Beth told you? That you have to drink her blood as a mortal to turn?"

"Yeah," Law said, suddenly uncertain. "She said we had to drink her blood for a while before we were ready to take the bite."

"Aw, son," Patrick said, shaking his head. "She's playing you like a guitar. You have no idea what you stepped
in. She lied to you to addict you to her blood. Drinking
her blood enslaves you, it doesn't prepare you for shit.
She's controlling you."

"Uh-uh," Law said, shaking his head. "She wouldn't do
that to me. She's—"

"Lying to you," Patrick said. "You yourself said she was
fucking with Duce. She's fucking with you too. Keeping
you under control. I can prove you don't need to drink
her blood to be turned. Find me any motherfucker who
hasn't tasted vampire blood, and I can do him, right here
and now."

Patrick prayed Law wouldn't take the bluff, even if he
was telling the truth.

"Ask yourself, Law. Have you felt this way for anyone
else in your life?"

"Nah," Law said, quietly. "Never."

Law fell silent a moment. He looked at the kitchen door
and Patrick suddenly realized Charles was standing there,
listening. Charles shook his head and walked away.

"Help me," Law said, a simple statement robbed of energy.

"What?"

"You keep saying I don't know what's what. And if what
you're saying is true about Beth, then maybe I don't. So
help me figure this shit out, cause I ain't backing away.
Not from this."

Patrick shook his head. "I—I can't. Duce—"

"Look, I got much love for Duce, but the brother isn't
here. You are. You came here to help him, and I respect
that. Now I'm asking for help. One brother to another.
We're part of the same Afrikan community, and whether
you like it or not, we're going to be sharing two communities. Now the last thing I want is to be another fucking
statistic, another victim of the systematic abuse against our
people. Aren't you tired of seeing your Afrikan brothers
fucked this way?"

lucien soulban

A kernel of panic welled up inside Patrick. He stood, heading for the door. "Look," he said, "this isn't what I was looking for. I shouldn't have come here."

"Aren't you tired of standing outside the community?" Law said, following him. "Don't you think that maybe the reason folks call you Chocolate Milk isn't only because of who bit you?"

Patrick spun around, ready to clock Law, but he held his temper in check. Charles was watching them very carefully, his hand on his gun.

"What the fuck's that supposed to mean?" Patrick said.

"It means you turned your back on the Afrikan community, turned your back on your people."

"That's bullshit!"

"Oh, and you're gonna front like you don't miss it, huh? You don't miss your own people, and I'm not talking about vampires. You were Afrikan for longer than you were bit."

"Yes, you're right, okay? I miss my community! I miss my people! But I'm not willing to jeopardize them so I can stop feeling lonely! I'm not willing to be the pusher who brings an addiction of blood into their lives!"

"Well, brother, that shit's about to change. You don't have to be alone any more. The community's coming to you. Your people are here. Do you still want to be left on the outside?"

"I gotta go," Patrick said, his mind a field of broken glass. Law was far better at reading people than Patrick gave him credit for. He turned to leave, hesitating between wanting to run and wanting to stay.

His people. His community. Those words contrasted with the loneliness he endured from years of self-imposed exile. They felt like words of salvation for a hungry man denied bread, a dream he never thought would come. Patrick didn't move. *Stay* he thought. *Say something, anything*...not to obliterate that hope. *Walk*, another part of him said. *Walk, not for yourself*...but as Duce's friend.

He couldn't do either, his hand caught reaching for the door knob, lingering. Finally, he looked over his shoulder at Law.

"You want a piece of advice?" Patrick said, unsure. "I can smell the blood in here. Someone spilled a lot of it. Kindred will notice if they come."

"Violent neighborhood."

"Whatever, man. Someone's already been feeding here. Someone died here."

"I'm listening."

"My point is, if anyone else finds out you're pulling this shit—"

"You're talking about the Invictus."

"Or the boys from Longinus...if either of them figures out a group of humans knows about the Masquerade and is harboring a vampire, they will gut your ass."

"All right," Law said. "Any suggestions?"

"Clorox this fucking place down. It reeks of vampire."

"So, you helping us now?"

Patrick hesitated; was this something he wanted to get involved with? Did he want to get caught holding the can opener when this ugly can of worms blew open? And with each indecisive, cautionary word urging him to retreat, Patrick grew angrier. There was a time when he wouldn't hesitate to help the community, when he wasn't standing outside in the cold. There was a time when he felt needed...wanted. These were his people, and smart or dumb, good or bad, there was a time he took care of his own. They took care of each other; and they sheltered each other from the wolves. They took responsibility....

"You helping us, brother?" Law asked again.

"I'll help," Patrick said, turning around.

Law held out his arm and waited for Patrick to clasp it.

"On one condition," Patrick said, keeping his hands by his side. "Find out who the fuck's gunning for Duce. You do that, and I'm in."

"Word," Law said, extending his hand out. Patrick took it and Law drew him in, clapping him on his back. "Welcome back, brother," Law said. "Welcome back."

Patrick didn't say anything. Instead, he noticed Charles talking on the cell phone and giving him a hard stare.

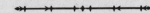

The apartment went beyond Spartan in its selection of furnishings; mattress on the floor for a bed, raggedy-ass brown chairs and sofa with stuffing missing, and a wobbly table with a gimp leg...all courtesy of local street corners. Duce hated living like this, but he couldn't buy furniture yet, not without new credit cards and someone to receive his shipment during the day while he rested elsewhere.

Otherwise, the emergency haven was a comfortable affair with its four rooms and clean eggshell-white walls. Only one room had windows, but that was easy enough to close off. It held plenty of potential, and Duce swore up and down to himself that once he had a free moment, he was going to make this place cozier than the last. The fact that he'd left his last haven so easily with nothing tying him to his past was disconcerting. He wanted a sense of being settled; of having a home that served as his emotional sanctuary. Naturally, he also needed a new fake identity and all the peripheral paperwork. Each haven he owned represented a new façade to minimize the chances of someone tracking him down. With his last haven destroyed, he needed a new emergency refuge should something compromise this location as well. New emergency retreat meant new identification.

None of that was on tonight's itinerary, however. Instead, Duce paced around the apartment, eager for Persephone's return. And when she finally walked through the door, there was nothing subtle about their need. They spoke through mouthfuls of one another....

"How'd it go?" Duce asked, pulling Persephone's shirt up over her head. He didn't bother unbuttoning it.

"Griffin's a snake," Persephone said, fumbling for Duce's belt "Going around telling people I'm betraying the Invictus."

"Never trusted the fucker."

"Lost some support, but—" Persephone hesitated.

"What," Duce said, pausing long enough to search her eyes for trouble.

Persephone shook her head and undid his fly and button. "But, ah, I convinced Halliburton to stick with us."

"Cool," Duce said, pulling Persephone out of her pants while squirming out of his.

"What about you?" she asked, biting into Duce's bare chest.

"I, uh—" Duce said, distracted, "think Daurice will help me. Ah! Need proof."

"Of what?" Persephone said between piercing bites.

"Later!" Duce said with a growl, dragging them both down into the mattress.

No foreplay tonight. No routine. Duce tore into her, and she into him, their pain another level of pleasure that bled into the other. The sensations intense, their words descending into guttural growls as Duce wrestled her for dominance and bit his way out of submission. Pinches of flesh torn away and devoured; razor slices across naked skin with their teeth; smeared in their own blood because they couldn't drench each other in sweat...in any other situation, this would have been a fight of survival. Here, however, Duce and Persephone were falling into one another. They searched for that moment of ultimate consumption when they were one in the cannibal sense of harmony. But it never came. They fell deeper and deeper into each other, and never hit bottom. It was always mere inches away, and the torture of that gap drove them into a greater sexual frenzy.

Finally, they pushed off each other, bruised, cut deep, missing tatters of flesh and mentally numb. Duce focused on stitching his body back together, his ribs aching as a fracture fused. His head throbbed from the effort of repairing the harm he'd invited upon himself. He looked over to Persephone's blood-caked body and could see she was focused on fixing herself.

lucien soulban

Lying there, they said nothing. Whatever reasons kept Persephone quiet, Duce wasn't sure, but he knew why he was silent. He wasn't shocked by the cruel passion to their intercourse or the acts themselves. He was more frightened by the thought that he could have gone further than biting her flesh; much further.

Persephone had good peripheral vision, enough to notice Duce studying her. Could he read her? Smell the betrayal in her blood? Did he know she'd given up his secret to save herself? She focused on mending her body. Seemed like a good place to get lost, like she did with the sex.

Feeding from Duce, being eaten by him, it was easy to let her passion overwhelm her and forget. But her self-inflicted distraction had its costs, in this case payment in bruised ribs, lacerated flesh and a hunger for more blood. It was too easy to fall into Duce, and she wasn't sure she could fall back out. There was a physical hunger to their obsession that went beyond primal. They needed each other, needed to wear each other's skin.

Persephone had never felt this way before, and the emotions it engendered were overwhelming. Now, however, that critical need tore her one way while her betrayal threatened to tear her in the opposite direction. She felt dizzy, caught in the funnel of a bloody cyclone that played off her primitive nature. There was no reason here, no logic. She wanted, she lusted, and she despised herself for allowing that need to override her conscience.

A weight pressed down on Persephone's chest and she couldn't breathe; as idiotic as that sounded, she couldn't inhale anymore, her lungs frozen.

"I have to go," she said, heading for the bathroom. She nearly stumbled in her flight from the room.

"You okay?" Duce asked, calling after her.

"Yes," she replied, closing the bathroom door. Relief rushed through her, the door a knife severing her from her anxiety.

"All right," Duce said from the bed. "I got somewhere to be as well. Don't take too long."

"I won't," Persephone said, running the shower at full steam. She didn't want to hear Duce's voice. She wanted to run away, collect her thoughts.

And she wanted to fall into him again, bite the soft from his flesh...

...get lost in the raging sea.

Charles was upset, that much Law knew in the way the big man had been pacing in the apartment; in the way his eyebrows knotted together and announced he was ready to go off on some violent tangent. He'd been brooding since Patrick left. Law was hoping Charles would cool off, but Charles wasn't going to let this matter slide either.

They were driving to KFC, just him and Charles, when the big man suddenly erupted into a tirade.

"Man, what the fuck's wrong with you?" Charles said.

"Best watch that tone, Charles. I won't be dissed by anyone. That includes you, dawg."

"What the fuck am I supposed to say, huh? Letting that punk bad-mouth Bethany. That inviting Duce's bitch into the crew was a good idea? That waiting for Duce to put the bite on you is smart? They're looking to fuck you up, and you just bending over like a punk."

Law slammed his foot on the brakes, fishtailing the Chevy to a stop in the middle of the street. Cars screamed past them, drivers heavy on their horns and the curses.

"Motherfucker," Law said. "You want out? Then get the fuck out!"

"Fuck you," Charles said, not budging. "You want me out, you gonna have to drag my fat ass out of the car—"

"Don't think I won't do it, motherfucker!"

"—or you can listen to what I got to say, for once in your goddamn life."

"I listen to you all the time."

"You listen, man, but you don't hear me."

"What?" Law said, laughing. "You getting all philosophical on my ass now?"

"Fuck you," Charles said, opening the door. "I *will* get out." He teetered his way out of the car, but kept the door open. "You go on, now," Charles said, bending over to talk to Law. "Go get yourself fucked over. Duce punked out on you once...punked out on his entire set, his family, and you don't think he'll do it again?"

"Man, you don't understand shit about Duce!"

"I know you got much love for the brother, I know that. But that means you're blind to his shit. He's using that against you, sending his bitch Patrick to spy on you. To spy on Beth."

"Man, Beth's fucking us over! She's got us hooked on her blood."

"Bullshit! I've been into enough shit to know when I'm fucked up, but my shit's never been clearer than now. Man, Beth gives me clarity, enough to know Duce sent Patrick to fuck you over."

"Ain't Duce's style."

"Oh, but it is his style to help the Establishment? He betrayed the race."

"He betrayed an insignificant fucking set poisoning our community! Duce is righteous. He's what the BG fucking Family needs!"

"And how the fuck you know? He's a biter now. He don't think the same. He's going to protect what's his, and that means, he ain't gonna turn your ass into folk like him!"

"That's why I had Terrell bit, in case Duce doesn't turn me. But you know what? You watch. He'll come around."

Charles snorted and shook his head, "You don't get it. Beth didn't give Terrell the bite so you could have insurance. He's her insurance in case you fucked up. Even *I* can see that. You should have let me get bit first."

"I didn't know how dangerous it was."

"Or is it you don't want me having something over you? Being your sire and shit."

"You're buggin'," Law said, shaking his head in disbelief. "You're jealous of Duce and Terrell?"

"Fuck you! You trust Duce more than me."

"He's my road dog!"

"He *was* your road dog. You don't run with him no more. But you can't see that. It's blinded you to the cause."

"You're telling *me* I'm blind to the cause? Motherfucker, I brought you into the BGF."

"Yeah, you did. But now, you acting like Duce is more important than the cause."

"Nobody's more important than the cause, not even me."

"Then why haven't you told them about vampires and the bite yet, huh? Why you keeping this shit to yourself?"

"I'm waiting for the bite first. Then we can show them what we can do."

"But Terrell can do that, can't he, motherfucker?" Charles said. "No, you want that privilege for yourself...the great and powerful Law...savior of the Black Guerilla Family...hero of the motherfucking revolution." With that Charles slammed the door shut.

Law gunned the engine, leaving a smoking trail of rubber behind him on the street. He watched Charles recede in the rearview mirror, all the while gripping the wheel tight and exhaling in expletives.

Charles watched as Law's car vanished down the block. He stepped to the sidewalk and dialed his cell phone.

"Where the fuck you at now?" he asked. "You still following that bitch? Cool. I'll be there. Let's wrap this shit up."

Chapter Seventeen

Duce walked up the front steps of the brownstone building and pressed the intercom button. He waited for folks
to review the security feed from the camera above his head;
waited for the anticipated argument to get in. Around him,
Chi-town's mortal denizens tucked their chins into their
jackets and slogged through the surprisingly crisp evening.
A few pulled their barking dogs away from Duce, not that
he cared. He was used to this treatment.

A moment passed, followed by two. The intercom crackled.

"May I help you?" a voice asked.

Duce recognized Samuel's voice. While not a chief aide
to Prince Maxwell, Samuel managed his royal highness's
receiving haven, where the Prince made himself available
for business matters.

"Here to talk to Max."

"*Prince* Maxwell isn't here at the moment," Samuel replied with his typically starched-collar aplomb. "Perhaps
if you return later?"

"No," Duce replied. "Doesn't work for me. But I tell
you what, Jeeves. I'll wait right here, at the door, till Max
comes back. I'll even entertain the good folks that come
here to talk to the Prince, how's that? Tell them how me
and Max are *tight*. I'm sure, given my current popularity,
Max really wants me hanging with them."

"I will call the police."

"You do that. But the longer I'm standing out here getting my nuts chipped off by the cold, the more people are
going to be talking."

The wait was brief; the door buzzed open and Duce walked through, into the building's spacious lobby. It was larger and more lavish than the entirety of his new apartment. Two security guards in black suits eyed Duce, but he ignored them, instead watching the elevator roll into the lobby with a loud whine. He already knew Prince Maxwell wasn't in the box. The door-shutters opened and out stepped Robert, wearing a gray flannel sweater and matching trousers.

"Prince busy?" Duce asked with a mocking smile.

"Mr. Carter, what are you doing here?" Robert asked, walking up to Duce. He kept his voice low, but then Duce never knew Robert to raise the decibels.

"What do you think, Rob? I got people trying to fuck me over from every different direction, and Max thinks he can—"

"That's *Prince* Maxwell to you," Robert said, impatiently.

Duce almost proffered an apology, but he fought the instinct. That was the Vinculum talking, his blood bond with Maxwell that engendered feelings of loyalty and a need to please. "Fuck you," Duce said, drawing upon his anger toward Maxwell for strength. "I'm not Invictus. Time y'all remembered that. It's Max to me until his lordship holds up his end of the bargain."

"Oh, and you think he's going to respond well to this tactic?"

"I don't give a shit anymore. I drank his blood because I thought it guaranteed me a few rights for my people. But I see now that Max was jacking me around. Using me."

"Oh, really?"

"Yeah, really. C'mon Robert. If he didn't want the Carthians getting all ethnic on his ass, he should've helped me. But now, because he fucked me over, left me there holding my dick, the Carthians are mobilizing."

"Mobilizing? What do you mean mobilizing?"

"Oh, I'm sorry. Are you talking to me now? A minute ago, I had to threaten y'all to get in."

lucien soulban

"Look, Mr. Carter. I'm sure you understand that the current situation is difficult for all of us."

"Really?" Duce said looking around the lobby. "Did some bloods roll up in here and start shooting your asses off, too? No?"

"You know what I mean."

"Yeah, I do. So don't fucking feed me this 'difficult for everyone' bullshit. I got motherfuckers trying to cap me, but that's cool. I'll handle my own shit. The real bitch here is that I find my ass dangling over the shark pool while his *majesty* protects his political ass at my expense."

"You really expected otherwise, Mr. Carter?"

"I did—that's my bad. But you know what, I'm gonna change that now. Tell Max that I'm losing control of the Carthians. I don't want to, but it's going to happen. And all that blood and time he invested in keeping Chi-town peaceful is going to vanish."

Robert refrained from responding. Instead, he walked around the hall, his footsteps echoing off the wall. He bit the tip of his thumb in thought. "I'll drop the attitude in relating the information, Mr. Carter, because I know you're angry," Robert finally said, "but what would you recommend I tell Prince Maxwell?"

"You gonna help me, Robert?"

"I'll pass along your concerns, but be very specific in your request. Prince Maxwell will give you neither carte blanche nor an open endorsement."

"Wasn't expecting either, Rob. What I need is a significant peace offering to make the Carthians feel like there's progress. Like I haven't been steering them wrong."

"Any recommendations as to what that might be?"

"I know exactly what I want," Duce said. "Two concessions. I want a Carthian of my choosing among the Primogen—"

"The council members will never go for that. It's—"

"Max's choice, not the Primogen's. And he won't be setting precedent, either. Atlanta, New York, New Orleans, Los Angeles...the Princes there all have Carthians in the Primogen, or so I'm told."

"I'll bring it up to Prince Maxwell," Robert said. "Your second concession?"

"We want Cicero."

"The town of Cicero?"

"Yes, the town of Cicero. We want the Prince to acknowledge it as Carthian domain. Invictus-free. Crusader-free."

"That'll be difficult...."

"Fishing for compromises, Rob?" Duce asked. "I was promised those concessions some time ago, but y'all were blowing smoke up my ass. Well, you backed yourselves into a corner. You. Not me. And it isn't a threat. It's the reality. Now I gotta give the Carthians something to keep the peace. Give us a seat on the council and give us Cicero, and I can avert a war."

"I'll tell the Prince, but I can't make any promises."

"Like y'all even want Cicero? It's mostly Latino and foreigners and under the national average in education and income. Not many Caucasian Kindred ready to invest in the area, if you know what I mean?"

"But it has a high population density. Several vampires feed from Cicero, alleviating the pressure from Chicago's feeding grounds."

"We can haggle feeding rights later," Duce said. "But I'm on deadline here, and so are you."

"Very well, but I should warn you. If Prince Maxwell agrees to those terms... if... then he will likely insist upon a *caveat emptor*. It means—"

"I know what it means. Go on."

"That the liberties your ilk have enjoyed in Chicago are conditional on your management of the covenant. If the Carthians replace you or cause problems, Prince Maxwell will revoke any and all concessions he's made in your favor."

"No shit," Duce said, laughing. "Figured that out myself."

"Was that all?" Robert asked.

"Yeah. That was about it."

"Good, then I do have a question for you. How's Persephone doing?"

lucien soulban

Duce noticed the pained expression crossing Robert's face. It hurt him to ask that, Duce figured, given that Robert was the shoulder Persephone leaned on early in her Embrace, before she became stronger.

"Shouldn't you be asking her that yourself?" Duce asked. "Oh wait. I forgot. You left her out in the cold when someone attacked her haven."

"Persephone can't monopolize the Prince's time and she knew the risks of fraternizing with you. She must be responsible for her own actions. I—we can't be there for her as much anymore. In any case, please say hello to Persephone, for me?" Robert asked, a small plea in his voice.

"Yeah," Duce said, "I will."

"And tell her to watch out."

"For what?"

"The rumors," Robert said, waiting for Duce to acknowledge his statement. "You don't know?" He walked back to Duce, face to face with a lowered voice. "They involve you implicitly."

"Really," Duce said. "She didn't say much, except...." Duce trailed off, remembering his brief conversation with Persephone before they tore into one another. "This got to do with Griffin? About her betraying the Invictus? She said it wasn't serious. Is it?"

"It depends on their validity. And the longer Persephone remains in your company—"

"What? You saying this is my fault?"

"Yes, Mr. Carter, I am," Robert said as he walked away. "And I know she cares about you enough to help you. Can you do the same for her by staying away?" Robert boarded the elevator cage, the doors closing behind him.

Duce stood in the lobby long after the drone of the lift rose and ebbed. Thoughts of Persephone wreaked havoc in his mind, concern mixed with explicit and lurid flashes of their sexual encounters. He wanted to help her, but another part of him wanted to tear into her, drink blood from the goblet of her flesh. He didn't want to hurt her in the traditional sense of pain and emotional injury, but something about her demanded he consume her, body and soul.

Patrick waited by the concrete column of the mostly empty car park, hidden away in shadows, feeling ridiculous. A few minutes later, Demetria appeared from a nearby maintenance door and made her way to Patrick's location.

"What's with all this spy game shit?" Patrick said. "I don't like creeping around in the dark."

"Sorry," Demetria said, uncharacteristically reserved and looking around with the conviction of someone who expected to find something. "I'm being cautious."

"What's wrong?"

"I found out who's following Persephone. He's Nosferatu, and he's one of Barlow's men."

"Ike Barlow? One of the Sanctified?"

"Yes!" Demetria said impatiently. Her manner showed she wanted to be elsewhere. "Member of the Spear on Longinus and party Inquisitor," she continued.

"I thought he was an interrogator for the Prince."

"Semantics. 'Inquisitor' is a way of avoiding friction with the Sheriff. It also makes Barlow more palatable to the Invictus when they require his skills."

"So what's it mean?" Patrick asked. "That Ike Barlow has it out for Persephone? Why?"

"Take one step up the ladder, and I think you have your answer."

"Solomon Birch? Oh fuck!"

"Oh fuck, is right—if it is Birch. And even if it isn't, Barlow isn't much better. Both are fucking psychopaths. Not enemies I want to make."

"You're backing out?" Patrick asked, making eye contact with Demetria enough that she stopped glancing around and focused on him.

"I'm sorry," she said, sighing. She cradled Patrick's cheek, affectionately. "It was fun, but this is too rich for

lucien soulban

209 blood in, blood out

my blood. Consider it a freebie, but I'm out. Whatever Persephone did to annoy Birch or Barlow, I want nothing to do with it."

"All right," Patrick said.

"And consider yourself lucky that I came here at all."

"No, no," Patrick said, trying to calm her. "I understand that and I appreciate it. I don't want to be mixed up in this shit any more than you do."

"Then back out," Demetria said, shrugging like the solution was simple enough. "Persephone can't mean much to you. I mean, you're only doing this for Duce Carter, right?"

"Yeah?"

Demetria shrugged. "Well. Been following Persephone around, and that includes her pit stops."

"I don't get you."

"Think about it carefully. If I've seen her and Duce together..."

"Then Barlow and Birch know about it as well," Patrick said. "Shit."

"Yeah. And whatever either of them is tangled in—Duce and Persephone, I mean—they're going to drag the other person down with them. Them and everyone around them."

"Thanks, Demetria," Patrick said. "I think, maybe, it's time I talked to Duce."

"Good idea. Tell him to get the hell away from ground zero."

"Persephone?"

"Miss Hiroshima herself."

"Thanks, Demetria."

"Good luck, Patrick. I don't want to be in your shoes right now," Demetria said with a sad twist to her mouth.

"Yeah, me neither. But hey, wait. Don't go yet. I could still use your help on something."

"Sorry, Patrick. This is too dangerous," Demetria said, shrugging. She vanished into the shadows.

"Wait! Don't go yet. Hear me out first. This has got nothing to do with the Sanctified." Patrick waited a moment, but Demetria didn't reappear. "Remember I told you about Law," Patrick said. "The Carthians are going to Embrace him, but he's got other plans. There's already a vampire in his crew, and I need help figuring out what he's up to. We think he broke the Masquerade with that shit out in Joliet."

Patrick heard nothing for a moment, then a sigh.

"No Sanctified?" Demetria said, her voice drifting out from the shadows.

"Shouldn't be. This is a separate issue. And if you spot one, you can walk away and never talk to me again."

"Already considering that option."

"Please?"

"All right," Demetria said. "But this, you're paying for. Tell me more."

"What the fuck were you *thinking*?" Duce said, nearly livid. He felt like he was burning a hole in Patrick's carpet just standing there. Patrick remained seated and calm, just staring and waiting for Duce to stop ranting. That annoyed Duce even more. "Well? You gonna say something?"

"Didn't want to interrupt," Patrick said.

"Don't fucking patronize me, Pat. Why'd you see Law? That wasn't your business."

"Look, man, I respect your pride, but it's getting in the way. There. I'm saying it. You're pride's fucking you over."

"My pride?"

"Half the shit happening wouldn't be biting you on the ass if it wasn't for your pride. If you'd talked to Law...just *talked* to him, then you might have found out what the Carthians were planning much earlier."

"It wouldn't have solved shit. The situation is what it is."

"That's your pride talking again."

"Look, what the fuck am I supposed to do?" Duce said, struggling to contain his frustration. "I can't turn this shit off. It's who I am."

lucien soulban

"I know that, Duce. But you gotta do something, because I tell you what...Adrian and Beth are using your pride against you. Whether you Embrace Law or not, it's all good for them. Don't you think it's time you robbed them of that tool?"

Duce fell into the chair with a heavy weight, his strength gone, his will sapped. "I don't know if I can," he said, almost whispering. "Half the shit I say comes out of my mouth before I can stop it. I feel angry, all the time, and I know that anger wasn't part of me before the bite."

"It's difficult," Patrick said, trying to offer a comforting smile. "It's what being a vampire means. All that passion struggling to find voice."

"I had a voice once. Political ideals, freedom, equality... all of it. I could see it once, taste it like it was there on my lips. It was all so real that I knew I—I could just reach out and grab it."

"And now?"

"And now? It's all about the game. All of this shit with Adenauer and Fulsome and Law—all of it, was never about ideals. It's all about position, status. It's politics without the ideals. Fulsome and Adenauer going for the crown and me trying to hold on to it. And all of us spinning election promises we probably won't keep."

"Hm," Patrick said, a sudden grin spread wide across his face.

"What? What's so funny?"

"Just remembered a story my college professor told me when I was at Chicago U. I was taking a class on Comparative Religions when he told us about an old covenant called the Mithrites. He goes..." Patrick said, lowering his voice an octave, "in Roman times, the Mithrites worshiped the God Mithras, but they were pretty much like the Christians. They followed one God; they called their priests 'fathers,' which Christianity stole from them; and they preached living a good and humble life to get into heaven, doing right by others along the way."

"I reminded you of *this*?"

"No wait. Listen," Patrick said, then resumed using 'the voice.' "The Mithrites and the Christians were competing for Rome's attention, but the Christians were still in hiding while the Mithrites enjoyed the patronage of Senators and politicians. Eventually, however, Christians prevailed and became the dominant religion of ancient Rome. And do you know why?"

Duce shook his head, bemused by Patrick's story.

"They lost because while they both advocated the same thing," Patrick said, "the Mithrites demanded their followers conduct themselves as exemplary human beings throughout their entire lives. But Christianity said you could be the biggest, most rotten bastard on the planet, but as long as you genuinely asked for absolution before you died, you could enter Heaven. Essentially, Christianity trumped the Mithrites by appealing to people's inherent laziness. They won by being a religion of slackers."

Duce laughed, finally breaking into a rare smile. "Shit," he said, still chuckling after a few minutes, "I hadn't heard that before."

"Look, man," Patrick said. "The point is, people will only respond to what they want to hear. And Adrian's giving that to them. He's giving them the promise of an easy life, not the hard truth."

"You're saying I should play his game."

"No, not at all. But you better be prepared for an uphill battle. You don't want to play Adrian's game, then I suggest you find that original passion that made you prefect. That made the others *want* to follow you."

"And what if I don't have it anymore," Duce said. "Patrick, man, what if I'm not what's right for the Carthians, that I'm only doing this to protect my status and not my beliefs."

"Do you want to step down?"

"I don't know anymore. I don't know if this shit's worth it. I don't know if we're all living a fantasy just to avoid facing the truth of our existence. That we're stalled... no hope of progress. No evolution. No growth. Just an eter-

lucien soulban

nity of sucking blood like the world's fattest mosquitoes."
Duce let out a short laugh. "Y'know. When I feel like this,
I always want to eat. Eat, y'know, like real food," he said,
pretending to hold a giant sandwich in his two hands. "I
see people eating, and I want to miss it. I sometimes even
buy myself a big ole' sloppy burger, just dripping in grease
with the fat tomato slices and the crispy fries, all smoth-
ered in ketchup. And I bring it to my lips, y'know, antici-
pating that rush of good vibes, remembering how good it
was all the other times when I was breathing. But even then.
I want to miss eating, but I can't, 'cause the only thing my
mouth remembers is the taste of blood. And suddenly, that
burger looks all wormy, like a clot of grease and fat. That's
when it hits me. I'll never be the same again and I'll never
miss food, even if I want to.... And I'm right back. Back
where I started. Pat, why the fuck am I doing this?"

"Maybe," Patrick said, "maybe you're doing things for
the wrong reasons now. But I remember that, once, you
were fighting the fight for the right reasons. You believed
in something. Call it equality or freedom, but you believed."

"So what happened to me, Doc? Where'd I lose it?"

Patrick smiled. "I don't have all the answers, Duce.
Hell, man, I don't know if I'm offering you bad advice
right now."

"Better than nothing, man."

"Well. I think you said it. You lost your way when the
position of prefect became more important than the message. Remember Martin Luther King, even Malcolm X.
They were great men, greater than those times had a right
to. But they were humble in their own way. They may have
enjoyed their popularity among their own people, but they
were never greater than the message. And they knew that."

"Yeah. They also knew they were going to die young,"
Duce said. "They weren't afraid to die if it meant one more
soul was going to hear their message. I've been too concerned with my own survival and my position that I forgot
that. Yo, Pat. What happened to these Mithrites anyways?"

"Stamped out. Once the Christians became the official religion of Rome, they destroyed the Mithrite cemeteries and burned their churches."

"So much for the meek inheriting the Earth."

"The meek will never inherit the Earth as long as mankind is around."

"Amen," Duce said. "All right, brother. Let's do this. If I'm going to lose the vote, then I'll lose true to who I am. No more games and shit."

"All right," Patrick said, smiling. "Let's do it then. What's the plan?"

"I need to talk to Law. Clear some shit up and find out if he's the kind of man we need. Maybe put the past behind us."

"Yeah, Duce, about that," Patrick said, slow consideration each word. "Some things you got to know."

"What?"

"I think Law's harboring a vampire. Someone from his set was already Embraced."

"What? Are you sure?"

"I could smell the blood. Someone had fed there, not too long ago, and they weren't too neat about it."

"You know who was Embraced? Who gave the Kiss?"

"No, man. But I think it was probably Beth who did the biting, or someone in her crew. It sure as hell wasn't Adrian."

"Doesn't sound like his style. Shit, we already figured Adenauer's gonna use Law against Fulsome, but the fact that that crazy bitch is Embracing brothers is another nail in her coffin."

"Maybe. But you're also right about Law being under the Vinculum, maybe Charles too. Beth sold them the idea by saying it was integral to the Embrace."

"Fuck, Law deserves better than to be some doped-up blood fiend. But it might also explain where Rasta comes from."

"I'm not sure," Patrick said. "That means Law is gunning for you, which doesn't make sense. Rasta could just be an outsider, attached to an unaligned vampire. Not everything has to tie up nicely."

"Maybe. But I don't buy it. A ghoul sending out a crew to cack a vampire...too much of a coincidence. I don't think it's Law pulling that shit, but it could be Adenauer. We need to talk to Law. Get the straight dope."

Duce's SUV was waiting in the street in front of Patrick's apartment building, though not in the condition Duce had left it.

"What the fuck," Duce said, racing up to his car. The tires were slashed and flat on the asphalt. Scratched into the car hood was: H.N.I.C.

Nobody else was around.

"Mother*fucker*," Patrick whispered.

Duce, however, was dead silent, trying to contain the rage festering just beneath his skin. His vision contracted into fierce points as he stared at the word...

...H.N.I.C...

...Head Nigger in Charge...

...nobody used *that* word against him. At least, nobody that ever walked straight, afterwards.

But if H.N.I.C. was vile, it was more than for the connotation of one word. The entire acronym was used for African-Americans who supervised and punished other slaves for their white masters; it meant someone who was a traitor to his culture. It meant he was the worst kind of Uncle Tom.

"This can't be Law's doing?" Patrick said.

"It isn't," Duce said. "He'd never do something like this. We better go see Law."

"Not in this car," Patrick said. "No way I'm rolling up in the Jets with that scratched into the hood."

"I'll park the car elsewhere. But we gotta go. And we gotta go now."

Chapter Eighteen

Law opened the door, looking genuinely surprised to see Patrick and Duce on the other side.

"Shit, come on in," Law said.

"Is Charles around, man?" Duce asked, walking into the apartment with a measured step and examining his surroundings. The smell of Clorox permeated the air with an almost overwhelming stench. Duce saw Patrick nodding in approval of something, but he wasn't sure of what. Law escorted them into the kitchen.

"Big Boy? Nah, man. He went all crazy on me, crawling up on my ass n' shit. Probably somewhere sulking. Brother does that a lot. Why?" Law asked. He looked at Duce and Patrick, studying them carefully.

"Somebody marked up my ride," Duce responded. "Keyed H.N.I.C. on the hood."

"Shit. Did you catch the motherfucker?"

"Not yet."

"We're thinking Charles did it," Patrick said.

"What? Man, Charles is Afrikan. We don't use slave words to identify each other."

"Not even as a dis?" Duce asked. "It doesn't slip out?"

"By accident. Sure, a lot of brothers still can't speak without using that particular word. I mean shit, it's in our music. It's part of the voice Afrikans think they should be using. But Charles scratching that into your hood? That shit's nickel and dime. Not his flavor."

"Charles has flavor," Duce said, immediately recognizing the cruelty in his own voice. He regretted the slight as

lucien soulban

soon as it came out; Law wouldn't understand where the comment came from. Patrick, however, stepped in quickly.

"Look," Patrick said. "Some brothers attacked Duce."

"Twice. Once outside a club and another at my crib. Both crews belonged to sets. At first, I thought you were responsible, you know what I'm saying?"

"Like I said. I'm B.G.F. now. No more brother-on-brother violence."

"Except against race traitors?" Duce said. "Right?"

"Anyone who conspires with the Amerikan government loses his privilege to be considered a part of the Afrikan community."

"Like me," Duce said.

"Nah, that's different—"

"Why?" Duce asked. "Because we're friends?"

"Because I wouldn't do you like that," Law replied, shaking his head. "I know why you escaped. Shit, *I* would have bounced too if I could have."

"Look," Duce said. "I believe you, man. I know you didn't send those gangbangers after me."

"But I'm not saying you're doing right, either," Law said. "I think you've been gone from your people for too damn long. I understand why you turned your back on the set, but you shouldn't have turned your back on the community."

"That's a discussion for later. Right now, I got a problem, and I'm thinking Charles is sending all this shit my way."

"What? Big Boy? Uh-uh," Law said, shaking his head. "Charles wouldn't play that game. Not without my say."

"You said you protected Duce's secret, right?" Patrick asked. "But I bet you told Charles."

"Charles's my boy. I bet you told Duce why my place smells like Clorox," Law said.

"Look, the motherfucker never liked my ass," Duce said, "and now he finds out I betrayed family. You saying he no longer hangs with anyone from his set? Nobody he could have told?"

Law hesitated in responding and Duce recognized the uncertainty in the face of his old friend. "Well—I mean, we all got homies still hanging with their old crews," Law said. "Sometimes, we try bringing them into the Black Guerilla Family."

"And sometimes?" Duce asked.

"And sometimes...we know better."

"Like a player named Rasta?" Duce asked.

"Yeah," Law replied. "Why?"

"Who's Rasta?" Patrick asked Law.

"Drug dealer poisoning our community," Law said. "Him and Charles used to hang together before Rasta turned all ghetto star and Charles went NARN 24-7."

"Excuse me?" Patrick said.

"Charles and me are with the New Afrikan Revolutionary Nation."

Duce nodded. "Heard about you cats. Intelligence gathering and studying data for the BGF, right?"

"That's us."

"Jesus," Patrick said, "that's why you're so eager for the Embrace."

"Did Charles ever try indoctrinating Rasta?" Duce asked.

"Nah, he knows better. We wouldn't accept Rasta."

"But Charles still hangs with him?"

"It's against BGF policy."

"But that hasn't stopped him before, has it?" Duce said.

"No," Law said, simply. "Rasta's got enough bling bling and beautiful sisters on his arms to be a 'community hero.'" Hard to fight capitalism when you're on a Marxist diet. Why you asking about Rasta?"

"Because someone had Rasta under a Vinculum...drinking vampire blood like you. Did your boy do this, Law?"

"No! Terrell's new n' shit. Brother barely knows what's what."

"Well, Rasta sent some motherfuckers after my ass. Him and I had a few words. Rasta's dead."

lucien soulban

"Shit! Man, if Charles found out what you did...." Law said, shaking his head.

"I don't think it'll make much difference," Duce said. "Motherfucker still wants me dead. Rasta sent one group of gangers against me, and I'm damn sure Charles sent the others. Law, you still got peeps in Black P-Stone?"

"A couple. Grooming some."

"Ask them what they heard about me. I want to know if it's open season on my ass. I need to know if my Pops is safe."

"We helping each other now?" Law asked.

"That depends, dog, that depends. I need your help with this shit 'cause if Charles is still riding with his old crew, it means we both got problems. Means Beth's playing all the goddamn angles to win, cause I bet you she enthralled Rasta too. Problem is, you're also under her blood."

Law studied Duce for a few seconds before shaking his head. "That hurts," he said. "You still treating me like I wronged you."

"Pat," Duce said, "can you give us a few minutes?"

"Sure thing. Actually, I got some things to clear up, including that shit we talked about with Persephone. She doesn't know who's following her." Patrick nodded to Law and headed out the front door.

"I'm listening," Law said.

"I know why you want the bite. You're not doing this for the Carthians. You're doing this for the BGF. I know about that shit out in Joliet."

"What about it?" Law said with a shrug.

"If you're planning what I think you are, you're playing a dangerous game. Beth's manipulating you into playing for her stakes, making you think you're getting yours."

"I ain't playing at shit, D. But if you know what I'm planning, then please, educate me."

"You're going to Embrace members of the BGF. You want to empower them."

"I'm planning on equalizing the situation for our brothers and sisters. Isn't that what the Carthians are about?"

"You're playing with words. The Carthians are about change, but within vampire society. It doesn't include over-throwing the U.S. Government!"

"Whatever freedom takes, D. Why you sweating the petty bullshit when you could be helping all people of color from this repressive regime? You gotta admit, it's been damn near 400 years coming."

"Law, dog, it doesn't work like that. We survived by keeping shit quiet and coming down hard on anyone who threatens that secret."

"Don't give a shit. About time someone dragged your asses out of the sandbox. We're at war, but you've become blind to that. You haven't seen the shit I've seen. Fuck, even Beth gets that—"

"Look, I don't need this 'Blacker than thou' speech. I love my people, but I don't need anyone telling me what it takes to be African-American, including some cracker-ass bitch."

"I'm talking about becoming *Afrikan*. These Amerikan motherfuckers never invited you into their country."

"No. We earned the right to be called American. There's a reason my Pops hung an American flag over his door. There's a reason he fought in Vietnam."

"Look, I respect your Pops for being something most Afrikan males forgot to be, a father. But he didn't spend ten years behind bars, and neither did you. The dictator-ship ruining this country claims to have abolished slavery, yet they're still running plantations."

"Man, what are you on about?"

"Prisons are being run like factories, with the prisoners being used as cheap labor. The cons do all the work and receive no medical, no vacation, no retirement, nothing to give them hope for the future," Law said, listing the points on his fingers. "But what really burns my ass is that the communities and corporations making money off hard-working Afrikans and Latinos in prison are cracker-ass white people! None of the money goes back into the ghettoes that need them! Take Joliet. These fucking white-ass towns take in Afrikans as prisoners and count them as unemployed citizens. That drives down the town's 'average' income and qualifies them for government aid programs... money that should be going to the fucking ghettoes that need them!" he said, falling full rage into a familiar and sensitive speech that never stopped angering him. "Goddammit, Duce! They know you can prevent more crime by spending the same amount of money on high-school graduation incentives than on 're-educating' prisoners! But the cocksuckers won't do that because they ain't making money off it and because it won't break the backs of the Afrikan people as effectively! Now how the fuck am I supposed to stand back and watch this shit happen? How the fuck am I supposed to watch my people die from guns and drugs they circulating on my streets? These motherfuckers want a war?" Law said, muscles straining from his furious pitch, "then I'll bring them war."

"Jesus," Duce said. "Adenauer doesn't know what she's done."

"No," Law said. "She thinks she controls me, but she don't got nothing on me!"

"And you don't think you're contributing to the problem by bringing vampire blood into the community? By letting punks like Adenauer turn you and Rasta and Charles into a new kind of addict?"

"I know," Law said. "I get that now. But I swear to Jesus it'll stop with us. Once I get the bite, I'll make sure that Beth or Adrian or the regime never takes advantage of my people again."

"Just so long as you can, right?"

"What?"

"You don't get it. Once you get the bite, you'll need to protect your secret. So you'll addict a couple of peeps to your blood just so they can watch your ass during the day and do shit for you while you sleep. You'll also give one or two the bite so you aren't fighting the fight alone. Then all of y'all will need to feed. And again, y'all will stick to the familiar and keep to hunting within the community. Eventually, you'll fall in love, and God save those sisters when the loneliness creeps in. You'll become the new plague of your people."

"I wouldn't do them like that," Law said. "Now that I recognize the dangers—"

"You won't have a choice. It's going to happen, intentions aside. It's the nature of what you've become."

Law said nothing, and Duce recognized the growing despair welling up inside his former friend.

"Where can I find Charles and this other vampire?" Duce asked softly.

"I'm not giving them up. They're family...my burden."

"Not anymore. Y'all stepped in my sandbox. Now I gotta fix the shit they started."

"They're Afrikan, like you."

"Law," Duce said, heading for the door. "You got no idea what happens to you after you're bit."

"Maybe you changed," Law said, "but you changed before the bite. Don't blame it on anything else. You got free will. The right to change back. The right to rejoin your brothers and sisters as an Afrikan."

"That time's gone," Duce said, opening the door.

"You're lying to yourself, playing games with vampires cause it's easier than facing the truth. Whether you like it or not, war is coming."

Duce looked at Law a moment, then left, saying nothing as he walked through the door.

Duce stared up at the apartment building before he made his way to the shadows of an adjoining alley. Stepping over the fetid garbage, he checked the alley with long glances before speaking.

"When did you leave?" Duce asked nobody in particular.

"Well..." a voice said, shattering the illusion of invisibility. Justin Hoff appeared, materializing from thin air. He was Nosferatu in the creepy sense of the word. It meant there was something frightening about his demeanor, a sense of *not right* in him, whether it was because his emaciated limbs seemed too long by an inch, or because his eyes were hollow sockets that Duce had to fall into just to see his irises, or because his hair grew in chemotherapy patches.

"I left," Hoff said, "when you told Patrick to leave."

"Good man," Duce said. "Did you see anything in there?"

"Nothing much. Somebody died in there...place reeked of blood and Clorox. Otherwise, there was no indication a vampire had been there recently or where they might be hiding him."

"Damn. Well listen, I still need your help."

"Glad to be of service, boss."

"Cool. Keep an eye on the place. Follow Law, but if you spot Charles, tail him."

"Charles. Walking refrigerator?"

"The guy I described, right."

"Will do, boss."

Duce patted Hoff on the shoulder and made his way out of the alley. He glanced back once, but Hoff was already gone.

The winds pushing off Lake Michigan were bitterly cold, like a knife drawn across the rag of Persephone's soul. Not even the barren, skeleton-fingered trees could shield her from the chilling gusts, not that Persephone cared for such considerations. Instead, she wandered through Lincoln Park's meandering paths, retreated into herself. Though she wanted to sort through her thoughts, she found it easier to remain numb and let everything wash over her, let the waves crash over and smooth down her jagged spirits. She offered no resistance and found the numbing tranquility comfortable.

At least she didn't have to think about Duce; to consider how she'd betrayed a pivotal, crucial secret that he'd kept hidden; how she'd peeled back his flesh to reveal his Achilles heel.

Only the first dropping snowflakes slowed her ambling trudge. She reached out and allowed a snowflake to settle on her outstretched palm, waiting for it to melt. It didn't. Persephone realized she was colder than concrete. She crushed the petal of snow and continued walking, not bothering to brush the accumulation powdering her shoulder.

Small patches of white grew and spread, refusing to melt quickly, and night adopted a strange twilight cast from falling snow. Even sound grew muted, and the traffic noise from the street dimmed into distant hushes. It would have been serene and beautiful, but in the open stillness of the park, Persephone realized she was no longer alone. Whether by some primal impulse of the Beast or lingering prehistoric skill of her survival instinct, Persephone was acutely aware of her vulnerability.

She looked around, able to see further thanks to the ambient twilight accompanying the falling snow and lightening even the deepest, darkest night. Two men walked directly towards her, sidestepping trees, youthful arrogance to their steps, heads swiveling around. No plumes of frosted breath to tinge the air around them; they weren't breathing. Persephone recognized the black-haired one from the Safe Harbor where she'd confronted Garin; he was one of the faces staring back at her in the crowd, openly belligerent. The other, brown-haired one appeared equally young, both sporting long unfettered hair and leather jackets. One wore a bandanna, the other did not. Both sent goosebumps up and down Persephone's neck.

The two men walked towards her, cocky, intent for harm in their eyes. Persephone recognized the look and understood the sentiment.

"I don't suppose you boys are just out for a stroll?" Persephone said, stepping backwards slowly.

"Maybe," the first man said, fangs exposed, "if that means strolling up and down your ass!"

lucien soulban

The black-haired one nodded and the two men split apart, trying to flank Persephone to her left and right. She smiled...

...and then pulled out her Glock.

The expressions on the two men's faces were priceless, not that Persephone had time to savor the moment. She opened fire, switching targets with every shot and backing away. Seven reports rang out and three bullets found marks. It wasn't enough to incapacitate her foes, but everything Persephone did was predicated on keeping her opponents off balance. This maneuver was the first in a small repertoire of moves she'd practiced and learned following Solomon Birch's assault back at her old apartment. She swore nobody would ever get that opportunity again. She was through feeling victimized and tonight was minor retribution for that evening.

While her gunplay wouldn't be enough against the likes of Solomon Birch, Persephone's twin attackers were far easier to handle. Both men stumbled forward, surprised and hurting. Persephone "pushed out" hard with her voice, issuing a one-word imperative that her target would be forced to obey... if it worked. "Run!" she said with a roar, trying to push one of them away through sheer force of will. It was enough to frighten the brown-haired vampire, who stumbled backwards with a scream and fled full dash from the fight, snarling in panic.

Persephone had little time to gloat. She turned to the black-haired vampire, who was almost upon her, and aimed her gun.

Until someone tackled her from behind....

Patrick looked up once at the sky and let out a small sigh. The flakes were small, but they heralded an early winter. Sure, it was darker earlier, giving him more hours in the night, but there would be fewer humans out on the streets as well. It would be harder to intermingle with them, lose himself in the dynamic summer crowds and pretend he was anything other than unliving. Winter was the dead time for Patrick, a depressing reminder that he was isolated.

The echoing metal shriek of the Blue Line train pulling into Racine station off in the distance shattered Patrick's reverie. He shook his head at the snow and made a silent vow to enjoy the next summer. He'd go out more, he promised himself while crossing the street; he'd ignore every vampire in the city and spend the warm evenings watching the pulse of crowds as they ebbed and waxed.

Lost in thought, Patrick didn't see the car until it was too late. Its headlights were off, and in the second before it struck him, it accelerated. Patrick's shins snapped against the fender, two matchsticks under a hammer's blow. He fell against the car, his legs swept out from beneath him, and bounced his head with such force that he left a deep dent in the hood and hairline fractures across his skull.

Patrick rebounded off the hood and briefly soared through the air, knocked senseless by the blow. He skimmed across concrete, leaving a smear of fabric, flesh and blood along the street. Somewhere in coming to a rest, both arms snapped and his shoulders popped out of their joints. His ribs were pulped. He screamed at the sudden influx of pain from the broken bones dancing free and stabbing his innards. Patrick couldn't stop the wave of fear from washing over him, and in that frightened moment, the Beast tore itself free. It only understood pain. It didn't understand physiology, that it couldn't stand up on shattered legs.

Patrick roared in pain, trying to stand, and hit the street again. He flopped around, a live fish in the frying pan, before bright lights caught his attention. His head snapped up in time to see the car hit him again. The car's grill caught him full in the face, and the wheels ground him under as the car rolled over him. The wheels spun, ripping open his stomach and shredding the flesh from the back of his skull.

The Beast was spent. It retreated back into its cage, whimpering. It left Patrick to the pain, to the paralyzing injuries. He was blind, his eyeballs knocked loose or perhaps crushed against bone. He only heard voices that swam in and out of his head. The muscle and bone stitching together slowly, far too slowly, brought even more pain.

"What up with you now, bitch?" one voice asked.

"Man, why we fucking with him? Thought you wanted Duce's ass?"

"'Cause this bitch talking shit about my Beth! And now… Duce's all alone, just like she said."

"*Shit*, he still moving."

"Nah, he done. Ain't that right, Patrick? Watch me cap his ass. I hear these bitches turn to ash."

Patrick struggled hard, trying to move, trying to lash out, swing at anything, everything around him. He barely lifted his arm. He flopped to the ground.

"Sayonara, bitch!"

Charles' voice was the last thing Patrick heard before gunfire and shotgun blasts tore through him, spreading more of him across the street.

Bodies tangled together, limbs interlocked. Elbows flying, nails scratching, a sharp heel into someone's thigh….

"Never again!" Persephone screamed, driving her knee into someone's stomach. She received a fist in her face for the effort, but it didn't hurt much thanks to the blood that turned her innards into stone and her bones into steel.

The fight played out in a sequence of raw, angry snapshots taken as blows connected. Persephone fought hard, a fury to her swings her assailants didn't expect. There were three of them, not counting the one who'd fled. Two black-haired punks and a bald-headed man in his mid-thirties who looked like a casting reject from *Easy Rider*. The punks were green, but Baldy was more experienced. Then again, so was Persephone.

"Fuckers!" Persephone raked her fingernails across Baldy's face, blinding the older man; the two other vampires tried pummeling her. One of them yelped in pain, his hand broken against Persephone's marble-hard skin. He rolled off as well, giving Persephone the quick respite to target the black-haired bastard who'd tackled her from behind. She slammed her fingers into his windpipe, breaking off two nails in the soft flesh of her assailant's throat. He reared back, enough for Persephone to fire two more shots into his stomach, sending him flying into his bald-headed ally.

The burning shots must have hurt, because the black-haired assailant roared in pain, his eyes instantly contracting into feral points. The Beast was loose in him, and he lashed out at the closest target: His friend. It was all the distraction Persephone needed. Baldy was trying to subdue him while the Beast-ridden vampire lashed out with every available limb, no rhyme or reason to his attacks. The last man was grimacing in pain as the bones in his hand stitched together, but he was also charging in to restrain his ally.

Rule 101 of the undead: Never leave a frenzied vampire unchecked.

Persephone ran.

Nobody saw anything. Just the way it goes, in some parts of town.

The few cars driving down the street saw the misshapen lump lying in the road, but when they slowed, they registered something that looked too decomposed to have died recently. The ashen, shriveled innards lay exposed, there was too much bone showing through ripped patches of desiccated skin, and the soft tissues were missing, revealing hollowed out eye sockets and a sunken nose. Only the clothing looked new, beyond the tears and tire marks.

Cars drove by, drivers convinced someone had dug up a corpse and left him in the street for amusement. Within a half-hour, a squad car showed up thanks to an anonymous tip concerning gunfire. All they found was a pile of ash and bits of bone in and around jeans, a not-so white

lucien soulban

sweater and a pair of hush puppies. No blood, so no foul play, and no stench either. The cops sent for the meat wagon and chalked up the incident to a poor practical joke.

Still, they couldn't explain the wallet and cell phone they found or why they belonged to a man who lived nearby but was nowhere to be found. They couldn't explain the 11 slugs scattered in the ash, nor the shotgun pellets. They never found from where the body was stolen, and they never found the wallet and cell phone, nor clothing, nor bagged ash again. Officially, the remains and personal effects were lost on route to the District 12 evidence locker and the Medical Examiner, though Internal Affairs never investigated the matter fully.

Unofficially, vampires took care of their own kind.

Chapter Nineteen

Persephone remained hidden until the last possible second, when she ran from the cab, up the stairs to Maxwell's brownstone building and stood under the camera. Somehow, she didn't feel as safe as she thought she would, but it was a far sight better than traversing town, looking over her shoulder for the next ambush.

Her thumb on the intercom button, Persephone continued pressing for several seconds. Samuel answered.

"Prince Maxwell is not—"

"Someone tried to kill me!" Persephone said, hoping she looked pitiful enough to carry her claim. There was no response, so Persephone pressed the intercom button again, this time rattling the door with a solid kick.

The intercom clicked on again, this time with the door opening. "It's Robert, come in."

Persephone pushed her way into the lobby and nearly collapsed from relief. One of the bodyguards came to her rescue, offering her a hand and escorting her to the stairs where she sat. From upstairs, she could hear Robert racing down the steps. He settled down next to her and took her in his arms as Persephone leaned against him, taking a moment to smell the Drakkar perfume that lingered on his sweater.

"Thank you," Persephone muttered. "I didn't think Samuel would open."

"I outrank him," Robert said softly. "What happened? Are you okay?"

"Four men attacked me," Persephone said. "They were Kindred. They called me a traitor."

Robert shook his head and pressed Persephone deeper into his chest, taking a moment to clear the strands from her face. "Ah, Persephone," he said with a sigh. "I warned you about this."

"I'm not a traitor—"

"I know. I believe you."

"—and it doesn't give anyone the right—" she said, then stumbled to a stop.

"No, it doesn't," Robert replied. "Can you give me a description of these men?"

"Yes," Persephone nodded. "I'll give their description to Sheriff Nguyen."

Robert continued holding Persephone a few moments longer before asking: "Did you give them hell?"

"Oh yes," Persephone said, smiling. "Four men, and they couldn't take me down. I was fierce!" she said with a whisper.

"Of that I have no doubt. But I'm glad."

"Of?" she asked, sitting up straight.

"You. I'm glad you stood your own ground. But I'm exceptionally happy you came here instead of going to Duce first."

"He's a good man," Persephone said.

"I—it's not my place to say, dear. Not when it comes to affairs of your heart."

"But?" Persephone asked.

"But, when it comes to Duce, he threatens your position within the First Estate. It didn't take much for people to turn against you with nothing more than allegations."

"I won't be bullied," Persephone said.

"No, I know you won't. You are smart, though, smart enough to question if Duce is a benefit or a hindrance. That is, if you plan on remaining Invictus."

"Of course I do," Persephone said, almost pleading for Robert to believe her.

"Then is Duce a safe investment... as an asset or lover?"

Persephone tried to answer, but she stopped herself. She didn't know what to say. She loved Duce... or at least she thought she did. But since they'd fallen back into each other's orbit, there'd been nothing but difficulty and trial.

"Think about it," Robert whispered, kissing her on the forehead. "Meanwhile, give us a few moments to prepare you a guest room." He rose to his feet, hand extended to help her up. "You're staying here, of course, unless you have somewhere else to be?"

Persephone shook her head. She was too tired to consider anywhere else tonight, though one matter concerned her as she stood. "Won't Maxwell—"

"He'd approve," Robert said, his smile a welcome dash of optimism. "You're his childe, and anyone who tries to harm you is flouting his rule over the city."

"All right," Persephone said, half-laughing. "I won't refuse. Where is he, by the way?"

"He's dining with Halliburton tonight. A private meeting."

"Ah," Persephone said, barely concealing a coy smile. At least something was going well this evening.

Duce was back in his rental car, a nondescript blue Toyota hatchback that was far too small for his shoulders. He'd been driving for a couple of hours now, with the radio off, mired in thought and considering his options now that Law was in the picture. Could he afford to let his old friend run rampant, pursuing mortal agendas with vampire muscle backing him up? Was Law right, though? Had he become so enmeshed in vampire policies and games that his own community had become a distant concern? Or was Law wrong in believing that any good could come of their accursed gifts?

Certainly, the prospect of longevity, strength, cunning, speed and the various disciplines of the Kindred mind were alluring...intoxicating, even. What Law didn't get, however, was the accompanying cost, the constant hooks and barbs that would chain his soul to the dirt floor. He didn't realize that callous words slipped through more readily, or that he'd be more willing to inflict suffering thanks to some cruel undercurrent circulating in his blood. Worst of all, Law didn't understand the Hunger. It was unlike anything he could comprehend except through experience; it was an addiction like no other. No matter how much blood he'd ingest, the Hunger would remain unappeased and unimpressed by such offerings. It was more than just satiating thirst; the curse was ultimately about the act of consumption, the need to gorge on something in its entirety. And it extended into all facets of his existence, including his emotions. Duce was already passionate, but the Hunger drove everything into such keen-edged focus that existence itself was one giant razor blade across which Duce dragged himself.

This was especially true in Persephone, Duce realized, where curse and blessing were all rolled into one. Duce cared for Persephone, he knew that much, but the Hunger robbed him of the ability to distinguish that fine line between his passion for her and his need to *consume* her. It was one big tangled ball, and Duce couldn't stop thinking about being with her, tasting her, devouring her. And he always stopped himself from imagining what it would be like to drink her absolutely, body and soul, till she was part of him.

Duce slammed his fist on the wheel. Love was already difficult enough to navigate without the Hunger adding its own cruel twists to the course. Did Duce truly love her? Was his need to consume Persephone an extension of that love? Was it an extension of that absolute desire to devour? Or was it a new twist to the curse that so muddled distinctions that passion and Hunger were now synonymous with one another?

I understand, Duce thought. He tilted his head back against the seat's headrest and almost laughed. That was what Patrick could never articulate properly, but inherently understood. Vampires couldn't partake of their mortal lives anymore because they could no longer protect their loved ones from themselves. And that was why being among other Kindred was simultaneously so dangerous and so essential.

Law didn't realize he'd eventually victimize the very people he was trying to help. He'd become a blight on his community the way Patrick infected his because, whether Law realized it or not, his perspectives would change.

The cell phone rang, startling Duce. He fumbled for it, quickly glancing at the number before flipping it open.

"Yo, Pat," Duce said. "What's up?"

The line crackled, but the voice on the other end wasn't Patrick's. "Hello, Duce," the voice said. "This is Sheriff Nguyen."

Puzzled, Duce quickly checked the number again, a sinking feeling hitting his throat and express-dropping its way down past his stomach. "Sheriff," Duce said, very slowly. "What're you doing with Pat's phone?"

"I'm sorry, Duce, but there was an incident. Please meet me at Prince Maxwell's receiving estate. You know the one."

"Fuck that! What's this about?"

"Patrick's dead," the Sheriff said, "and that's all I'm saying until you get here."

Before Duce could ask another question, Nguyen hung up the phone. Duce quickly pulled to the side of the road and punched redial, then Pat's home and then the cell number again, but in all three cases, there was no response. Swearing loud enough to catch the attention of nearby pedestrians, Duce tore back into the street, driving with the accelerator pushed to the floor, heading for Prince Maxwell's brownstone building.

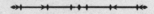

The upholstered window seat was comfortable, offering Persephone a quiet view of the pristine snowfall outside the building. She studied the street, watching traffic drift by and listening to hushed wheels pushing through the thin slurry. No pedestrians in these late hours; just drivers trying to get home to their warm beds. Persephone envied them that. She missed sleeping at night, like normal people, and waking up with the rest of the world. The hours between 4:00 AM and sunrise were the hardest, because that's when the world was asleep and the Kindred cleaved together to remind themselves they weren't alone.

Convenient lie, that is, Persephone thought. The Kindred were alone, frightened of humans discovering their secrets, frightened of the thirst in each other, frightened of themselves if they faltered....

Fear propels us, Persephone thought, *and we are right to be afraid.* She couldn't think about Duce without seeing him in visceral snapshots, her teeth digging into his flesh, his mouth sucking out her blood. That they were bonded to one another was a given, though Duce's bond was tempered by the stronger Vinculum to the Prince. Her love for him, however, also provided no bulwark against betrayal. She could justify her duplicity in revealing Duce's secrets, but when it came down to it, she was his Jezebel. Her disloyalty was easy too, just the right motivation required.

Take away her power, however, and Persephone was right back to a few years ago, right back to that feeling of helplessness when Solomon Birch overpowered her and beat her to a pulp.

"Never again," Persephone said to herself in a soft whisper that filled the quiet. After Birch, she'd taken steps to protect herself, learned tricks people wouldn't expect of her kind as Ventrue. She expanded her influence as well, anything to empower herself. Unfortunately, fear still steered her decisions. Case-in-point: Scrambling after Halliburton for his support. Case in point: Betraying Duce and, in effect, betraying her own ethics.

I lied to myself, Persephone realized. *I thought I could skirt the edge of both worlds without suffering the consequences.* Well, the consequences were now apparent through her situation with Griffin, with the rumors and with Duce. Exist in one world or the other—Carthian or

Invictus. Trying to bridge both communities was an invitation for disaster, a collision of interests and agendas that had already pinned her in the middle.

Persephone finally recognized that a choice existed, a choice she needed to make. While the nature of the decision allowed for a spectrum of responses, the real question was simple enough. *Where do you stand? Is it with both feet in the First Estate? With the Carthians? Or one foot in each domain and damn the consequences?*

The First Estate offered power and upward mobility. More importantly, it offered security and privilege for its members, a very attractive prospect for someone drifting further from the era of her birth into the uncertain future. The Carthians, however, fought the status quo and tried to change a stagnant and sometimes fetid system. They almost represented hope among Kindred, a belief in a better society, a better future. What attracted Persephone to the Carthians was that they fought to shape tomorrow rather than regret its arrival.

Persephone also found the Carthians attractive because of Duce, even though that was no longer a viable reason for affiliating with them. She had to protect herself—protect her hard-earned investments—but whether that included Duce was another issue.

A knock at the door interrupted Persephone's thoughts. "Who is it?" she asked.

"It's Robert."

"Come in," she said, standing from the window seat and moving for the door.

Robert entered, looking grave and a little troubled. He offered a half-smile reserved for apologies.

"What's wrong?" Persephone asked.

"Patrick Morneau was murdered this evening."

"What?" Persephone said, grasping the lapel of her gown. "How?"

"Drive-by, maybe? Police found bullets, and locals reported hearing screeching tires."

"What happened?"

"The police responded to a call. They found ash, clothing and personal possessions in the middle of a street. They radioed it in. We intercepted the ashes and the contents. We just confirmed it was Mr. Morneau. I'm sorry."

"Oh, God," Persephone said, sitting on the corner of her bed. "Does Duce know?"

"Sheriff Nguyen is bringing him here to speak with Prince Maxwell."

"I have to talk to Max," Persephone said, getting up.

"He isn't to be disturbed."

"This isn't Duce's fault!"

"Perhaps. Perhaps not. Prince Maxwell will decide that himself."

"Then let me talk to Duce."

"I'm sorry, Persephone," Robert said, shaking his head. "That's for the Prince to decide."

"What am I supposed to do here, Robert?" Persephone said. "I can't stand by. Patrick was Duce's best friend. He wouldn't hurt him."

"Persephone," Robert whispered, "you'll find that as Kindred, your actions bear greater significance. Everything you do has a wider scope of consequences. Maybe Mr. Carter didn't pull the trigger, but he's undoubtedly responsible for bringing Mr. Morneau to whatever situation ended his existence… and for besmirching your reputation. The best thing you can do right now is stay here."

"I—"

"You can't help him. Leave it to Mr. Carter and Prince Maxwell. They're grown men, and they'll handle it as such."

"I can't," Persephone said. "Please, tell Maxwell that I'll abide by any decision he makes concerning me if it means he'll be more lenient on Duce."

Robert studied Persephone for a long moment. "Are you certain, Persephone? There could be much to answer for."

"I don't care. Tell Maxwell I'll fall in line with the Invictus, a true daughter of the First Estate. Someone worthy of his blood."

Robert nodded. "You know he'll ask you to stop associating with Kindred like Duce."

"I know."

"All right, but consider your promises carefully. They could be harder to keep than you know."

"Time will tell," Persephone said with a sad smile.

Robert kissed Persephone on the forehead before turning and leaving the room.

It was late in the night when Charles stumbled back into the apartment, a big bottle of Colt 45 in his hand, well on its way to being emptied. He flopped down on the sofa, bleak-eyed and brooding, and Law wondered, for a brief moment, if you Embraced someone while they were drunk...would they stay drunk?

Despite appearances, Charles was never a big drinker. He handled enough alcohol to shut people up, but on the whole, it tore his stomach ragged. He reserved liquor for truly dark moments in his life, and Law suspected that their little fight earlier was not the cause of his latest drinking bout.

So Law sat there reading, on the lounger across from the sofa, waiting for droopy-lipped Charles to speak first. It was a few minutes in the coming, but Charles finally said:

"Rasta dead."

Law closed his copy of Soul on Ice and avoided the obvious, clichéd responses that came to mind. *I warned you about associating with Rasta... Rasta had what was coming to him...What the fuck were you thinking, helping Rasta get blooded... Did you set Rasta on Duce... Damn, I sound like my mother.* He stayed silent, letting Charles unburden himself. This wasn't the time to be chastising him, though damn if Law wasn't angry. If half of Duce's allegations were true, then Charles was in deeper than he should have been.

"Motherfucker blew Rasta's head off. Both barrels. Booya, motherfucker, booya!"

"I'm sorry," Law managed with little sympathy.

"Dude said the fucker who did Rasta and his crew was a monster, all bloody and fast. Mean bitch tore brothers' throats out like a mad dog. He had teeth and was strong 'n shit—a biter. Bit one deep and hard. Shot others up good. Said he looked like Duce. Duce is Shaft-ass bad, huh? Ain't he, *Law*?"

Law shook his head. He hated self-pity, especially pity born out of hypocrisy. He also had no patience for this anymore. "Tell the whole story, bitch," Law snapped, fixing Charles with a hard stare. "What about the motherfuckers you told Rasta to set on Duce?"

Charles looked up slowly, a blend of surprise, resentment and alcohol mixed in the martini glasses of his eyes.

"Yeah," Law said, "you can stop playing *playah*. I know what you did. I know you told Rasta about Duce and I know Rasta sent those motherfuckers after him."

"All right. Yeah. I did it," Charles said, sitting up straight, acting proud. "I went after Duce to protect your ass!"

"My ass?"

"Yeah, because I knew you're blind to his shit!"

"You went after Duce because you're jealous, and besides, it was Beth and Adrian who wanted me to get the bite from Duce. What's Beth going to say now that you're fucking with her plans?"

"Shit, Law. That *was* her plan, man. Beth never wanted Duce giving you the bite. That shit was all Adrian thinking he was maneuvering Duce n' shit. Beth, though... Beth got it right. She wanted Duce ashed. Who you think gave me his cell number?"

"What? What are you on about?"

"Duce's motherfucking cell phone. The one with that GPS shit in it. The one that all new cell phones got. Beth gave me his number and Rasta got his boy in Chicago PD to trace the calls. Duce makes a call, and bang! We got his home address."

"I gotta talk to Beth," Law said, fumbling for his cell phone.

"Too late," Charles said. "Too fucking late. Beth started worrying when you were all 'I want Duce with me.' Thought you were stronger than that. But she got me now, and Terrell. She don't need you no more."

"I don't give a shit about Beth," Law said, standing and throwing the phone into the wall. It splintered into plastic shards and components. "What about you and Terrell? You took an oath to the BGF!" Law said, angry now, his patience slipping in long yards.

"Look it, Law," Charles said, standing. "The Family is noble n' all, but this Marxist shit won't fly. The Black Panthers failed because they didn't recognize. Money makes the world go round. You need money to make shit work. To buy the guns, to buy the votes, whatever. Rasta knew that and Beth made me see that."

"The Black Panthers failed because the government drove them into the ground with their jackboots, Charles. But finally, man, we got a weapon that puts us eye-to-eye with the regime. Don't turn your back on that."

"Y'all ain't living in the real world! Look around you, Law. Everybody's fucking each other over, man. It ain't just us. It's the way of the world! You eat the dog before the dog eats you! And the motherfuckers doing the eatin' are the motherfuckers with the Benjamins. Shit. Even terrorists are fucking bankrolled these days."

"I see how it is," Law said. "So then, *brother*. What about me, huh? Am I just another dog to you to? What happened to *never let a brother fall to a knee?*"

"Nah, man," Charles said, whispering and punching his chest. "It ain't like that. You're my boy. I was just trying to protect you against Duce. But...the longer this dragged out, the more I realized this shit ain't working. Duce is going to go all Judas on your ass because of what he is, and you ain't gonna see it coming because you're too busy dream-

lucien soulban

ing. You blind to too much shit. How's a blind man supposed to lead me, huh?"

Law was ready to hurt Charles, ready to beat him to a bloody mess, but Charles had his hand on the grip of his gun. Law held his temper in check.

"And what are you dreaming about, Charles? Huh? Fine honeys, bling bling and Cristal?"

"Nah, man. I still believe in the cause, and that shit out in Joliet was just the beginning. I don't agree with the process, though. Beth made me see that. See, she needed someone with money and weapons, and Rasta provided that shit if she promised him the bite. She respected Rasta… Rasta was keeping it real. We gonna do what you hoping to do, only with money," Charles said, moving for the front door.

"You think you're just gonna walk out of here?"

"That's exactly what I'm gonna do, dog," Charles said. "You ain't got shit. We got Terrell, and we got the blood. I talked to Beth tonight. We don't need you no more." Charles walked past Law and headed for the door. "I'll pick up my shit later," he said.

"Duce is gonna come after you, you know that, right?" Law said.

"I know," Charles said, heading out the front door. "Beth and me made sure he did."

"What's that mean?" Law said, calling out from the living room, but Charles was already heading down the corridor.

The room was conservative with its deep brown wall panels and carpeting, and the red-brown of its rosewood table and chairs. Duce was pacing around the table, trying to calm himself, desperately wanting to lash out and hit something, anything. But he couldn't. The first blow wouldn't placate him or soothe his savage temper. It would only fuel the flames, the first blow followed by another and another until the Beast rode out in his rage.

Finally, Duce managed to calm himself by focusing on Patrick, what he meant as a friend...his kick-you-in-the-head advice. It was enough to settle Duce for the moment and steel himself for what would undoubtedly be an unpleasant conversation. Only when he sat down did the door to the meeting room unlock. Four large ghouls, sporting shades and likely tanked on blood, walked in. They wore charcoal gray jackets and the same buzz cut they probably had when they left the Marines or Army or whatever mercenary outfit Maxwell recruited them from.

A few silent moments later, Prince Maxwell walked through the door. Barrel-torsoed with a thick streak of white to his dreadlocked hair, Maxwell was an imposing-looking brother with an arrowhead beard and Fu Manchu mustache. He wore a dark brown sweater with a jacket and matching slacks; conservative clothing reflecting the rich, but conservative surroundings.

Duce struggled hard not to fall into the role of fawning thrall, but it was difficult. His anger over Patrick's murder almost evaporated, and Duce found apologies and pleas for forgiveness forming on his tongue. He fought the urge to debase himself for one accepting glance, one supportive smile from the Prince. The hold of Maxwell's Vinculum was strong, but not so strong that Duce couldn't struggle against it...struggle to be heard. Duce focused on Patrick's death and used that to cut his way through the forest of webs hampering his thoughts. It was difficult, nonetheless.

"Mr. Carter," Maxwell said, sitting at the head of the table. "I've seen far too much of you this month. I can't say I'm happy."

"I'm sorry," Duce said, almost muttering, before grimacing. "Patrick was my friend. Someone murdered him. I want their asses! I want to rip their fucking heads off!"

The Prince looked surprised that Duce still had some fight in him. Duce, however, was trying to appear strong by channeling his anger towards whoever killed Patrick.

Whoever? Duce thought. *More like Charles. That bitch is dead!*

"You have enough worries for the moment."

"So the sheriff said," Duce replied, redirecting his anger at Sheriff Nguyen to sound stronger. "But this is my mess. I'll take care of it."

"Well," Maxwell replied. "I'm glad you realize this is your mess, though you may have forced me to intervene."

"No," Duce said, quickly.

"No?"

"I'm sorry. It's just that…you'll be shooting yourself in the foot."

"How so?" the Prince asked.

"You'll undermine my position with the Carthians."

"From what I heard, you're already losing control."

"I know, I'm sorry," Duce said, desperately fighting the effects of this forced love. "But I know how to recover the situation."

"Your time has come and gone, Mr. Carter," Maxwell said, moving to stand. "You've proven you can't control them."

"No!" Duce said, forcefully enough that the guards casually reached for their weapons. "I failed because of you," Duce said, his heart sinking at the comment. He didn't want to blame Prince Maxwell, but he was fighting for everything at this moment. To be rendered *persona non grata* was, in itself, a death sentence. He'd never be safe again; this was survival talking.

Maxwell looked surprised and amused at Duce's outburst. He'd probably inflicted the Vinculum on enough people to find this amount of self-determination, this level of stubbornness, curious. With a simple nod to the guards, he sank back into the chair; the four goons relaxed. "Explain yourself," Maxwell said.

"You didn't keep your promises," Duce said. "You gave me nothing to work with and now Patrick's dead."

"You're blaming me for his death?" Maxwell said, almost laughing before a thought occurred to him. "Wait.

Are you saying the Carthians are responsible for his destruction?"

"No, I'm not," Duce replied quickly. "I think I know who killed Patrick. He's human and he's involved with that shit out in Joliet. If I take care of him and his vampire buddy, then I weaken Adenauer and Fulsome."

"So the Carthians *are* involved," Maxwell said with a growl. "Who are they? I'll have the Sheriff deal with them, and with you for withholding that information."

"Maxwell, man, you don't get it," Duce said, almost sighing. "If you do that, you'll fuck up everything. The Carthians will see this as a move against them and retaliate with violence. There'll be blood in the streets, and while I have no doubt that you can squash the movement for now, you'll make martyrs of everyone you destroy. Chicago will become a rallying point for every Carthian shit-kicker out there. The vampires you'll draw to your city won't be the ones you got now. You'll pull in the *vatos* from LA and the political freedom fighters from Atlanta. You'll pull in every vampire trying to prosper from the chaos in Chicago, and you know what it's like when our kind smells blood in the water. You know how we get. But if you let me handle the problem, in-house, then we can keep this quiet, our deal intact and Chicago peaceful."

"But only if I agree to Cicero and a seat among the Primogen," Maxwell said. "Isn't that what you told Robert? Given how you've lied to me, I see no reason to make those concessions."

Duce locked eyes with Maxwell, feeling stronger in his presence for the first time in a long while. "If you *agree*?" Duce said. "You already agreed to those terms. You agreed to them six fucking years ago!"

And Maxwell blinked. He must have felt it, the false trust he'd instilled in Duce slipping a notch. Duce certainly felt it and felt strong enough to launch into a rejoinder.

"Everything's fucked up because you *lied* to me," Duce said. "You strung me along, and now the Carthians are fed up with shit. Joliet's the result of that. Now you can fucking bury me or stake me or UV my ass, but it doesn't change the situation. Unless I stop them, the Carthians are going to start crawling up people's asses and start nesting!"

"Mr. Carter," Maxwell said, "that's enough!"

"No it's not enough. Fuck! Why didn't I see it before? I should have seen it!"

"Sit down and behave!"

"I thought I needed you, but the real bitch is, you need *me*!"

"That is enough!" Maxwell said, slamming his fists down on the table. The bodyguards surrounded Duce, waiting for him to try something.

"You need me," Duce said, quietly now. "Without me the Carthians will run wild. But I can stop them *and* give you the fucker responsible for the breach in Joliet. Give me three days. And if shit isn't under control by then, then you can call it Duce-hunting season."

The room was silent, a turbulent pool waiting for the ripples to calm. Prince Maxwell and Duce watched each other carefully. Duce, however, was no longer angry. He was calm; more so than he'd ever been.

"Three days," Maxwell said.

"With Cicero and the Primogen seat still on the table."

"Fine," Maxwell said, his eyes narrowing, "but on one condition. Stay the hell away from Persephone."

And as simple as that, Duce nodded. "Done," he said.

Duce stepped back out into the street, his body numb. The snowfall had slowed and everything was quiet, the world asleep and ignorant of the monsters lurking in the shadows. Duce pushed a trickle of Vitae through his system; it saturated his chest and spread warmth throughout his body. It was like a shot of Irish coffee on a cold day, suffusing him with false heat. Another trickle of blood, and Duce inhaled, his lungs breathing cold air with a rhythm and pulse, ebb and flow. Still more slivers of vitality invigorated Duce's corpse, reviving his dead autonomic functions. And he thought about Patrick, trying to see if he could still grieve the way mortals do—the way he once did. Could he cry saline tears, or inhale sharp, mournful breaths that failed to fill the void? Could his throat ache? Did his beating heart struggle through its paces? Could he lament Patrick like a human and not some cold dead thing?

The answer was no.

Duce was on automatic, his breathing and heart rate slow, deliberate and divested of passion. The tears flowing down his face were melted snow muddied with trickles of blood, and his throat didn't ache. The emotional pain was there—Duce still felt the sharp stab of grief—but the human expressions of it were lacking. Only the Hunger lingered, and it was cunning. His grief expressed itself in bloody fantasies of revenge, spilling Charles's blood, gorging on Charles's blood... Charles was simply convenient to his thoughts. The Hunger knew how to disguise its intent, however thin the excuse.

The cell phone rang and Duce abandoned any pretense of grieving as one living. His breath guttered out, his heartbeat died in mid-beat and the cold overtook his extremities, driving the heat inward till it was a pale ember in his chest.

"Hello?" Duce said, not bothering to study the number.

"Hi," Persephone responded, her voice dusked. "I'm so sorry," she said.

"Thanks," Duce replied. "Look. This isn't such a good time."

"I know," she replied. "Turn around."

Duce turned around, but there was nobody on the stoop. Movement in a third-story window drew his attention there. Persephone had her hand pressed against the glass. She was a ghost smiling down on him and he, he was still hungry for her. Not even the grief could suppress that. Duce put his hand up briefly before bringing it back down

lucien soulban

and wiping the blood from his eyes. They stared at one another.

"We can't be together, anymore," Duce said finally.

"I know, but I don't know if I can. I love you—"

"No you don't," Duce said. "And I don't love you either."

"I know you're saying that just to—"

"No!" Duce snapped. "I'm tired of feeling this way. I'm tired of fighting the urge to drink you dry."

"It's called passion," Persephone said, an odd sigh following her statement. "I feel it too."

"This ain't right. I can't be with you," Duce said. "This can't be love. Not if the goddamn Beast in me is trying to consume you."

"I know," Persephone whispered. "I—I don't want to betray you."

"I trust you, Pea," Duce said. "I know you wouldn't do that."

Duce was surprised by Persephone's sharp laugh.

"No," Persephone said. "Maybe you're right. Maybe we aren't meant for each other."

"I don't know," Duce admitted. "I want to walk away right now," he said. "But I also want to taste you again, just once."

"Duce, go," Persephone said, moving away from the window. She vanished. "If you don't leave now, we'll never leave each other."

"I love you," Duce said, "and I don't want to kill you."

"You'd never do that," Persephone whispered.

"Yes," Duce said, imagining the fiery taste of her blood. "Yes, I would."

"Goodbye," Persephone whispered. The line went dead.

"Give the Invictus hell," Duce said to the dead air, then turned and walked away.

The room was dark; perfect for brooding. Robert walked into the study and waited for Prince Maxwell to acknowledge his presence; a smile was perched on Maxwell's lips. He was content with himself. After a quiet ten-minute wait, Maxwell finally spoke.

"Call Halliburton," the Prince said. "Tell him I reconsidered his request. I'll do him this favor."

"Yes, sir."

"Schedule a meeting with him for tomorrow night to discuss the terms."

"Yes, sir," Robert said.

"And tell Persephone, I'm giving her this last chance to prove herself. Tell her I've been more than fair in this matter and that... I let Duce walk as a favor to her."

"Of course," Robert said, before leaving Maxwell to his small victories.

About forty miles of tunnels still survived, much of it never having been recorded on any map. One such segment of tunnel linked to the basement of an abandoned apartment building south of Clark and 18th, or at least, that's what Hoff told Duce.

Getting into the building was easy enough, as was slipping through a forgotten coal chute in the basement that accessed the abandoned network below. Duce was glad he wasn't claustrophobic, however, given that the dark tunnel measured six feet wide and seven feet high.

"I love this place," Hoff whispered in Duce's ear. "Can I keep it?"

"You sure they came down here?" Duce whispered.

"Oh yeah," Hoff replied. "After Charles stormed out of Law's place, I followed him here. Trust me, we're in the right spot."

Duce nodded. Ahead, the corridor curved toward an active light source. Someone had a flashlight or lamp around the bend, though the light fluctuated through a kaleidoscope of splotchy colors, from red to green to blue. Duce could hear the hum of a generator and voices talking. He checked behind him, his acuity in the dark sharper than those of his compatriots, and nodded to the others. They moved forward silently to the lip of the curve, the corridor widening into what might have been a room or large junction. The voices were more distinct now. Duce recognized Charles' voice, but the others—three at least— were strangers. It sounded like they were drinking.

Duce nodded to Hoff, who vanished like mist on the wind. He returned a moment later, whispering.

"Six people, including Charles and our vampire, all armed. Large room, maybe 15 by 15, with a generator in the furthest left corner and a couple of cots on the right wall."

Duce looked to the others. "All right," he whispered. "Charles is mine."

The others nodded and waited for Duce to count off with his hand.

3...

2...

1...

Duce and his crew burst into the junction room, all hell breaking loose in a single, terrifying instant....

The six men were seated in a circle on wood boxes and milk crates. A large cooler sat in the middle, while on the surrounding floor lay piles of empty beer cans and bottles. Christmas lights had been hooked to the generator and were strewn on all four walls. There was also a television set and a PS2 with an NBA game on pause.

Charles was the first to react, suddenly aware that they were no longer alone. He had a sawed-off Ithaca shotgun with *Booya!* written on both barrels, which he brought to bear. Duce was on the big man in a blur, however, shoving the shotgun down so it discharged into the floor.

Hoff entered, locking eyes with one man in a wife-beater, and froze him in place with a horrific gaze. He then bit into the man's neck and drank deep. Next up was Marco Chavez, a bald-headed and tattooed Latino wearing a leather vest and white tee beneath. Chavez had some gang ties to his human past; Duce figured Los Solidos, though Chavez never said and Duce never pried. Chavez moved fast with a Glock in his grip. Speed and firepower were deadly combinations, but he refused to kill these days. Instead, he went straight for Terrell in his drooping jeans, oversized Bears sweat jacket and Uzi, shooting him in the legs and shoulders at point blank range.

Daurice was there as well. The stout man took a step back and used one-word imperatives that sent two men running at top clip back into the tunnels. Accompanying Daurice was Liz Kim, a young woman who was Daeva in every sense. Lithe and slight of frame, she wore a leather bustier to great effect and low-slung leather pants that always left the straps of her thong exposed. Pure distraction for her quick darting movements and the surprising strength of her brawl-house style punches. She waited in the corridor, catching any runners that Daurice sent her way.

Duce had never been a great fighter, which he already knew. Charles, however, was a brawler, and far more capable of handling himself in a fight. Duce's only edge in this skirmish was the Vitae coiled inside him.

Charles butted Duce in the face with the shotgun. Duce stumbled back, shaken, but he continued moving, barely avoiding a second shotgun blast that sent pellets ricocheting down the narrow tunnels.

Duce went low, grabbing Charles by the legs with both arms. He pulled and sent the big man crashing on his back. The shotgun flew from his hands. Big Boy locked his legs around Duce's waist and twisted, bringing him down as well.

Charles was a strong man who used his weight in fights. Several times he rolled on the ground with Duce, trying to get atop him. Duce was nothing if not nimble, however, squirming out of the way and trading hard punches with Charles. Finally, Duce managed to roll away completely, coming up with Daurice at his shoulders. Charles looked

lucien soulban

around and panicked, trying to locate Terrell, but both Chavez and Hoff were on the neophyte vampire, keeping him pinned with a gun to his skull. Kim walked into the room, licking blood from her fingertips. Charles went to grab the shotgun a few feet away, but Duce was quicker, pressing the barrel of his Beretta against Charles's temple.

"Stand up, bitch!" Duce said.

Charles said nothing, but he rose to his feet.

"When we bury Patrick," Duce said, "I'm going to throw your teeth on his casket."

"Bury him?" Charles said. "Shit, there wasn't enough of him to flush down a damn toilet!"

"You got balls to admit killing Patrick," Duce said. "Now, tell them about Adenauer and Rasta and Law and all that good shit," Duce said, indicating the assembled Kindred with a nod.

"Fuck you, cocksucker!" Charles replied. "I ain't saying shit."

Duce pulled the hammer back on the gun and pressed it harder against Charles's temple, tilting the man's head.

"Do it," Charles said. "It won't change jack. Your boy's still a skid mark over on Monroe, and you won't get shit from me."

"Duce," Daurice said, stepping forward. "Allow me?"

Duce hesitated a moment. He wanted the satisfaction of hurting Charles, making him suffer. But then...he'd be pulling the exact same shit he'd done in the past, trying to handle the matter on his own and making everyone feel superfluous to the process. He knew he had Hoff's support. The other three were still unsure, which was why he'd brought them along, to hear the truth straight from Charles' mouth. Showing them he could change was necessary to earn their trust.

"Yeah," Duce said, keeping his gun trained on Charles but giving Daurice the nod. "I do need your help."

"All right, then," Daurice said, walking up to Charles. He locked eyes with the big man and smiled. "I'm gonna stick my fingers in your brain and wiggle them hard for what you did to Pat."

"Blood is family," Chavez added from the back. "Blood is all."

"Fuck you!" Charles said, starting to struggle, but Hoff stepped forward with a carved pumpkin's grin.

"No, no," Hoff said, his voice like spider webs and cotton candy, "you stay put, my little lamb." In that moment, they locked gazes and Charles's eyes went wide. His mouth dropped at whatever horror Hoff inserted into his thoughts, and for a moment, Duce thought he would start screaming. Charles remained rigid, however, frozen and shaking, the terror never leaving his face.

"I can save you from that," Daurice said, nodding to Hoff, "if you tell me what I want to know."

Duce felt it, the push in Daurice's voice that turned grown men into puppets, the words that carried hooks in their unstated promises. Charles felt it too, firsthand. He managed to nod, but was unable to look away from Hoff.

"Good," Daurice said. "Start from the beginning."

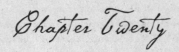

Chapter Twenty

The Aurora Movie Theater was long abandoned, having traveled down the chain of importance from a legitimate theater to an old-style, one-screen movie house to repertory cinema to peep show. Its decline mirrored the urban slide of the neighboring community, with the establishment's closure a sad punctuation ending the area's history.

The Carthians had cleared the alternating rows of seats and worked at restoring the Art Deco flourishes and Americana mosaic panels found molding in the basement. It was their meeting spot and sanctuary, and tonight, it was their assembly hall, though people were slow in gathering. Most of the vampires present stood near the walls and corners of the theatre, which suggested to Duce they were still undecided about matters. There was less than a half-hour left, but Duce hoped that Adrian had taken his invitation seriously.

Duce waited in one of the two surviving private opera boxes overlooking the theater floor. With him were Hoff and Brown. Joseph Brown was a black-haired Caucasian with a slender build and angular features. He studied Duce's floral print vest, which the prefect wore without a jacket, and brushed imaginary lint from the burgundy fabric.

"D'ya mind not touching the threads?" Duce said with a slight smile. "Fucking with my flavor."

"You are removing those sunglasses, aren't you?" Brown responded.

"Why don't you touch me?" Hoff said, smiling with his Jack-o-Lantern grin.

"You still carrying a spider on you?" Brown asked.

"He's around here somewhere," Hoff replied, relishing Brown's sudden discomfort.

"Then no. I'm not touching you again."

Duce shook his head and deposited his sunglasses in his vest pocket. "Y'all are strange fuckers. I'll be fine. Y'all go on and send Daurice up."

Brown and Hoff nodded, making their way past the moth-eaten curtain as Adrian arrived.

Fulsome was dressed conservatively, in a white, untucked dress shirt with the top button undone, casual jeans and a black jacket.

"You wanted to see me?" Fulsome said. "I hope you've reconsidered Embracing Law. He told me he approached you."

"I've come to settle shit, once and for all. I'm giving you a chance to back out and save face."

Fulsome laughed. "You've got some balls, Duce. I'm calling for a vote of no confidence that I know is in the bag, and you're giving *me* a final chance? No, here's the deal. Either Embrace Law and help the Carthians become a force of reckoning in the city, or move aside."

"Are you sure those are my only options?" Duce asked.

"Look, play games if you want, but this is your last chance to salvage your situation. It's time we struck out in a new direction. You were a good leader, but in keeping us safe, you made us complacent. Now, I appreciate your efforts to reach mutual compromises with the Invictus, but the fact remains that we've made little gains over the years. In fact, you've been overly cautious in pursuing the future, stifling our fires with the same uneven hand of the so-called First Estate. You've made us into the very thing we're struggling against, a stagnant collection of vampires no further in our goals than five, ten, fifteen years ago."

"That so?" Duce said. "Well, let me lay it down for you. *Keep it real*, as they say. You fucked up and you fucked up

lucien soulban

good. One, you shouldn't have gone after me in the way you did—"

"Look, this isn't a popularity contest, it's what's best for the Carthians. I'm giving the covenant a decision in *their* future."

"Save the speech for someone who doesn't know you better. The fact is, you stepped in it."

"All right, what is it I'm supposed to have *stepped in*?"

"Let me lay it down for you. I know you been using the no confidence vote to advance yourself, making it seem like you're moderate."

"So?"

"Wait, hear me out. Better I say what I gotta say in here, than down there. You been letting Adenauer use words like *revolution* and *change through force*, letting her take the heat as the political agitator in case your shit goes south. I know y'all approached the BGF looking for some hardcore revolutionaries to help the Carthians, and I respect the fact you blooded your contacts to keep them from talking to the Family. Only, I gotta ask. Did you sanction that shit down in Joliet with the murders?"

Fulsome was caught off guard, hesitating a moment too long. "I have no idea what you're—"

"Don't fuck with me!" Duce said. "I get using Adenauer to draw the heat and I get using Law against me, but why the fuck did you let her pull that shit in Joliet?"

Fulsome shook his head as Daurice and Kim walked through the curtain.

"What're you doing here?" Fulsome said.

Daurice looked at Duce, who nodded. "Chavez, Kim and me helped Duce capture Charles and Terrell. I questioned them directly…to prove to Duce he was wrong about you. I've since changed my mind and I'll publicly withdraw my support for you if you go public against Duce. I'll quit the Carthians before I see you in power."

Kim smiled and nodded as well.

Fulsome's eyes went wide, his gaze flickering nervously from Daurice to Kim and back again. Duce used his stunned silence to press forward.

"Look," Duce said. "It's just us here. I'm trying to save you from this shit, cause right now, the Prince has Charles and Terrell. He's calling a Blood Hunt on Adenauer that I'm supporting to show the Invictus has the full cooperation of the Carthians."

"*What*?" Adrian said, his eyes wide. "How could you betray one of your own like that?"

"Shut the fuck up," Daurice said. "You started this shit rolling. Because of you, Patrick's gone."

"I had nothing to do with Patrick."

"Yes you did. Indirectly, but you did," Duce replied. "Beth and Charles murdered Patrick and they've been gunning for me from the beginning! Right now, the only thing I haven't done is implicate you. So come clean, man. Or we're all walking away and leaving you to hang."

"Christ," Fulsome said. "Look, I didn't know about Joliet until it was too late, all right?"

"What happened? You were using Beth and Law against me, right?"

"Yeah, but Beth went too far."

"How far was she supposed to go?"

"We were trying to corner you with Embracing Law. I was counting on the fact you wouldn't go for it."

"So you could claim I didn't have the Carthians' interest at heart?" Duce said.

"Yeah. But also, I told Beth we could use Law's connections with the BGF to make things uncomfortable for the Prince. Then, we'd step in and clear up the problems for Maxwell in exchange for some concessions."

"Only that wasn't what Beth had in mind," Duce said.

"No. I didn't expect them to go after those correctional officers and their families. I spoke to Law last night. He told me how Beth okayed the attacks out in Joliet and how she enthralled a criminal named Rasta. Seems she was planning on killing you all along. Then she was coming after me. They left Law out in the cold because he was no longer useful. She was trying to highjack this entire thing out from under me."

"I warned you," Duce said. "What about Law?"

"I—I sent two men to find him, but he vanished. I don't know where he is."

"Jesus," Duce said. "He knows about our kind, and whether the BGF believes him or not, he knows how to start looking for us."

"What for?" Fulsome said. "He's done with. Everyone's betrayed him."

"He still wants the bite," Duce said. "And he'll find a way to get it. Once he does, he'll give it to the BGF."

"We started looking for him already," Daurice said.

"You let me know when you find him," Duce said.

"The Assembly will come to order," Kenneths called from the stage below the opera box, her voice filling the theatre. She looked up and nodded to Duce and Adrian.

"We're coming down," Duce said. All four of them entered the rear corridor, out of sight when Duce turned to Fulsome.

"What am I supposed to do here?" Adrian asked.

"Support me," Duce said. "I've lost too many Carthians these last few months, and I need your help. I got an offer for you."

"Why? Why you helping me after what happened?"

"Because I may not like you, but I need you to bring the Carthians together. We can't have dissension in the ranks. Not now. I humiliate you publicly and I alienate your supporters. I need your help, and you're more useful to me as an ally than an enemy. Trust me, threats aside, I can make it worth your while. But if you fuck with me again," Duce said, "you'll be eating sunlight for breakfast."

"Thank you," Kenneths said, studying the hall. "For those of you who don't know me, I'm Annie Kenneths, and both Duce Carter and Adrian Fulsome asked me to arbitrate in the matter of who should lead the Carthians. Now, two things before we begin. First, is there anyone who's got a problem with me adjudicating this matter?"

Silence. People swept the room with their eyes slowly, studying one another for some telltale betrayal. Nobody spoke up, however.

"We'll continue, then. The second matter concerns formality. While I'm acting as Myrmidon for tonight, I'm not deciding Duce's fate. I'm just giving both parties the chance to speak and state their case before we deliberate on the matter of no confidence. Once they do, you'll have a chance to vote on who you want as prefect. We set up a booth at the back of the hall, and yes, it was once a peepshow booth...you should recognize it, Dillon," Kenneths said, drawing laughter from the crowd. "After *both* speeches, you'll have a chance to vote on whether Duce remains our prefect or if we need to call for a general election. Duce has the floor to state his case, after which, Adrian Fulsome can offer rebuttal before we cast our votes."

Duce walked up the stairs on the side of the platform and made his way to center stage.

"First off," Duce said, keeping his voice clear and enunciating his words. He looked at everyone while he spoke, making sure each person earned eye contact and a reassuring smile. "I want to thank Annie Kenneths for stepping in as Myrmidon in what's been a trying time for many." He nodded to her.

She bowed her head in a slight tilt.

"I'd like to ask for a moment of silence as we remember Patrick Morneau," Duce said, bowing his head. The room fell quiet, and while Duce thought about Patrick, he used the moment to gather his strength and prepare for what lay ahead. This was it, the crucial minutes he'd been preparing for this past week amidst the hellish events. It was the journey to this moment that killed Patrick. Duce could offer no apology, no thanks to his friend except for making him proud of what he himself would say and do. It was the least he could offer Pat.

Duce raised his head. "Thank you," he said, waiting a moment. "When I was first planning this," he continued, "thinking about what to say, I was trying to figure a way of convincing you y'all were wrong, I'll be honest. But it took me a while to realize that while we don't see eye to eye, it was actually my fault. I should have involved you more. I should have trusted you more. I thought I was protecting you by assuming responsibility. I made y'all feel ineffectual as contributing members of the Carthians because I thought I had to save you from yourselves—protect you. Well, I fucked up. I can't say I didn't, or Adrian Fulsome wouldn't have found reason to call for this vote."

"That said, I learn from my mistakes and I'm not planning on stepping down unless that's the wish of the majority. I still want to run the Carthians, if you'll have me, but I need your help. I can't do it on my own. I tried, and I've been shot at and had my best friend killed. Now, I'm used to death, y'all know that, and I'm not afraid to shed blood to achieve my aims, but I recognize a senseless death when I see it. And Patrick's death was senseless. It shouldn't have happened."

"Now, I don't want your pity and I won't beg for my position, but I will remind you why I am the right man for the Carthians, now, more than ever. Despite what Fulsome claims, we are not a force of change. We are a force of *evolution.* Change for its own sake is reckless and it won't withstand the test of time. And neither will we if we charge into this blindly. But we don't share the same vision of tomorrow, do we? Fulsome talks about the future, but he never talks about *which* future. Is it democracy, Socialism, benevolent fascism, Libertarianism? You don't know. Fact is, he's stumbled on the same problem I've been wrestling with since I became prefect. How do you guide the Carthians into the future when they can't agree on that vision?"

"If you can't guide us," someone yelled out, "then step down."

"Quiet!" Kenneths barked. "Or I'll kick your ass out of these proceedings and you'll lose your right to vote."

Duce was impressed. Kenneths was better at this than he anticipated. He continued undeterred. "I need your help. To let me or Fulsome decide on your future is no better than the First Estate or the Crusaders doing such for you. We have to decide, together, what we want. Adenauer's call for a revolution isn't the answer. Blood for the sake of spilling blood is a waste of time, a waste of life. But you've been hearing that from me these last few years, so how about I illustrate my point with action instead of words. I may not stop fighting you folks on issues, but I'll never stop fighting for y'all. I've been trying to bring us forward, and I can finally say that tonight, we made a big step.

"Maxwell has agreed to give us representation among the Primogen," Duce said. "We have a seat on the council."

Everyone spoke at once, an excited chatter of disbelief, happiness and congratulations. Kenneths called for order again, and after a moment an expectant silence fell.

"Hold up," Duce said, laughing. "That's not all. I didn't struggle all these damn years to walk away with a *chair*."

More people laughed, but a few were eager for more news in what had definitely felt like a dry season.

"We have Cicero."

"What?" a few people asked.

"The district of Cicero is ours. Carthian territory. Our power base to back up our seat among the Primogen."

"Maxwell agreed to this?" Kenneths inadvertently asked, stunned.

"Yeah, he did. Cicero and a seat on the council."

"Why?" someone asked, her suspicions drawing uncertain murmurs from the crowd.

"Because we proved that we could be a force for change without the bloodshed and the bullshit," Duce said. "Look, I'm not saying the Invictus loves us, but we're now a quantity they know. We proved we could keep the peace while staying true to ourselves. Well, guess what, we have a place where we can explore, as a covenant, what it means to be Carthian."

"Is this legit?" Chavez asked.

"Yeah, man," Duce said. "It is."

The crowd looked at Duce. He shrugged and smiled back at them. "That's it. I'm done. Adrian," he said, looking at Fulsome. "Your turn, my brother."

It was getting late, but the votes were in and Duce had to wonder. Did he get through to them? Did he retain his title as prefect because the system worked, or were the Carthians being true to their nature? Being true to the growing stagnancy that preferred the status quo over the promise of change? When the separation between life and unlife grew by the measure of years, decades, vampires become more entrenched in their opinions and the way things were. The world was less frightening that way, the future a false certainty.

That's maybe one reason why we play these games, Duce thought, *the fucking Danse Macabre. Schemes are nothing more than imposing our will on the future—pretending we have some control over its direction when the truth is... we don't control shit. We're just fucking rocks in a river that's moving by us at a fast clip. Patrick was right to hate the game. It's deception of the worst kind. It's deception of self.*

At the very least, however, that part was over. Fulsome supported him in public and he offered Fulsome the position of Primogen. While it seemed that the reward far outstripped the nature of Adrian's actions, Duce cast Fulsome into the same role to which Adrian had consigned Adenauer—that of troublemaker. Duce was glad to step away from the spotlight in that case and let Fulsome take some heat from what would undoubtedly be a hostile council.

Next would come talk of Bethany Adenauer's actions, with word of her betrayal spreading across the city. Meanwhile, Kenneths stepped down as Myrmidon, leaving Duce to award the position to Daurice, while the remaining Carthians began to debate the future of their new domain in Cicero.

Duce waited in the nearly empty theatre, sitting on a chair, when Chavez walked up to him.

"Congrats on Cicero," he said. "But you and me, we grew up in barrios. We both know a ghetto when we see it."

"I know, Chavez. But look, man, if we can't control and run Cicero, what makes you think we can run or control this city?"

"True," he said. "Look, me and a couple others are gonna try and find Beth."

"Don't destroy her. I think we should judge her first among the covenant instead of having some outsider destroy her."

"All right. You got Law?" Chavez asked.

"Yeah, I got things on this end. Go."

Duce watched Chavez make his way out, finally leaving him alone with his thoughts.

"Congratulations," came a woman's voice.

Duce jumped out of his seat to find a beautiful, black-haired woman standing in the aisle. She had olive skin, and a white floral tattoo ran down the side of one leg that peeked out from the slit of her black dress.

"Who the fuck are you?" Duce said.

"Easy," Demetria said. "I know Patrick and Persephone."

"Wait, shit," Duce said, clicking into matters. "What the fuck's your name?" This was more to himself than to her. "You're their spy, right?"

"I worked for Persephone," she said, "but I'd like to think I was a little more with Patrick. He was a nice man."

"Yeah," Duce said. "He was. What are you doing here?"

"Came to pay my respects."

"Well, we're having a wake for him—"

"Not what I meant," Demetria said. "Patrick hired me to do something, so you and Persephone are now the beneficiaries of that."

"What d'you mean?"

"I already told Persephone about her little problem. Nothing she can't handle now that's she's in Prince Maxwell's company. As for you, Patrick had me follow Law around. I know where he's gone to hide."

"Where?"

"Well, first there's the matter of a fee. Patrick only paid me for half the job."

"I thought you and Pat were friends?" Duce said, sneering.

"Patrick was, but you don't have that privilege yet. Two thousand dollars for the information, or I walk."

"Fine," Duce said. "I'll have the money wired to you."

"Great," Demetria said. "For an extra five grand, I can take care of Law."

"No," Duce said, trying to conceal his surprise. "He's my friend, my responsibility. Where is he?"

"I can show you," she said.

"No. I have another matter to deal with. Just tell me where he is."

Duce followed Sheriff Nguyen into the basement of the building, the air rank with the smell of congealing blood. Fat, black flies droned lazily in the dank air. They stopped at a steel door. The Sheriff studied Duce a moment.

"You sure you want to do this?" he asked.

"Y'all are through questioning him, right?" Duce said. "The Prince was planning on destroying him, right?"

"That's correct," the Sheriff said, unlocking the door. "You have special dispensation for this."

"And Terrell?"

"The Prince wants to see if we can rehabilitate him. Otherwise…" Nguyen said, trailing off.

Duce walked into the cell, the interior austere except for a chain that suspended the prisoner from the ceiling, his feet barely touching the floor. A single light bulb showed ugly purple bruises across his naked, fly-covered body. He glistened with sweat and blood, his eyes swollen shut.

Whatever they'd done to the man, Charles was now a shell, his mind snapped by his ordeal. Duce almost felt pity for the man…

…almost.

"You dumb bitch," Duce said, shaking his head. He went right into Charles's face, even though Big Boy was a head above him. "What am I supposed to do here?"

Charles said nothing. He blinked, slow and cow-like, though Duce could see brief glimmers and flashes of lucidity.

"Say something," Duce said. "Tell me how you murdered Patrick."

"I hit him with Kenny's car," Charles said, his speech slurred. "And then I ran him over. And I shot him."

"Tell me he suffered," Duce said, trying to work up the nerve to kill him.

"He suffered."

"Tell me you enjoyed killing him," Duce said, trying to build himself into a rage.

"I enjoyed killing him."

"Tell me you're just repeating my words."

"I'm just repeating your words," Charles said.

"Motherfucker!" Duce's scream filled the cell, shrinking Charles under the echo. "Is there anything of you left in there?"

Charles blinked.

"Anything I can kill?"

Charles said nothing. He looked confused and horribly bewildered.

Duce studied Charles, trying to find something of the bastard that killed Patrick, any sliver of the personality he could latch onto so he could justify a violent revenge. But the frightening fact was, Duce didn't need a reason. The Beast was there, in him, ready to provide any excuse Duce required to carry forth the deed. Even before the Beast, he'd killed people, and was capable of doing it again.

In both cases, though, the situation had dictated his responses. In both cases, Duce was as much a victim of things as the people he murdered.

Duce headed back for the door and pounded on it. Sheriff Nguyen said nothing as he let Duce out and escorted him back outside.

"Don't worry," the Sheriff said. "We'll take care of him."

It snowed again, the weather conspiring to bring an early Winter Wonderland to Chicago's streets. It was still early evening, but the night was gaining ground over daylight, its reach growing a little longer with each sunset.

Duce was surprised at how empty the building felt. It was another high-rise cinder block, the lives inside choked on poverty. The elevators didn't work, but that was expected, and the stairwells were empty and strewn with trash. What Duce didn't expect was nobody to stop his march upstairs, to the nondescript hallway with its rows of nondescript doors, up to Law's hiding place. No room full of BGF brothers and sisters, either; the only person inside the apartment was Law himself.

"Was expecting you," Law said, leaving the door open for Duce to walk in. Law went back to the empty living room where an M16 stood propped up against the wall. "I'm glad you showed up."

Duce looked around, half distracted by the hunger raging inside him. "Me too," he said. "I came to tell you that it's over. Adenauer's on the run and the Kindred got Charles and Terrell."

"Figured," Law said. "So where's that leave me?"

"Up to you, brother," Duce said. "You can walk away or I can give you the bite, but you can't ever associate with or tell the BGF about us."

"I can't do that," Law said. "The BGF is my life. I swore an oath to them."

"I can make this easy," Duce said, extending his forearm. "I can blood you to me. Take that burden from you." It was another lie. Beth's grip on him wouldn't slip until she was destroyed, but part of Duce was willing to say anything if Law would just come around. *It never stops*, he thought bitterly. *It just never fucking stops.*

"Thought you called it a drug? You pushing that poison too, now?"

"It's better than the alternative," Duce said.

"Nah," Law said, shaking his head, leaning against the wall within easy reach of the M16. "I ain't about to be used like that again."

"You're making a mistake," Duce said. "Shit isn't that simple anymore."

"Keep hearing that shit from you, but you've forgotten who *you* are."

"Bullshit, Law. For a long time I thought I had lost my way, lost my community. But the thing is, I'm no longer who I was. I can't be part of that community anymore because who I was and who I am now...they don't mix."

"Brother, *please*," Law said. "I look at you and still see a fellow Afrikan who lost his way. But I can show you the road back."

"That's the problem, Law. I'm not lost. I know exactly where I belong. And it ain't with the community. I gave up my place at the table. I can't bring anything but misery to the people I love, and that includes my Pops. Better he doesn't have me in his life anymore, especially now that the Black P-Stones know I turned on them. I'm a marked man."

"We'll protect your Pops," Law said, almost imploring. "We protect our own. We'll keep you legit. We could use a brother like you. You're strong, smart. You got your shit together. I'd sponsor you, man. It'd be like old times, you 'n me, just a couple of road dogs out to change the world, *look out*!"

"You don't get it," Duce said, shaking his head. "It's a nice illusion, but when you get bit, you *die*. Fact is, when you get bit, your perspectives change. You saw it in Terrell."

"Yeah, but Terrell was willing to help us until that bitch fucked him over."

"She only accelerated shit, man. Eventually, Terrell was gonna realize you're no longer folk. And it's not because he's better. It's because you've grown and evolved and left his ass behind. It's because you're food and your concerns don't seem all that important anymore. He'd have found us eventually, because we're the only stable thing left in the

lucien soulban

world. We're the only ones who get his pain. Try telling rich people what it's like living in the hood. They'll hear ya, but they'll never understand. It's the same with us. Do yourself a favor. If you truly respect your Afrikan brothers, don't let them get bit. Don't tell them about us," Duce said, gritting his teeth against the knot of hunger in his gut.

"Man, I thought you'd understand," Law said, shaking his head. "But you too scared to see the truth. I know about the curse. Seen it work in Terrell. Seen the hunger. But I got something to keep me legit, knowing that my sacrifice will provide the BGF with the weapons to fight back. I'm keeping it real."

"Yeah," Duce said, "well, you're about as far from real as it gets. You want to know the truth…Tupac's dead."

"What?" Law said, caught off guard.

"Tupac's dead. Nobody Embraced the motherfucker. George Jackson, dead. Malcolm, dead. Elijah Muhammad, dead. Eldridge Cleaver, dead. And nobody's Embracing Farrakhan either."

"Your point, aside from dissing the brothers?"

"I'm not dissin' them! I'm saying they ain't vampires 'cause nobody was willing to take that risk. Like you, they wouldn't understand the differences separating the two worlds until it's too late, or until they or a shitload of the people they cared for were dead! Vampires and humans don't mix, especially when we start interfering in their business. You think you're the first motherfucker to come along and want to change the mortal world by using Kindred? Please! People have tried it and been staked and left to suntan. It happened during the Inquisition, when humans found out we existed and fucked us over. We led nations once. Now look at us…we're fucking scavengers living in mankind's shadows. Ain't that a bitch!"

"We ain't gonna make the same mistakes as you. We got plans and goals. All we need now are the weapons. We need your bite."

"We're not weapons!" Duce yelled. "We're a plague. We don't discriminate! We don't care! We hurt what we touch, and we kill what we love! And if you try using vampires to fight your battles, you'll be their first victims."

Law shook his head. "Even plagues have their uses."

"Shit..." Duce said, suddenly tired of the arguments, tired of the debate. Law wasn't listening. He didn't want to hear. And even if Duce Embraced him to make the point, Law still wouldn't understand the divide separating humanity from vampires. He wouldn't understand the dangers and the dormant stopgaps emplaced to prevent the very thing Law was talking about. Hell, Duce was still learning the ropes himself. There were creatures older than him, especially within the Invictus, and they sure as hell instituted measures to protect mortal governments from the kind of interference Law was talking about. Not out of the goodness of their hearts, but because vampires survived by protecting the status quo.

Better the times they knew than an uncertain future.

Better humanity remain ignorant of their kind than turn on them in fear.

Duce had no choice. Law was threatening that in every conceivable sense, and not because he had a chance to pull it off. It was because he didn't understand the dangers enough to surmount them. He had no idea what it meant to be a vampire, and he wasn't going to learn in time. He knew what it meant to be Afrikan, and that was all that mattered to him. There was no other perspective.

Duce focused on the Hunger, the one he deliberately fueled by having starved himself. The Beast, sensing the opening in its cage, rushed forward to express itself in Duce. Duce cringed in pain, fighting the frenzy for a moment longer, forestalling the inevitable rage. He was about to betray his friend for a second time, a man whose loyalty shamed him. He was about to do everything he fought so hard against by achieving his aims through nonviolence, fighting the Beast to retain his dignity, not hurting another person deliberately. Only, he didn't see another choice. He couldn't bind Law to him. And he couldn't let Law live without jeopardizing the community of the

lucien soulban

damned. To have believed he could do otherwise was foolish.

"What's wrong?" Law said, shocked at the sudden look of pain and desperation on Duce's face.

"I'm sorry," Duce said, tears of blood streaming down his face. "I don't want to remember killing you."

Duce screamed and let the Beast rush forth in that torrent of crimson rage, that moment of weakness. The last thing he saw was Law's look of terror as the man scrambled, too slowly, for the M16.

Duce broke free of the whirlpool's drag, free from the fang-laced currents that threatened to shred and drown him in his own crimson rage. Blood's thunder roared in his chest, but he breached the bestial shell surrounding his consciousness. He stumbled along the edge of the horrible madness of those afflicted by the terrible lucidity of their actions.

His hands were his own again, not the jagged, lightning-like claws of the Beast within. Duce was bloody and torn. He felt weak as he stumbled outside into the cold. He collapsed to one knee, the iron-tasting bile of blood still bitter and slick in his mouth.

He vomited a stream of brown viscera, and watched it melt the early snow. No gagging cough followed, but his stomach muscles pushed and cramped against vacating cavities. The images flooded back into his thoughts, Duce ripping mouthfuls of flesh and blood from Law's neck; Duce ripping away skin by the handful. The images flitted and flashed in his skull, but Duce made no attempt to chase after them.

He didn't want to remember what he'd done. He wanted none of this.

Epilogues

The gathering in the brownstone building's main, marble-floored hall was well attended, perhaps the largest in some months. With recent events, including the drive-by on Duce, the murder of Patrick Morneau and the allegations of Persephone's questionable loyalties, the assembled Kindred were drawn by curiosity and the sense that greater events were at play.

The evening, however, was not without its surprises. The Carthian delegation arrived with Duce Carter leading and Adrian Fulsome in tow. They looked more unified than rumors claimed, though they wore black armbands. The delegation waited patiently until the Primogen adjourned their session and Prince Maxwell walked down the stairs.

At that point, the gathered met with their second surprise. Persephone was on Prince Maxwell's arm. On the upper floor landing, the Prince took a moment to kiss his smiling daughter on the cheek, before she continued down the stairs in her long silver-satin dress like some 1950s starlet on the red carpet.

It was a quiet statement, one that said Persephone was and remained a daughter of the First Estate; any word or action against the childe of the Prince was an attack against the Prince himself. The message was clear.

Nobody, however, caught the cold stare Persephone fixed on the Herald Sebastian Garin as he made his way up to Prince Maxwell, nor the fact that he kept his head bowed to avoid her eyes. Nor did they see Halliburton and

Persephone exchange quick smiles. Persephone and Duce all but ignored each other.

Standing next to Prince Maxwell, Garin made three announcements, each a bombshell. The first was that Adrian Fulsome would have a seat among the Primogen as the Carthian representative, acting on behalf of Duce Carter and the covenant. Everyone spoke at once, the hall erupting into a cacophony of murmurs. Garin silenced everyone after a couple of tries, moving on to the next bit of news...

...the Carthians were being given Cicero, in an attempt to create a city that celebrated diversity, equality and unity. Stunned silence replaced the murmurs, with Kindred searching the impassive faces of Prince and Primogen for some reaction, some reason behind the news. No explanation was forthcoming.

Finally, Garin made his third announcement; the formation of a Blood Hunt to contend with four rogue vampires responsible for attacking Persephone, and one against Bethany Adenauer for murdering Patrick Morneau and orchestrating the drive-by on Duce Carter. Said vampires, Garin said, were trying to destabilize the city by disrupting the peace accords between the Invictus and the Carthians. As such, their existences were forfeit.

With the final announcement, Duce Carter and Prince Maxwell retired to a private chamber, to ratify the accord between the two covenants. The remaining Carthians spoke to some of the other Kindred, but for the most part remained aloof until Duce emerged with the signed charter. The Carthians broke into a cheer, and left the building to celebrate.

The rest of the Kindred watched in stony silence, their cold eyes calculating.

Persephone made a point of walking among the other Kindred, fixing the ones she recognized from the Safe Haven and blood parlor with a hard gaze. *Don't you ever*

fuck with me again, she said with a stare and a cruel smirk on her lips.

It didn't take long for her to find Griffin. The smaller man acted as though nothing had changed, now that she was back in vogue. He offered a hollow smile and put his arms forward to embrace Persephone, but she laughed in his face and continued laughing as she walked away.

That felt good.

Still, the right to laugh, the right to walk away in triumph, came at a heavy cost. She was partly saddened by Patrick's death, though she couldn't call it grief, really. No, the true cost was her realization of just how little freedom she truly possessed. The Prince's cage was expansive, certainly, but it was still a cage. Outside it, she was vulnerable to the turn of someone's whim—someone, in this case, being Ike Barlow and Solomon Birch, if Demetria was to be believed. Persephone was vulnerable because of her role as daughter to the Prince, and she would never be safe anywhere except under his shadow. Not even Duce could protect her, despite his strengths. So she chose the shorter leash because it was closer to the Prince and his aegis. She had less room to run, but by default, fewer places where she'd get hurt and fewer opportunities for Birch and Barlow to attack her.

It was a compromise she was willing to make, until she could turn the situation to her advantage.

Pesephone continued smiling as she moved through the crowd, slowly picking up in her orbit a growing collection of admirers and sycophants.

It was a quiet spot along the Des Plaines River southwest of Chicago. The church was in the Gothic Revival style with its arched windows, whitewashed exterior and steep-gabled roofs; the cemetery in the back was surprisingly spacious. Two black hearses and a gray Buick kept their headlights on as workers finished digging two deep pits. They then lowered four coffins into the ground, two in each hole, with a priest watching over the midnight burials. Nobody approached Solomon Birch or Ike Barlow, who watched from the shadows, just beyond the wash of headlights.

"A rather harsh end for them, don't you think?" Barlow asked.

"They let Persephone escape," Birch replied. "They drove her right back to Prince Maxwell."

"You can't say that you're surprised?" Barlow asked.

Birch considered for a moment before replying. "No. No, I'm not surprised. I didn't think Persephone would get away so easily, though. I expected better from you and your allies."

Barlow shrugged. "You roll the dice and you take your chances."

"I suppose it doesn't matter. At least they were sufficiently deniable."

"Total dead-ends."

"Nevertheless, it's fortunate we got to them before the others did. All in all, this was a good test run."

"Test run?"

"Of course," Birch said. "I wanted to see how far I could stretch the elastic bond between Persephone and Maxwell before it snapped back. I was just testing the waters."

"And?"

"Now I know. Now I can prepare for the next time."

"You think Persephone will stray from her sire again?"

"It's inevitable. Next time I'll make sure all my pieces are in place. Next time, I'll get Persephone to sever the umbilical cord completely so there's no return."

"And how will you accomplish that?"

"Two words, rhymes with Achilles Heel..." Birch said, grinning as the workers buried the last casket, "...Duce Carter."

"And then you nail them both."

"Not at all," Birch said. "Then I nail *everyone*."

Sheriff Nguyen watched as the black-robed executioner lowered Charles to his knees, but kept him suspended on the chain. The executioner bit deep into Charles' neck. Instead of feeding from him, however, the executioner's nostrils flared and he inhaled...

...blowing hard mouthfuls of air into Charles' jugular.

The executioner quickly licked the wound closed, sealing the air inside his victim's blood vessels, and then moved back. Charles stood up, his body trembling. He clutched his neck with his shackled hands and screamed. Air bubbles were working their way to his brain, lodging themselves in the smaller veins and capillaries along the way. He continued screaming, his voice tortured before he choked on vomit and emptied his stomach's contents on the floor. Charles clutched his abdomen in pain and then his chest, his lungs struggling to draw breath. He fell, his body snapping on the chain and convulsing, his limbs locked. The air bubbles found their way to his brain, and Charles was dying in small, excruciating steps. He foamed, his mouth opening and closing like a fish caught out of water, trying to draw a breath that wasn't there.

Sheriff Nguyen watched Charles shudder one last time before his body went still. He left the executioner to handle the disposal.

The hiss of compressors and monitoring equipment filled the hospital room. Tania Bentley's eyes fluttered open, juiced on morphine and pain. She saw Duce standing near the curtain dividers between the beds. She struggled to focus on him.

"Duce?" she said, a small, tired grin creeping across her face.

"Heya," Duce said. "I'm sorry I haven't been around."

"S'okay," she mumbled, falling back under. Duce watched her for a few minutes, before her eyes fluttered open. "Sorry."

"Don't apologize," Duce said. "You go on, now, and get some sleep."

She nodded and drifted back under. Duce watched her for a few minutes more, offering her a thousand silent apologies for bringing her into this. He finally stepped past the curtain.

An elderly white woman with sharp green eyes was in the adjoining hospital bed. She offered Duce a matronly smile. "Might be best if you came back later," she said. "I don't think the dear will remember your visit."

"Maybe that's for the best," Duce said, walking for the door.

"Well, who should I tell her visited her?" the woman asked.

"A shadow," Duce said, walking out the room. "Tell her to have a beautiful life, will you please?"

And with that, Duce vanished back out into the corridors; out the building and into the night...his world, where Chavez and Hoff were waiting near his SUV with its re-buffed hood.

"What up, boss?" Chavez asked.

"Hoping you could tell me," Duce responded.

"Still looking for Beth, though she's covered her tracks pretty well," Hoff said. "Rumors say she's still in the city, but nothing definite."

"Keep your ear to the ground. What about the BGF?" Duce asked.

"No fucking clue where to start," Chavez said. "We're pretty sure Law never told them about us, but we don't know for certain."

"That's the problem," Duce said. "I'm not worried about them knowing. I'm afraid of Beth striking a separate deal with them now that she's had an in with Law and Charles. Nothing we can do but wait."

"For what?" Chavez asked.

"For the dead, drained bodies of prison guards to start showing up again. Then we move and hope we can find her before the Invictus or the Sanctified get their hands on her and she tries implicating Fulsome."

"Not much of a plan, boss," Chavez said.

"It never is," Duce replied.

"Do we dust her?" Hoff asked.

Duce shrugged as he got into the SUV. He waited for the others to enter.

"You know the rule of our kind," Duce said after some consideration.

"What rule?" Hoff said.

"Blood in, blood out," Chavez said.

"Amen, motherfucker," Duce replied, "Amen."

About the Author

Lucien Soulban is a writer with over 90 roleplaying game credits as author, editor and developer. Having written for such companies as White Wolf, Wizards of the Coast, Guardians of Order, *Inquest* & *Inferno* magazine and Alderac Entertainment, Lucien truly believes he's been blessed with singularly unique experiences despite himself. He designed and developed White Wolf's acclaimed **Orpheus** roleplaying game and helped create the Silver Age Sentinels superhero game. He's written for several fiction anthologies, including *The Book of Final Flesh* and Dragonlance's *Search for Power*, and is currently working for Ubisoft Entertainment as a videogame scriptwriter. He also penned the script for Relic Entertainment's well-received **Warhammer: Dawn of War**.

If you're really dying to exchange ideas about *this* novel, start a thread at http://www.worldofdarkness.com.

Enjoy the following preview of Rock Jones' **Werewolf: Heart of the Hunter**, the first novel in the all-new series based on **Werewolf: The Forsaken**. This series takes place in the same World of Darkness as the novels based on **Vampire: The Requiem** and characters can and will carry over from one to the other.

Look for **Heart of the Hunter** this spring.

Heart of the Hunter
Rick Jones

ISBN 1-58846-867-4; WW11310; $6.99 US

The werewolf sat in a crowded bar, patiently waiting for his prey to pay and leave. He had a table to himself, where he nursed a draft beer and ate peanuts. The place was packed, but nobody dared sit at his table, or even ask for his extra chair. The air reeked of cigarette smoke and the stink of too many humans in one small space at a time.

The band made the unpleasant situation somewhat bearable, but they had just finished their last number. They were some unknown Celtic rock band called The Dark Ladies. The werewolf didn't much care for all that "we will drink and die and piss and moan and die some more for we are Irishmen" in the lyrics, but the singers knew how to harmonize, and that appealed to him. During the set break, he had followed the prey back to the bathroom, and picked up the band's CD while waiting for the prey to come back out. Buying the CD had meant the difference between a better drink and the American beer he was currently nursing, but the werewolf had a long drive ahead of him. The werewolf took another sip and smacked his lips. He suspected there was a tube from the urinal to the taps.

The werewolf pulled a few crumpled bills from his well-worn jeans and glanced at a small mirror behind the bar. He could see the prey anxiously tapping a credit card against the table. The waitress came back to the werewolf's table. He didn't smile when he paid her. People didn't like his smile. She didn't treat a scruffily dressed man in well-worn clothes like a homeless bum, though, so he left his change on the table and pulled on his coat. It was army surplus, with numerous patches and scars of long use. He patted the pocket holding the CD and rolled his shoulders. They popped and cracked from the night of sitting still.

"*Sayonara,*" she said.

He turned and looked back at the waitress. He cocked his head to the right and replied, "I'm not Japanese."

She blanched. He suspected if the air were not so thick with smoke he would have smelled fear. He was hunting. She sensed it. Some werewolves would have smiled a human's smile, or used some supernatural trickery to calm her. This werewolf didn't much care. He had paid his bill and tipped her, if poorly. That was more than he usually did. He wasn't concerned about how well she slept that night.

The werewolf easily moved through the crowd of people towards the exit. He risked a direct glance back to the prey. At the table, the man held out his hand to the woman, and she wrapped herself around him in an embrace more suited to the bedroom than a bar. The werewolf noted all of the different glasses and bottles on one side of the table, and the untouched glass of wine on the other, and shook his head. He wondered if anyone else in the bar noticed. Certainly the waitresses must have?

The crowd parted before the werewolf, as he sidled towards the exit. He was trying to be nonchalant, but the crowd subconsciously sensed some wrongness about him, and cleared a path. The werewolf hoped the prey didn't notice it, but there wasn't much chance they would with the way they were kissing. People studiously avoided looking at them, because a part of them wished someone would kiss them like that. To the untrained eye, it looked like new love, full of raw passion. The werewolf saw it was nothing but hunger on one side, and need from the other. The werewolf lowered his head slightly, keeping his eyes on the prey's backs. He just wanted them to go back to their damn car.

The lights of the city made it impossible to see more than a handful of stars, but he could see the moon. He felt Mother Luna's power wash over him. The full moon had been a few nights ago, and he smiled at the memories it drew forth. He quickened his pace, eager for the hunt to begin again.

The bar had a tiny parking lot where people who came early enough to find parking spaces were now trying to negotiate their way out of them. Everyone else parked wherever they could, and the streets for two blocks around were packed with cars. The werewolf walked purposefully down the street. He saw the prey's car, parked on the road, a shiny black Lexus. The werewolf glanced at the tinted windows, the radar detector on the dash and the comfortable leather interior. He liked the car. He liked the parking spot even more. The man had parked at the end of one strip, near a small alleyway. If the streetlight had been working, it would have been brightly lit, but it wasn't. Some werewolves would have spoken with the spirit of the streetlight, asking it to burn out the bulb. This werewolf had used a rock.

The werewolf stepped back into the alleyway. He pulled off his coat, sniffed it once then started to throw it in the dumpster. He caught himself at the last second, pulled the CD from the pocket and then threw the coat away. He liked the coat enough to sew it up a few times, but the stale stink of cigarette smoke would drive him nuts, especially on the road. His shabby t-shirt and worn jeans followed the jacket into the dumpster. He'd have to shower at some point to get the smell out of his hair, but he would have multiple reasons for bathing in a moment. He kicked off his secondhand sneakers and shoved them under the dumpster. His keen ears caught the fevered whispers of the couple.

"How was your day?"

"Tedious. I wish you could have called."

"But then you wouldn't be so happy to see me now."

The werewolf heard a chuckle. "I'm always happy to see you. Or hear you." He heard a brief kiss. "Or taste you."

The two stopped to kiss again, and the werewolf could hear the wet smacking sounds. He rolled his eyes and wished the two would hurry up. He had a long drive ahead of him. On the other hand, it gave the werewolf time to change. The werewolf's already shaggy mane grew wild, and his beard thickened and spread further across his face. He grew six inches, and added heavy slabs of muscle to his wiry frame. His face became more feral, with harsher cheekbones and yellow eyes. His color perceptions muted slightly, but his other senses expanded. The dimly lit alley was now in sharp focus. He could pick out the panoply of smells in the fetid alley, and the click-clack of approaching footsteps became heavy thuds. He could even hear a heartbeat, racing with excitement. He flexed his fingers, and examined the ragged but elongated fingernails.

The werewolves had a name for each of their five shapes. They called this one "Dalu." He licked his lips, careful to avoid the now sharp fangs. The prey was almost here. He felt the predator within urge him to continue the transformation, to take the massive Gauru form, the war form. He ignored the impulse. The war form wasn't for hunting, it was for slaughter.

The couple walked to the car. The man pulled his keys from his pocket and turned off the alarms. He looked at the woman, who stared at him hungrily. "What is it?"

"I can't wait," she said. From the alley, the werewolf could feel the lust flowing off of her and it stirred something in him. He throttled that emotion and focused his attention. Raw hunger radiated from the necking couple, and it stirred the werewolf's appetite.

The man looked back and forth. Nobody was nearby, as far as he knew, and the darkness gave them privacy. "Come here, then," he murmured.

"Good boy," she said, and slithered up to him. They kissed some more, leaning against the car. The werewolf shuddered with anticipation, and felt even more strength pound into his muscles. Just a moment more and he could strike.

The couple kissed hungrily, their hands running all over each other. She kissed his cheek, and whispered in his ear. "I need it." She nipped at his earlobe and he gasped.

"Here?" asked the man. He looked back and forth. The darkness provided an illusion of privacy, but a twinge of modesty bubbled up through the fog of desire.

"Here." She licked his cheek and gently ran her fingers through his hair, tilting it a fraction. "Now." The woman smiled and her ruby red lips parted, showing a pair of razor sharp fangs. She nuzzled his neck. The fangs slid into his carotid artery, and he shuddered. The werewolf could smell his lust and hear his heart racing. He licked his lips again. The vampire's body made no sounds except for the quiet suckling of the blood as it poured into her mouth.

The werewolf couldn't wait any longer. He leaped from the alleyway, crossing the distance in less than a second. He landed by their sides. He could see the vampire's eyes widen in the dim light. He grabbed her perfectly styled hair in his hairy paw and yanked.

Blood spurted up in a fountain as, unable to release in time, her fangs shredded her victim's neck The werewolf's yank pulled her off of her feet and she stumbled to the ground, her face now awash in gore. Her lover started to scream, not only from the pain, but also in frustration that the ecstasy of her bite suddenly ended. The werewolf cut him off before he could object further, slamming him into the side of the car.

Instinctively, the vampire focused her will on the werewolf. Some still-human part of him cried out in response. Had he been entirely human, it would have overcome his reason, and he would be mad with lust and a slave to her will. But the werewolf was already a slave to his urges, and it wasn't lust that drove him. It was hunger. He snarled and rushed at her. The two tumbled into the alley, a mass of limbs and anger.

She took advantage of the momentum, and threw him into the brick wall. The werewolf growled at the pain and launched himself at her again. She became a blur of motion and leaped straight up, trying to reach the roof of the dry cleaners. The werewolf caught her by the ankle, and slammed her against the dumpster. He heard bones in her back snap. She hissed and kicked him with her other leg. His left forearm broke cleanly and the predator urged again. He had hoped to avoid this, but saw no other choice for a quick victory. He gave in to the urge and shifted again. In an instant, he was a hulking creature of nightmares, the deadliest predator to ever walk the earth. He was well over nine feet tall. Brindled fur covered powerful muscles. He had the head of a wolf, and a mouth full of terrible teeth. His arms hung down like an ape's, though they possessed a fierce strength beyond any natural creature. He gripped the vampire's ankle tighter and swung her up and over his head into the other wall. The bricks and stone dented behind her, and her ribs shattered. She fell to the ground in a boneless heap. Already, the werewolf could see the wounds starting to heal. He looked down at his own left arm. The bones were knitting, but the pain was intense. His anger bloomed again and he reached down with his massive right hand, the size of a car's tire. His clawed fingers dug into her chest, slicing through tissue and muscle and gaining purchase on her ribs. She tried to scream, but couldn't muster the strength. Just to be sure, the werewolf covered her face with his left hand. Between his fingers, he could see her eyes, bloodshot from ruptured capillaries. He knew what she was wondering.

In the massive Gauru, human speech was difficult, but the werewolf made the effort. "Needed car," he grunted. He flexed his powerful limbs and pulled her head from her body.

He looked back to the car, where the vampire's victim quietly moaned. The werewolf smelled the rich red blood that covered his expensive jacket and shirt. He poked his enormous head out of the alleyway. No one had heard the sounds of the scuffle, or more likely, nobody wanted to check it out. Still, he had to hurry. He dragged the bleeding man into the alley by his feet. He shrank down to the Dalu form. He rubbed his arm and looked around. "Fucking vampires," he muttered. He heard the victim groan. He walked over and crouched down, standing on the balls of his feet over the bleeding man. He looked at the growing pool of blood and inhaled deeply, smelling the rich coppery smell. He looked at the face of the man. Nodding to himself, he pulled a thin wallet from the man's jacket pocket and sniffed the leather. He pulled the car keys from a pants pocket and placed it with the wallet above the man's head.

The werewolf's face never changed expression as he grabbed the man's chin and turned it gently, first left, then right. He could smell the vampire's lifeless scent all over the man. He put his other hand on the man's chest to steady him, then roughly shoved the man's chin to the left. The vertebrate popped and snapped. The werewolf's nose wrinkled at the fresh smell of urine and shit. He looked down and remembered to take the watch.

The vampire's jewelry joined the keys, watch and wallet in a pile on top of the dumpster. He wrapped them all in a newspaper, reminding himself to wash all the blood off later. If sunlight were to touch the vampire's black blood, that blood might ignite, ruining what he had taken. He reached under the dumpster, and grabbed his shoes, along with a rolled up blanket wrapped around something long and flat. He reached again, and found a pair of ratty cargo pants. He placed his swag on top of the blanket. He looked at the dead bodies. One was still cooling. The other appeared to have been dead for decades. He picked up the head and tossed it onto the roof of the dry cleaners. The body soon followed, now sounding like a bag of dry twigs as it landed. The morning sun would take care of her. He tossed the dead man into the dumpster, and covered him up with more trash. He slipped back into human form, and pulled on the pants. No sirens in the distance, so even if anyone had heard, they didn't call.

He collected the pile of loot, his belongings and the CD and got in the car. The werewolf popped in the CD and pulled out. He had to be in Denver in 36 hours. More than enough time to pawn the loot and hit the road.

The werewolf looked up at the moon and then at his hands on the steering wheel. The man's blood was caked under his fingernails. His stomach rumbled with hunger. His hand started to move towards his mouth. He shook his head and gripped the steering wheel tightly. The werewolf didn't want a burger, but it would have to do.

World of Darkness Novel Contest
$20,000 in prizes!

The World of Darkness is home to vampires, werewolves, mages and other supernatural mysteries not so easily labeled. While we're delighted for you to join us as we recount some of these stories, we'd also like to hear your story. And we're going to make it worth your time with a $20,000 World of Darkness Novel Contest that will help us find the best new novel.

The contest will take place in three rounds. One hundred winners in Round One will be invited to participate in Round Two, and five winners of that round will be asked to complete their novels for consideration for the grand prize.

Round one closes on March 31, 2005 so hurry up!

Full rules and contest details available at:

http://www.worldofdarkness.com/novelcontest/